Praise for
Joe Haldeman
Winner of the Hugo, Nebula, and John W. Campbell Awards

"If there was a Fort Knox for the science fiction writers who really matter, we'd have to lock Haldeman up there."

—Stephen King

"Haldeman has long been one of our most aware, comprehensive, and necessary writers. He speaks from a place deep within the collective psyche and, more importantly, his own. His mastery is informed with a survivor's hard-won wisdom."

—Peter Straub

Camouflage

"Haldeman's adept plotting, strong pacing, and sense of grim stoicism have won him wide acclaim . . . his prose is laconic, compact, seemingly offhand but quite precise . . . Like the grammar of cinema, it is a mode that looks natural and even easy but requires exacting skill." —*The Washington Post*

"Joe Haldeman has quietly become one of the most important science fiction writers of our time . . . Fresh and original . . . [Haldeman] is a skillful storyteller worth your time . . . *Camouflage* is an addictive read, one of the strangest love stories around. If you haven't discovered the appeal of Haldeman's unique brand of science fiction, it's time you did." —*Rocky Mountain News*

"There's a vapid movie about aliens and predators that, for millennia, have used Earth as a proving ground. Better to use your imagination and read Haldeman's book."

—*The Kansas City Star*

continued . . .

"Joe Haldeman has delivered an eminently readable, suspenseful, even touching novel here, one that's clearly state-of-the-art SF, yet which also pays affectionate homage to several classics of the field. Funny, tragic, shocking, insightful, this novel proves that the only behavior truly alien to the universe is that which ignores love and curiosity."

—Paul Di Filippo, *Science Fiction Weekly*

"Award-winning SF veteran Haldeman proves as engaging a storyteller as ever, especially given this book's irresistible premise and page-turning action."   —*Booklist*

"With his customary economy of words, Haldeman examines the differences and similarities between human and nonhuman nature as his protagonists face possible destruction. Superb storytelling and a panoramic view of history recommend this novel."   —*Library Journal*

"It's a fast-paced adventure with high-tech wreck recovery, an international 'man'-hunt, and lots of alien sex and violence. And it's fun."   —*SF Revu*

"This futuristic aliens-among-us tale is a terrific story line that hooks the audience from the moment the object is lifted from the sea . . . Russell is a fabulous lead human protagonist, but clearly, the mystery of the two ETs and their 'key' is what grips the audience in a fabulous thriller that needs a chlorine-based sequel."   —*Midwest Book Review*

"A great book . . . It is well written and the writer is able to make his scenarios seem possible and believable as well as crafting an exciting story. He succeeds in making the alien a sympathetic character as well as exploring fresh ideas, blending scientific fact with true science fiction. An excellent book which is thoroughly recommended."   —*SF Crowsnest*

Guardian

Chosen by Locus as one of the year's
Recommended Reads

"Eminently likable."
—*The New York Times*

"A series of brilliantly told adventures . . . Frontier Alaska is described with vivid and loving detail. Haldeman is a magnificent writer and the details and characters are superb. Reaching a place where the science fiction experience passes close to mysticism, *Guardian* doesn't try to fit into any of the conventional science fiction pigeonholes."
—*The Denver Post*

"An amazingly fine historical novel . . . Haldeman is a marvelous storyteller."
—*Rocky Mountain News*

"Joe Haldeman is an excellent writer . . . He does wonderful work."
—*The San Diego Union-Tribune*

"An elegant parable of many worlds and multiple possibilities . . . the tale of a courageous woman whose life spans most of a century and whose hopes and dreams cross the barrier between worlds."
—*Library Journal*

"Joe Haldeman's novels are as much about ordinary life as life's extraordinary elements . . . [he] vividly paints the experiences of a woman at the turn of the century."
—*The Davis Enterprise*

"Award-winning author Joe Haldeman has written a very simple story about a woman's fight to survive and triumph. What is not so simple is the way the protagonist has to learn those lessons, but what would defeat another person doesn't even faze Rosa. She takes what she learns and applies it to her everyday life and, in doing so, makes the world a better place."
—*Midwest Book Review*

"Engrossing . . . hard to put down."
—*Library Bookwatch*

continued . . .

"Haldeman is a skilled stylist. He writes thoughtful books, rich with characterization. But who knew he could so completely get into the head of a woman born in 1858? That this master of science fiction, who has made the interior of spaceships and the far reaches of space so believable, could also so readily bring to life the world of the Midwest and Alaska in the latter part of the nineteenth century? Trust me, he does. Haldeman conveys the voice of the character perfectly, so much so that you never really think about who's actually writing the book: a male professor at MIT and Vietnam vet. He also does a wonderful job describing this lost time, from train travel and railroad strikes to steamboats and life in the rough mining towns that provided the launching bases for prospectors on their way to the gold fields. Highly recommended."

—Charles de Lint

"Joe Haldeman has long been one of our more thoughtful and interesting writers . . . Masterfully done, a genuine pleasure, and Rosa is one of those characters you wish you knew in person. I commend this one to you highly."

—*The Reference Library*

"A superb historical tale."   —*Booklist*

"A compelling and economical narrative . . . Rosa Coleman is one of Haldeman's characteristically indomitable and competent women characters, and in some ways she may be the most humanly convincing of all of them . . . Haldeman manages Rosa's narrative voice with a brilliantly controlled sense of tone, and the tale of her cross-continent odyssey is strong enough to sustain the novel even without its late blossoming of SF conceits . . . *Guardian* is a compelling tale, demonstrating that Haldeman's vaunted skill at the integration of character and setting is equally at home in the past as in the future."

—Gary K. Wolfe, *Locus*

camouflage

joe haldeman

ACE BOOKS, NEW YORK

THE BERKLEY PUBLISHING GROUP
Published by the Penguin Group
Penguin Group (USA) Inc.
375 Hudson Street, New York, New York 10014, USA
Penguin Group (Canada), 90 Eglinton Avenue East, Suite 700, Toronto, Ontario M4P 2Y3, Canada
(a division of Pearson Penguin Canada Inc.)
Penguin Books Ltd., 80 Strand, London WC2R 0RL, England
Penguin Group Ireland, 25 St. Stephen's Green, Dublin 2, Ireland (a division of Penguin Books Ltd.)
Penguin Group (Australia), 250 Camberwell Road, Camberwell, Victoria 3124, Australia
(a division of Pearson Australia Group Pty. Ltd.)
Penguin Books India Pvt. Ltd., 11 Community Centre, Panchsheel Park, New Delhi—110 017, India
Penguin Group (NZ), Cnr. Airborne and Rosedale Roads, Albany, Auckland 1310, New Zealand
(a division of Pearson New Zealand Ltd.)
Penguin Books (South Africa) (Pty.) Ltd., 24 Sturdee Avenue, Rosebank, Johannesburg 2196,
South Africa

Penguin Books Ltd., Registered Offices: 80 Strand, London WC2R 0RL, England

This is a work of fiction. Names, characters, places, and incidents either are the product of the author's imagination or are used fictitiously, and any resemblance to actual persons, living or dead, business establishments, events, or locales is entirely coincidental.

CAMOUFLAGE

An Ace Book / published by arrangement with the author

PRINTING HISTORY
Ace hardcover edition / August 2004
Ace mass market edition / August 2005

Copyright © 2004 by Joe Haldeman.
A shorter version of this novel was serialized in *Analog* magazine.
Cover art by Craig White.
Cover design by Rita Frangie.
Interior text design by Tiffany Estreicher.

ISBN: 978-0-441-01252-7

ACE
Ace Books are published by The Berkley Publishing Group,
a division of Penguin Group (USA) Inc.,
375 Hudson Street, New York, New York 10014.
ACE and the "A" design are trademarks belonging to Penguin Group (USA) Inc.

PRINTED IN THE UNITED STATES OF AMERICA

10 9 8 7 6

for ralph vicinanza, faithful navigator

The author gratefully acknowledges the help of Chris Nelson, our guide through the alien world of Samoa, and Cordelia Willis, for her knowledge of forensic technology and DNA matters.

"Life is so peculiar,
all you really have to say is 'that's life.'"
—Louis Armstrong
(improvising on Johnny Burke's
"Life Is So Peculiar")

prologue

The monster came from a swarm of stars that humans call Messier 22, a globular cluster ten thousand light-years distant. A million stars with ten million planets—all but one of them devoid of significant life.

It's not a part of space where life could flourish. All of those planets are in unstable orbits, the stars swinging so close to one another that they steal planets, or pass them around, or eat them.

This makes for ferocious geological and climatic changes; most of the planets are sterile billiard balls or massive Jovian gasbags. But on the one world where life has managed a toehold, that life is *tough*.

And adaptable. What kind of organisms can live on a world as hot as Mercury, which then is suddenly as distant from its sun as Pluto within the course of a few years?

Most of that life survives by simplicity—lying dormant until the proper conditions return. The dominant form of life, though, thrives on change. It's a creature that can force its own evolution—not by natural selection, but by unnatural mutation, changing itself as conditions vary. It becomes whatever it needs to be—and after millions of swifter and swifter changes, it becomes something that can never die.

The price of eternal life had been a life with no meaning beyond simple existence. With its planet swinging wildly through the cluster, the creatures' days were spent crawling through deserts gnawing on rocks, scrabbling across ice, or diving into muck—in search of any food that couldn't get away.

The world spun this way and that, until random forces finally tossed it to the edge of the cluster, away from the constant glare of a million suns—into a stable orbit: a world that was only half day and half night; a world where clement seas welcomed diversity. Dozens of species became millions, and animals crawled up from the warm sea onto land grown green, buzzing with life.

The immortal creatures relaxed, life suddenly easy. They looked up at night, and saw stars.

They developed curiosity, then philosophy, and then science. During the day, they would squint into a sky with a thousand sparks of sun. In the night's dark, across an ocean of space, the cool billowing oval of our Milky Way Galaxy beckoned.

Some of them built vessels, and hurled themselves into the night. It would be a voyage of a million years, but they'd lived longer than that, and had patience.

A million years before the monster's man is born and its story begins, one such vessel splashes into the Pacific Ocean. It goes deep, following an instinct to hide. The creature that it carried to Earth emerges, assesses the situation, and becomes something appropriate for survival.

For a long time it lives on the dark bottom, under miles of water, large and invincible, studying its situation. Eventually, it abandons its anaerobic hugeness and takes the form of a great white shark, the top of the food chain, and goes exploring, while most of its essence stays safe inside the vessel.

For a long time, it remembers where the vessel is, and remembers where it came from, and why. As centuries go by, though, it remembers less. After dozens of millennia, it simply lives, and observes, and changes.

It encounters humanity and notes their acquired superiority—their placement, however temporary, at the top of every food chain. It becomes a killer whale, and then a porpoise, and then a swimmer, and wades ashore naked and ignorant.

But eager to learn.

Russell Sutton had done his stint with the U.S. government around the turn of the century, a frustrating middle-management job in two Mars exploration programs. When the second one crashed, he had said good-bye to Uncle Sam and space in general, returning to his first love, marine biology.

He was still a manager and still an engineer, heading up the small firm Poseidon Projects. He had twelve employees, half of them Ph.D.s. They only worked on two or three projects at a time, esoteric engineering problems in marine resource management and exploration. They had a reputation for being wizards, and for keeping both promises and secrets. They could turn down most contracts—anything not sufficiently interesting; anything from the government.

So Russ was not excited when the door to his office eased open and the man who rapped his knuckles on the jamb was wearing an admiral's uniform. His first thought was that they really could afford a receptionist; his second was how to frame a refusal so that the guy would just leave, and not take up any more of his morning.

"Dr. Sutton, I'm Jack Halliburton."

That was interesting. "I read your book in graduate school. Didn't know you were in the military." The man's face was vaguely familiar from his memory of the picture on the back of *Bathyspheric Measurements and Computation;* no beard now, and a little less hair. He still looked like Don Quixote on a diet.

"Have a seat." Russ waved at the only chair not supporting stacks of paper and books. "But let me tell you right off that we don't do government work."

"I know that." He eased himself into the chair and set his hat on the floor. "That's one reason I'm here." He unzipped a blue portfolio and took out a sealed plastic folder. He turned it sideways and pressed his thumb to the corner; it read his print and popped open. He tossed it onto Russell's desk.

The first page had no title but TOP SECRET—FOR YOUR EYES ONLY, in red block letters.

"I can't open this. And as I said—"

"It's not really classified, not yet. No one in the government, outside of my small research group, even knows it exists."

"But you're here as a representative of the government, no? I assume you do own some clothes without stars on the shoulders."

"Protective coloration. I'll explain. Just look at it."

Russ hesitated, then opened the folder. The first page was a picture of a vague cigar shape looming out of a rectangle of gray smears.

"That's the discovery picture. We were doing a positron radar map of the Tonga-Kermadec Trench—"

"Why on earth?"

"That part *is* classified. And irrelevant."

Russ had the feeling that his life was on a cusp, and he

didn't like it. He spun around slowly in his chair, taking in the comfortable clutter, the pictures and the charts on the wall. The picture window looking down on the Sea of Cortez, currently calm.

With his back to Halliburton, he said, "I don't suppose this is something we could do from here."

"No. We've chosen a place in Samoa."

"Now, that's attractive. Heat and humidity and lousy food."

"I tend to think pretty girls and no winter." He pushed his glasses back on his nose. "Food's not bad if you don't mind American."

Russ turned back around and studied the picture. "You have to tell me something about why you were there. Did the Navy lose something?"

"Yes."

"Did it have people in it?"

"I can't answer that."

"You just did." He turned to the second page. It was a sharper view of the object. "This isn't from positrons."

"Well, it is. But it's a composite from various angles, noise removed."

Good job, he thought. "How far down is this thing?"

"The trench is seven miles deep there. The artifact is under another forty feet of sand."

"Earthquake?"

He nodded. "A quarter of a million years ago."

Russ stared at him for a long moment. "Didn't I read about this in an old Stephen King novel?"

"Look at the next page."

It was a regular color photograph. The object lay at the bottom of a deep hole. Russ thought about the size of that digging job; the expense of it. "The Navy doesn't know about this?"

"No. We did use their equipment, of course."

"You found the thing they lost?"

"We will next week." He stared out the window. "I'll have to trust you."

"I won't turn you in to the Navy."

He nodded slowly and chose his words. "The submarine that was lost is in the trench, too. Not thirty miles from this . . . object."

"You didn't report it. Because?"

"I've been in the Navy for almost twenty years. Twenty years next month. I was going to retire anyhow."

"Disillusioned?"

"I never was 'illusioned.' Twenty years ago, I wanted to leave academia, and the Navy made me an interesting offer. It has been a fascinating second career. But it hasn't led me to trust the military, or the government.

"Over the past decade I've assembled a crew of like-minded men and women. I was going to take some of them with me when I retired—to set up an outfit like yours, frankly."

Russ went to the coffee machine and refreshed his cup. He offered one to Halliburton, who declined.

"I think I see what you're getting at."

"Tell me."

"You want to retire with your group and set up shop. But if you suddenly 'discover' this thing, the government might notice the coincidence."

"That's a good approximation. Take a look at the next page."

It was a close-up of the thing. Its curved surface mirrored perfectly the probe that was taking its picture.

"We tried to get a sample of the metal for analysis. It broke every drill bit we tried on it."

"Diamond?"

"It's harder than diamond. And massive. We can't estimate its density, because we haven't been able to budge it, let alone lift it."

"Good God."

"If it were an atomic submarine, we could have hauled it up. It's not even a tenth that size.

"If it were made of lead, we could have raised it. If it were solid uranium. It's denser than that."

"I see," Russ said. "Because we raised the *Titanic*. . . ."

"May I be blunt?"

"Always."

"We could bring it up with some version of your flotation techniques. And keep all the profit, which may be considerable. But there would be hell to pay when the Navy connection was made."

"So what's your plan?"

"Simple." He took a chart out of his portfolio and rolled it out on Russ's desk. It snapped flat. "You're going to be doing a job in Samoa. . . ."

San Guillermo, California, 1931

Before it came out of the water, it formed clothes on the outside of its body. It had observed more sailors than fishermen, so that was what it chose. It waded out of the surf wearing white utilities, not dripping wet because they were not cloth. They had a sheen like the skin of a porpoise. Its internal organs were more porpoise than human.

It was sundown, almost dark. The beach was deserted except for one man, who came running up to the changeling.

"Holy cow, man. Where'd you swim from?"

The changeling looked at him. The man was almost two heads taller than it, with prominent musculature, wearing a black bathing suit.

"Cat got your tongue, little guy?"

Mammals can be killed easily with a blow to the brain. The changeling grabbed his wrist and pulled him down and smashed his skull with one blow.

When the body stopped twitching, the changeling pinched open the thorax and studied the disposition of organs and muscles. It reconfigured itself to match, a slow and painful process. It needed to gain about 30 percent body mass, so it removed both arms, after studying them, and held them to its body until they were absorbed. It added a few handfuls of cooling entrails.

It pulled down the bathing suit and duplicated the reproductive structure that it concealed, and then stepped into the suit. Then it carried the gutted body out to deep water and abandoned it to the fishes.

It walked down the beach toward the lights of San Guillermo, a strapping handsome young man, duplicated down to the fingerprints, a process that had taken no thought, but an hour and a half of agony.

But it couldn't speak any human language and its bathing suit was on backward. It walked with a rolling sailor's gait; except for the one it had just killed, every man it had seen for the past century had been walking on board a ship or boat.

It walked toward light. Before it reached the small resort town, the sky was completely dark, moonless, and spangled with stars. Something made it stop and look at them for a long time.

The town was festive with Christmas decorations. It noticed that other people were almost completely covered in clothing. It could form more clothing on its skin, or kill another one, if it could find one the right size alone. But it didn't get the chance.

Five teenagers came out of a burger joint with a bag of hamburgers. They were laughing, but suddenly stopped dead.

"Jimmy?" a pretty girl said. "What are you doing?"

"Ain't it a little cool for that?" a boy said. "Jim?"

They began to approach it. It stayed calm, knowing it

could easily kill all of them. But there was no need. They kept making noises.

"Something's wrong," an older one said. "Did you have an accident, Jim?"

"He drove out with his surfing board after lunch," the pretty girl said, and looked down the road. "I don't see his car."

It didn't remember what language was, but it knew how whales communicated. It tried to repeat the sound they had been making. "Zhim."

"Oh my God," the girl said. "Maybe he hit his head." She approached it and reached toward its face. It swatted her arms away.

"Ow! My God, Jim." She felt her forearm where it had almost fractured it.

"Mike odd," it said, trying to duplicate her facial expression.

One of the boys pulled the girl back. "Somethin' crazy's goin' on. Watch out for him."

"Officer!" the older girl shouted. "Officer Sherman!"

A big man in a blue uniform hustled across the street. "Jim Berry? What the hell?"

"He hit me," the pretty one said. "He's acting crazy."

"My God, Jim," it said, duplicating her intonation.

"Where're your clothes, buddy?" Sherman said, unbuttoning his holster.

It realized that it was in a complex and dangerous situation. It knew these were social creatures, and they were obviously communicating. Best try to learn how.

"Where're your clothes, buddy," it said in a deep bass growl.

"He might have hit his head surfing," the girl who was cradling her arm said. "You know he's not a mean guy."

"I don't know whether to take him home or to the hospital," the officer said.

"The hospital," it said.

"Probably a good idea," he said.

"Good idea," it said. When the officer touched its elbow it didn't kill him.

mid-pacific, 2019

It worked like this: Poseidon Projects landed a contract from a Sea World affiliate—actually a dummy corporation that Jack Halliburton had built out of money and imagination—to raise up a Spanish-American War–era relic, a sunken destroyer, from Samoa. But no sooner had they their equipment in place than they got an urgent summons from the U.S. Navy—there was a nuclear submarine down in the Tonga Trench, and the Navy couldn't lift it as fast as Poseidon could. There might be men still alive in it. They covered the five hundred miles as fast as they could.

Of course Jack Halliburton knew that the sub had ruptured and there was no chance of survivors. But it made it possible for Russell Sutton to ply down the length of the Tonga and Kermadec Trenches. He made routine soundings as he went, and discovered a mysterious wreck not far from the sub.

There was plenty of respectful news coverage of the two crews' efforts—Sutton's working out of professional courtesy and patriotism. Raising the *Titanic* had given them visibility and credibility. With all the derring-do and pathos and technological fascination of the submarine story, it was barely a footnote that Russ's team had seen something interesting on the way, and had claimed salvage rights.

It was an impressive sight when the sub came surging out of the depths, buoyed up by the house-sized orange balloons that Russ had brought to the task. The cameras shut down for the grisly business of removing and identifying the sailors' remains. They all came on again for the 121 flag-draped caskets on the deck of the carrier that wallowed in the sea next to the floating hulk of the sub.

Then the newspeople went home, and the actual story began.

san guillermo, california, 1931

They put a white hospital robe on it and sat it down in an examination room. It continued the safe course of imitative behavior with the doctors and nurses and with the man and woman who were the real Jimmy's father and mother, even duplicating the mother's tears.

The father and mother followed the family doctor to a room out of earshot.

"I don't know what to tell you," Dr. Farben said. "There's no evidence of any injury. He looks to be in excellent health."

"A stroke or a seizure?" the father asked.

"Maybe. Most likely. We'll keep him under observation for a few days. It might clear up. If not, you'll have to make some decisions."

"I don't want to send him to an institution," the mother said. "We can take care of this."

"Let's wait until we know more," the doctor said, patting her hand but looking at the father. "A specialist will look at him tomorrow."

They put it in a ward, where it was observant of the other patients' behavior, even to the extent of using a urinal correctly. The chemistry of the fluid it produced might have puzzled a scientist. The nurse remarked on the fishy odor, not knowing that some of it was left over from a porpoise's bladder.

It spent the night in some pain as its internal organs sorted themselves out. It kept the same external appearance. It reviewed in its mind everything it had observed about human behavior, knowing that it would be some time before it could convincingly interact.

It also reflected back about itself. It was no more a human than it had been a porpoise, a killer whale, or a great white shark. Although its memory faded over millennia, past vagueness into darkness, it had a feeling that most of it was waiting, back there in the sea. Maybe it could go back, as a human, and find the rest of itself.

A couple enjoying the salt air at dawn found a body the tide had left in a rocky pool. It had been clothed only in feasting crabs. There was nothing left of the face or any soft parts, but by its stature, the coroner could tell it had been male. A shark or something had taken both its arms, and all its viscera had been eaten away.

No locals or tourists were missing. A reporter suggested a mob murder, the arms chopped off to get rid of finger-prints. The coroner led him back to show him the remains, to explain why he thought the arms had been pulled off— twisted away—rather than chopped or sawed, but the re-porter bolted halfway through the demonstration.

The coroner's report noted that from the state of de-composition of the remaining flesh, he felt the body had been immersed for no more than twelve hours. Sacramento said there were no appropriate missing persons reports. Just another out-of-work drifter. The countryside was full of them, these days, and sometimes they went for a swim with no intention of returning to shore.

Over the next two days, three brain specialists examined Jimmy, and they were perplexed and frustrated. His symptoms resembled a stroke in some ways; in others, profound amnesia from head trauma, for which there was no physical evidence. There might be a tumor involved, but the parents wouldn't give permission for X rays. This was fortunate for the changeling, because the thing in its skull was as much a porpoise brain as it was a human's, and various parts of it were nonhuman crystal and metal.

A psychiatrist spent a couple of hours with Jimmy, and got very little that was useful. His response to the word association test was interesting: he parroted back each word, mocking the doctor's German accent. In later years the doctor might classify the behavior as passive-aggressive, but what he told the parents was that at some level the boy probably had all or most of his faculties, but he had regressed to an infantile state. He suggested that the boy be sent to an asylum, where modern treatment would be available.

The mother insisted on taking him home, but first allowed the doctor to try fever therapy, injecting Jimmy with blood from a tertian malaria patient. Jimmy sat smiling for several days, his temperature unchanging—the body of the changeling consuming the malarial parasites along with other hospital food—and he was finally released to them after a week of fruitless observation.

They had retained both a male and a female nurse; their home overlooking the sea had plenty of room for both employees to stay in residence.

Both of them had worked with retarded children and

adults, but within a few days they could see that Jimmy was something totally unrelated to that frustrating experience. He was completely passive but never acted bored. In fact, he seemed to be studying them with intensity.

(The female, Deborah, was used to being studied with intensity: she was pretty and voluptuous. Jimmy's intensity puzzled her because it didn't seem to be at all sexual, and a boy his age and condition ought to be brimming with sexual energy and curiosity. But her "accidental" exposures and touches provoked no response at all. He never had an erection, never tried to look down her blouse, never left any evidence of having masturbated. At this stage in its development, the changeling could only mimic behavior it had seen.)

It was learning how to read. Deborah spent an hour after dinner reading to Jimmy from children's books, tracing the words with her finger. Then she would give Jimmy the book, and he would repeat it, word for word—but in *her* voice.

She had the male nurse, Lowell, read to him, and then of course he would mimic Lowell. That made the feat less impressive, as reading. But his memory was astonishing. If Deborah held up any book he had read and pointed to it, he could recite the whole thing.

Jimmy's mother was encouraged by his progress, but his father wasn't sure, and when Jimmy's psychiatrist, Dr. Grossbaum, made his weekly visit, he sided with the father. Jimmy parroted the list of facial nerves that every medical student memorizes, and then a poem by Schiller, in faultless German.

"Unless he's secretly studied German and medicine," Grossbaum said, "he's not remembering anything from before." He told them about idiots savants, who had astonishing mental powers in some narrow specialty, but otherwise couldn't function normally. But he'd never heard of anyone

changing from a normal person into an idiot savant; he
promised to look into it.

Jimmy's progress in less intellectual realms was fast.
He no longer was clumsy walking around the house and
grounds—at first he hadn't seemed to know what doors
and windows were. Lowell and Deborah taught him badminton, and after initial confusion he had a natural talent
for it—not surprising, since he'd been the best tennis
player in his class. They were amazed at what he could do
in the swimming pool—when he first jumped in, he did
two rapid lengths underwater, using a stroke neither of
them could identify. When they demonstrated the Australian crawl, breast stroke, and backstroke, he "remembered" them immediately.

By the second week, he was taking his meals with the
family, not only manipulating the complex dinner service
flawlessly, but also communicating his desires clearly to
the servants, even though he couldn't carry on a simple
conversation.

His mother invited Dr. Grossbaum to dinner, so he
could see how well Jimmy was getting along with the help.
The psychiatrist was impressed, but not because he saw it
as evidence of growth. It was like the facial nerves and
German poetry; like badminton and swimming. The boy
could imitate anybody perfectly. When he was thirsty, he
pointed at his glass, and it was filled. That was what his
mother did, too.

His parents had evidently not noticed that every time a
servant made a noise at Jimmy, he nodded and smiled.
When the servant's action was completed, he nodded and
smiled again. That did get him a lot of food, but he was a
growing boy.

Interesting that the nurses' records showed no change in
weight. Exercise?

It was unscientific, but Grossbaum admitted to himself

that he didn't like this boy, and for some reason was afraid of him. Maybe it was his psychiatric residency in the penal system—maybe he was projecting from that unsettling time. But he always felt that Jimmy was studying him intently, the way the intelligent prisoners had: *what can I get out of this man?*

A better psychiatrist might have noticed that the changeling treated everyone that way.

It takes a long time for cement to cure in the tropics, and the artifact stayed floating offshore, shrouded, for two weeks while the thick slab, laced with rebar, slowly hardened. They knew that no conventional factory floor could support the massive thing without collapsing. It was the size of a small truck, but somehow weighed more than a Nautilus-class submarine: five thousand metric tonnes. It would be three times as dense as plutonium, if it were a solid chunk of metal.

Halliburton had started to let his beard and hair grow out the day he retired his commission. The beard was irregular and wispy, startling white against his sun-darkened skin. He had taken to wearing gaudy Hawaiian shirts with a white linen tropical suit. He would have looked more dapper if he didn't smoke a pipe, which accented his white clothes with gray smudges of spilled ash.

Russell regarded his partner with a mixture of affection

and caution. They were waiting for lunch, sipping coffee on a veranda that overlooked the Harbour Light beach.

The morning was beautiful, like most spring mornings here. Tourists sunned and strutted on the dark sand beach, children laughed and played, couples churned rented dugouts with no particular skill in the shallows over the reef, probably annoying divers.

Russell picked up a small pair of binoculars and studied a few of the women on the beach. Then he scanned the horizon line to the north, and could just make out a pair of fluttering pennants that marked their floating treasure. "Did you get through to Manolo this morning?"

Halliburton nodded. "He was headed for the site. Says they're going to test the rollers today."

"What on earth with?"

"A couple of U.S. Marine Corps tanks. They went missing from the Pago Pago armory, along with a couple of crews. You want to know how much they cost?"

"That's your department."

"*Nada.* Not a damn thing." He chuckled. "It's a mobilization exercise."

"Convenient. That colonel we had dinner with, the Marine."

"Of course." Three waiters brought their meal, two piles of freshly sliced fruit and a hot iron pan of sizzling sausages. Halliburton sent away his coffee and asked for a Bloody Mary.

"Celebrating?"

"Always." He ignored the fruit and tore into the sausages. "The test should commence at about 1400."

"How much do tanks weigh?" Russell served himself mango, paw-paw, and melon.

"I'd have to look it up. About sixty tons."

"Oh, good. That's within a couple of orders of magnitude."

"Have to extrapolate."

"Let's see." He sliced the melon precisely. "If a two-pound chicken can sit on an egg without harming it, let's extrapolate the effect of a one-tonne chicken."

"Ha-ha." The waiter brought the Bloody Mary and whispered, "With gin, sir." Halliburton nodded microscopically.

"It's not exactly Hooke's law," Russell continued. "How can you get a number that means anything?"

Halliburton set down his silverware and wiped his fingers carefully, then took a pad out of his shirt pocket. He tapped on its face a few times. "The Wallace-Gellman algorithm."

"Never heard of it."

He adjusted the brightness of the pad and passed it over. "It's about compressibility. The retaining plates we drove down into the sand. It's actually the column of sand supporting the thing's mass, of course."

"A house built on sand. I read about that." Russell studied the pad and tapped on a couple of variables for clarification. He grunted assent and passed it back. "Where'd you get it?"

"Best Buy."

He winced. "The algorithm."

"California building code. A house built on sand shall not stand without it."

"Hm. So how much does an apartment building weigh?"

"We're in the ballpark. It's going to settle some. That's why the moat-and-dike design."

"If it settles more than five meters, we won't have a moat. We'll have an underwater laboratory." Once the thing was in place, the plan was to put a prefabricated dome, five meters high, over the thing, dig a moat around it, and then build a high dike around the moat. (If it settled more than a couple of feet, water would seep around it at high tide anyhow. The moat made that inevitability a design feature.)

"Won't happen. It was in sand when we found it, remember?"

Not volcanic sand, Russell thought, but he didn't want

to argue it. The coral sand wasn't that much more compressible, he supposed. He signaled the waiter. "Is it after noon, Josh?"

"Always, sir. White wine?"

"Please." He reached over the fruit and speared a sausage.

"So when do we expect the tanks?"

"They said 1300."

"Samoan time?"

"U.S. Marine Corps time. They have to get them back by nightfall, so I expect they'll be prompt."

The Marines were a little early, in fact. At a quarter to one, they could hear the strained throbbing of the cargo helicopters working their way around the island. They probably didn't want to fly directly over it. Don't annoy an armed populace.

They were two huge flying-crane cargo helicopters, each throbbing rhythmically under the strain of its load, a sand-colored Powell tank that swung underneath with the ponderous grace of a sixty-tonne pendulum. They circled out over the reef before descending to the Poseidon site, a forty-acre rhombus of sand and scrub inside a tall Hurricane fence.

Two men on the ground guided them in, the tanks settling in the sand with one solid crunch. The helicopters hummed easily as they reeled in their cables and touched down delicately on the perforated-steel-plate landing pad just above the high-tide line.

There were three Poseidon engineers waiting at the site. Greg Fulvia, himself just a few years out of the Marines, went to talk with the tank crews, while Naomi Linwood and Larry Pembroke did a final collimation of the four pairs of laser theodolites that would measure the deformation of the concrete floor while the great machines crawled back and forth on it.

A couple of workers rolled up in a beach buggy and set up a canopy over a folding table where Russell and Halliburton were waiting under the sun. They put out four chairs and a cooler full of bottled water and limes on ice. Naomi came over to take advantage of it, yelling "Bring you one" to Larry over her shoulder.

Naomi was brown from the sun and as big as Russell, athletic, biceps tight against the cuffed sleeves of her khaki work clothes, dark sweat patches already forming. She had severe Arabic features and a bright smile.

She squeezed half a lime into a glass and bubbled ice water over it, carbonation sizzling, and drank half of it in a couple of gulps. She wiped her mouth with a blue bandana and then pressed it to her forehead. "Pray for rain," she said.

"Are you serious?" Halliburton said.

She grimaced. "My prayers are never answered." She looked at the cumulus piling up over the island. "Good if we could get most of this done by two thirty." It usually rained around three. "Comes down hard, we may get sand in the mountings."

"Would that throw off the readings?"

She pulled her sunglasses down on her nose and looked over them at him. "No; they're locked in now. I'd just rather watch TV tonight than take down the tripods and clean them." One of the tanks roared and coughed white smoke. "All *right*." She set the glass down and jogged toward Larry with the rest of the bottle.

Russell and Halliburton didn't have to be there; the measuring was straightforward. But there wasn't anything else to do until the artifact was brought in the next day. Halliburton called the central computer with his note pad and gave it the Wallace-Gellman numbers, which were basically the number of millimeters the concrete pad flexed in three directions as the tanks wheeled from place to place. The artifact would eventually rest in the center of the slab, which was a little smaller than a basketball court, but it would have to be rolled or dragged there from the edge. They wanted to be sure the thing wouldn't flex the slab so much that it broke in the process.

Trouble came in the form of a young man who was not dressed for the beach; not dressed for Samoa heat. He belonged in an air-conditioned office, dark rumpled jacket and tie. He walked up to the yellow tape border—DANGER DO NOT PASS—and waved toward Halliburton and Russell, calling out, "I say! Hello?" A very black man with a British accent.

Russell left Halliburton with his numbers and approached the man cautiously. They didn't see many strangers, and never without a rent-a-cop escort.

"How did you get by the guard?" Russ said.

"Guard?" His eyebrows went up. "I saw that little house, but there was no one in it."

"Or just possibly you waited for the guard to take a toilet break, and snuck in. We really should hire two. You did see the sign."

"Yes, private property; that piqued my interest. I thought this was free beach here."

"Not now."

"But the gate of the fence there was open. . . ."

The guard came running up behind the man. "I'm sorry, Mr. Sutton. He got by—"

Russ waved it off. "We have a lease on this stretch," he told the black man.

"Atlantis Associates," he said, nodding. That wasn't on the sign.

"So you know more about me than I know about you. Work for the government?"

He smiled. "American government. I'm a reporter for the *Pacific Stars and Stripes.*"

A military newsie. "You in the service?" He didn't look it.

He nodded. "Sergeant Tulip Carson, sir." To Russ's quizzical look, he added, "In the middle of gender reassignment, sir."

It was a lot to absorb all at once, but Russ managed a reply. "We aren't speaking to the press at this time."

"You volunteered for the submarine rescue earlier this year," he said quickly, "and then claimed salvage on a sunken vessel you'd detected on the way."

"Public record," Russ said. "Good-bye, Sergeant Carson." He turned and walked away.

"But there's no record of a ship ever going down there. Mr. Sutton? And now you have that shrouded float waiting out there . . . and the helicopters and tanks . . ."

"Good day, Sergeant," he said to the air, smiling. This is the way they'd wanted the publicity to start. Something mysterious? Who, us?

By the time they unveiled the artifact, the whole world would be watching.

san guillermo, california, 1932

The changeling began to construct sentences on its own just after New Year's, but nothing complex, and often it was nonsense or weirdly encoded. It still "wasn't quite right," as Jimmy's mother nervously said.

The changeling didn't have to acquire intelligence, which it had in abundance, but it had to understand intelligence in a human way. That was a long stretch from any of the aquatic creatures it had successfully mimicked.

It came from a race with a high degree of social organization, but had forgotten all of that millennia ago. On Earth, it had lived as a colony of individual creatures in the dark hot depths; it had lived as a simple mat of protoplasm before that. It had lived in schools of fish, briefly, but most of its recent experience, tens of thousands of years, had been as a lone predator.

It had seen that predation was modified in these creatures; they were at the top of the food chain, but animal food had long since been killed by the time they consumed

it. It naturally tried to understand the way society was organized in those terms: food was killed in some hidden or
distant location, and prepared and distributed by means of
mysterious processes.

The family unit was organized around food presentation
and consumption, though it had other functions. The
changeling recognized protection and training of the
young from its aquatic associations, but was ignorant about
sex and mating—when another large predator approached,
it had always interpreted that as aggression, and attacked.
Its kind hadn't reproduced in millions of years; that
anachronism had gone the way of death. It didn't know the
facts of life.

At least one woman was more than willing to provide
lessons.

When it knew it would be alone for a period, the
changeling practiced changing its appearance, using the
people it observed as models. Changing its facial features
was not too difficult; cartilage and subcutaneous fat could
be moved around in a few minutes, a relatively painless
process. Changing the underlying skull was a painful business that took eight or ten minutes.

Changing the whole body shape took an hour of painful
concentration, and was complicated if the body had signif-
icantly more or less mass than Jimmy. For less mass, it
could remove an arm or a leg, and redistribute mass ac-
cordingly. The extra part would die unless there was a reason to keep it alive, but that was immaterial; it still
provided the right raw materials to reconstruct Jimmy.

Making a larger body required taking on flesh; not easy
to do. The changeling assimilated Ronnie, the family's old
German shepherd, in order to take the form of Jimmy's
overweight father. Of course Ronnie was dead when he
was reconstituted; the changeling left the body outside
Jimmy's door, and the family just assumed it had gone
there to say good-bye, how sweet.

The changeling had seen Mr. Berry in a bathing suit, so about 90 percent of its simulation was accurate. The other 10 percent might have made Mrs. Berry faint.

Similarly, the changeling could, in the dark privacy of Jimmy's bedroom, discard an arm and most of a leg and make itself a piece of flesh that had a shape similar to that of the nurse Deborah, at least the form she apparently had under her uniform, severely corseted. But it had no more detail than a department store dummy. The times being what they were, it could have had free rein of the house and not found any representation of a nude female.

It was still months away from being able to simulate anything like social graces, but to satisfy this particular desire, no grace was needed. Precisely at 7:30, Deborah brought in the breakfast tray.

"Please take off your clothes," it said, "and put them on the dresser."

Deborah may or may not have recognized the doctor's voice. She managed not to drop the tray. "Jimmy! Don't be silly!"

"Please," Jimmy said, smiling, as she positioned the lap tray. "I would like that very much."

"So would I," she whispered, and glanced back to see that the door was almost shut. "How about tonight? After dark?"

"I can see in the dark," it said in her whisper, husky. She slid her hand into his pajamas, and when she touched the penis an unused circuit closed, and it enlarged and rose with literally inhuman speed.

"Oh my God," she said. "Midnight?"

"Midnight," it repeated. "Oh my God."

Her smile was a cross between openmouthed astonishment and a leer. "You're strange, Jimmy." She backed out of the room, mouthing "midnight," and closed the door quietly.

The changeling noted this new erect state and experimented with it, and the unexpected result suddenly clarified a whole class of mammalian behavior it had witnessed with porpoise, dolphin, and killer whale.

The music teacher came for his twice-weekly visit, and was stupified by the sudden change in Jimmy's ability. The boy had been a mystery from the start: before the accident, he had taken piano lessons from age ten to thirteen, the teacher was told, but had quit out of frustration, boredom, and puberty. Or so the parents thought. He must have been practicing secretly.

This current teacher, Jefferson Sheffield, had been hired on Dr. Grossbaum's recommendation. His specialty was music for therapy, and under his patient tutelage many mentally ill and retarded people had found a measure of peace and grace.

Jimmy's performance on the piano had been like his idiot-savant talent with language: he could repeat anything Sheffield did, note for note. Left to his own devices, he would either not play or reproduce one of Sheffield's lessons with perfect fidelity.

This morning it improvised. It sat down and started playing with what appeared to be feeling, making up things that used the lessons as raw material, but transposed and inverted them, and linked them with interesting cadenzas and inventive chord changes.

He played for exactly one hour and stopped, for the first time looking up from the keyboard. Sheffield and most of the family and staff were sitting or standing around, amazed.

"I had to understand something," it said to no one in particular. But then it gave Deborah a look that made her tremble.

*　*　*

Dr. Grossbaum joined Sheffield and the family for lunch. The changeling realized it had done something seriously wrong, and retreated into itself.

"You've done something wonderful, son," Sheffield said. It looked at him and nodded, usually a safe course of action. "What caused the breakthrough?" It nodded again, and shrugged, in response to the interrogative tone.

"You said that you had to understand something," he said.

"Yes," it said, and into the silence: "I had to understand something." It shook its head, as if to clear it. "I had to *learn* something."

"That's progress," Grossbaum said. "Verb substitution."

"I had to find something," it said. "I had to be something. I had to be some . . . one."

"Playing music let you be someone different?" Grossbaum said.

"Someone different," it repeated, studying the air over Grossbaum's head. "Make . . . made. Made me someone different."

"Music made you someone different," Sheffield said with excitement.

It considered this. It understood the semantic structure of the statement, and knew that it was wrong. It knew that what made it different was new knowledge about that unnamed part of its body, how it would stiffen and leak something new. But it knew that humans acted mysteriously about that part, and so decided not to demonstrate its new knowledge, even though the part was stiff again.

It saw that Grossbaum was looking at that part, and reduced blood flow, to make it less prominent. But he had noticed; his eyebrow went up a fraction of an inch. "It's not all music," he said, "is it?"

"It's all music," the changeling said.

"I don't understand."

"You don't understand," the changeling looked at its hands. "It's all music."

"*Life* is all music," Sheffield said. The changeling looked at him and nodded. Then it rose and crossed the room to the piano, and started playing, which seemed safer than talking.

It was awake at midnight, when the door eased open. Deborah closed it silently behind her and padded on bare feet to the bed. She was wearing oversized men's pajamas.

"You have clothes," it said.

"I just got up to get a glass of milk," she said, confusing it. The fluid it produced that way was not milk, and to fill a glass would take all night.

She read its expression almost correctly and smiled. "In case I get caught, silly."

A little moonlight filtered through the curtains. The changeling adjusted its irises and made it bright as day, watching her slowly unbutton the pajama top.

It noted the actual size and disposition of breasts, not the way they appeared when she was clothed. The pigmentation and placement of nipples and aureoles. (It had wondered about its own nipples, which seemed to have no function.)

She slipped into bed next to it, and it attempted to pull down the pajama bottoms.

"Naughty, naughty." She kissed it on the mouth and moved one of its hands to a breast.

The kiss was odd, but it was something it had seen, and returned with a little force.

"Oh my," she whispered. "You're hot." She reached down and stroked the part that had no name. "Aren't you the cat's pajamas."

That was pretty confusing. "No, I'm not."

"Just a saying." It moved both hands over her body, studying, measuring. Most of it was similar to the male body it inhabited, but the differences were interesting.

"Oh," she said. "More." It was studying the place that was most different. Deborah began to excrete fluid there. It went deeper. She moaned and rubbed its hand with the wet tissues there.

She closed her hand over the unnamed part, and stroked it softly. It wondered whether it was an appropriate time to leak fluid itself, and began to.

"Oh no," she said; "oh my." She shucked off her pajama bottoms and slid up his body to clasp him there, with her own wet parts, and move up and down.

It was an extraordinary sensation, similar to what he had done alone earlier, but much more intense. It allowed the body's reflexes to take over, and they pounded together perhaps a dozen times, and then its body totally concentrated on that part, galvanized, and explosively excreted—three, four, five times, the pressure decreasing.

It breathed hard into the space between her breasts. She slid down to join her mouth with its. She inserted her tongue, which was probably not an offering of food. It reciprocated.

She rolled over onto her back, breathing hard. "Glad you remember something."

apia, samoa, 2019

They had a lot of company when two tugs began to tow the artifact toward the beach. Three military helicopters jockeyed for space with six from news organizations.

It was a perplexing sight. The artifact wasn't visible even from directly overhead, though the shroud over it had been removed. The titanium-mesh net that carried its mass kept it suspended a meter above the ocean floor, and the water was perfectly transparent.

A newsie photographer with diving gear jumped from a helicopter skid and went down beside it, and saw a sand-colored drape over a long cigar-shaped object. The drape fluttered once and revealed a shiny mirror surface. The mesh of the net was too fine for the newsie to reach through and expose it, but it was moving slowly enough for her to swim alongside and offer pictures and a running commentary, amusing for its lack of content, as the artifact hit the sandy floor and crunched through dead coral on its way to shore. It made a groove a meter deep in the sand, and the cables pulling it yanked tight and thrummed with the force of moving it.

When the tugs came gently aground, Greg and Naomi dragged a heavy cable through the light surf and dove with it, giving the newsie something to photograph. They cut through the mesh with a torch and pulled back the drape while the other two engineers worked their way down the cable with a large metal collar.

The collar, a meter round, supported four thick bolts. They slipped it over the shiny metal thing, and drove the bolts down with an air hammer, deafening in the water. When they were done, they took out earplugs and waved at the dazed newsie, and swam back along the cable.

A deeply anchored winch on the far side of the concrete slab growled into life, and the cable started to crawl out of the sea. When the cable sang taut, the growl increased in pitch and volume. People around the large machine could smell ozone and hot metal as it strained. But it won; the cable inched its way up the pad.

The artifact wormed slowly up through the surf. You wouldn't have to know anything about physics or engineering to see that there was something fundamentally strange going on—the thing's unearthly heaviness as it sledged through the damp sand; its mirror brightness.

The barrier of bright yellow DO NOT CROSS ribbon may have saved some lives. The cable started to fray where it was attached to the collar, then suddenly snapped, and a hundred meters of thick heavy cable whipped back with terrible speed. The broken end of it smashed through the window that protected the winch operator, Larry Pembroke, and sheared off his arm at the shoulder.

One of the Marine helicopters was down in less than a minute, and while the corpsman gave first aid they put the severed limb in a cooler full of beer and Cokes. They were in the air in another minute, streaking toward Pago Pago, where a surgical team was assembling. He'd be all right in a few months, though it would cost Poseidon, as the saying goes, an arm and a leg.

By the time the excitement had settled down, Russ and Jack had considered and discarded three plans for getting the heavy thing up on its slab. It lay there in the surf like a half-beached whale, weighing more than ten whales.

Since it seemed indestructible, Jack was in favor of using explosives—a large enough shaped charge would pitch it forward. Russ was totally against the idea, since there was no way of telling how delicate the artifact was inside. Nonsense, Jack said; the thing had gone through earthquakes under crushing pressure. If there was anything fragile inside, it was long since garbaged.

They asked Naomi, who had been a demolition engineer, and she said that intuitively it seemed impractical, and then did some numbers. No way. A free-standing shaped charge doesn't direct all its force in one direction. The side blast would make a crater so big it would swallow the concrete slab—and the explosion would probably shatter every window on this side of the island.

But she suggested a kind of explosive that is truly linear: a rocket engine. If they could strap a booster from a small spaceship onto it—if it were a kind they could shut off!—they could drag it up onto the slab by brute force.

And think of the visuals.

They got the other engineers together and hashed out the details. They'd need a kind of chute, to keep it going in a straight line, and the booster would have to be a kind that could be carefully controlled. The thing was pointed straight at Aggie Grey's Hotel, and it would be bad publicity to demolish a century-old landmark full of tourists, where Jack had finally taught the bartender how to make a decent martini.

But the scheme would be great publicity if it worked. They called the American, French, and British space agencies, but China underbid everyone by half: a mere thirty

million eurobucks. Jack called some people and found he
could underwrite a quarter of it by granting an exclusive
news franchise. By lunchtime the next day they were
joined by a Chinese lawyer with a short contract and a big
notebook of specifications.

They could have their rocket in eight days. Jack grum-
bled about that—they'd be old news by then—but it's not
exactly like buying a car off the lot. And the artifact wasn't
going anywhere.

- 8 -

San Guillermo, California, 1932

"Jimmy" had made a little too much noise during its sexual initiation, and although Mr. Berry was secretly relieved that his boy was doing *something* normal, he obeyed his wife's wishes and fired Deborah, slipping her a hundred-dollar bill as she left. That was a year's rent for her: more than adequate compensation.

The changeling was becoming human enough to be slightly annoyed to find her replaced by another male, but it had learned enough from the one encounter that its simulation of a woman would fool anyone but a thorough gynecologist.

Dr. Grossman wondered whether Jimmy's astounding musical performance extended into related areas of motor control, and so for the next meeting he brought along a friend who was an artist—and also a beautiful woman. He wanted to observe the boy's reaction to that, as well as his skill with a pencil.

Jimmy did show some special interest when they were

introduced. She was a stunning blonde who matched his
own six feet.

"Jimmy, this is Irma Leutij. Everyone calls her Dutch."

"Dutch," it repeated.

"Hello, Jimmy," she said in the husky voice she automatically used with attractive men. She calculated that
Jimmy was about five years her junior, wrong by a thousand millennia.

"We want to do an experiment with drawing," Grossbaum said. "Dutch is an artist."

The changeling knew the sense of the word "experiment," and was cautious. "Artist . . . experiment?"

"Do you like to draw?" Dutch said.

It shrugged in a neutral way.

Grossbaum snapped open his briefcase and took out two
identical drawing tablets and plain pencils. He gestured toward the breakfast-room table. "Let's sit over there."
Jimmy followed them and sat down next to Dutch. The
psychiatrist put open tablets and pencils in front of them
and sat down opposite.

"What shall I draw?" Dutch said. "Something simple?"

"Simple but precise. Maybe a cube in perspective."

She nodded and did it, nine careful lines in four seconds.

"Jimmy?" He pushed the pencil toward the boy.

The changeling was cautious, remembering people's reaction to the piano playing. It could have duplicated the
woman's actions exactly, but instead slowed down to a
crawl.

Grossbaum noted the speed. He also noted that Jimmy's
cube was a precise copy, even to its position on the page
and accidental overlap of two lines, less than a millimeter.
An expert artist could have done it if you asked for an exact copy. The slow compulsive precision would be appropriate for an idiot savant.

But as far as he could find, reading and talking to people, you had to be born with that condition—no normal

person had ever become an idiot savant from a blow on the head or a stroke.

"Let me draw him," Dutch said, "and see whether he draws me."

"It's an idea," he said doubtfully. The boy would probably just copy his own portrait, precisely.

Dutch turned the page back and picked up her pencil and stared at Jimmy.

It returned her stare, unblinking. She smiled and it smiled. When she began to draw, though, it didn't do anything but watch.

She finished the simple portrait in a couple of minutes, and turned the tablet around to show it to Jimmy.

The changeling studied the picture. The left ear was a half-inch low, and so was the chin. Having seen her use the eraser, it applied it and corrected her work, completely redrawing the whole ear and chin. It added a small mole she had missed.

"What is that all about?" Grossbaum said.

"Amazing. I made a slight mistake in proportion, and he corrected it. Added the mole I'd left off." She set the tablet down. "Do you spend a lot of time looking in the mirror, Jimmy?"

The changeling didn't quite understand the question, but nodded, and then shrugged.

Most people can't draw freehand circles. Dutch did three concentric ones, and then tapped on Jimmy's tablet.

Again it slowed down its natural impulse, and again made a perfect copy.

"Jimmy, do you know the word for those?" Grossbaum said.

"Drawing," it said.

Dutch tapped the center of the picture. "These?"

"Circle," it said. "Circles."

"I wonder how much he knows," she said, "and can't talk about."

"Well, he knows about sex, although he's never discussed it. They caught him with a nurse."

The changeling nodded. "Nurse Deborah. She is kind . . . *was* kind. To me."

"They let her go."

Dutch looked Jimmy up and down. "They should have paid her extra. Poor kid must be going crazy."

"Crazy." The changeling nodded emphatically. "They say I am. Crazy."

"Are you?" she whispered.

"I don't know." Jimmy pointed at Grossbaum. "He should know."

"I don't know what's wrong with you, Jimmy. You do some things so well."

"You should know," Jimmy repeated.

"Bruno . . ." She touched Grossbaum's arm. "I think you may be inhibiting him. Could you leave us alone for a while?"

He smiled psychiatrically. "Would you report . . . . everything to me?"

"You know me, Bruno." He did, in fact, very well.

He looked at his watch. "I do have a patient coming to the clinic at one. I could be back by two thirty."

"That should do."

He stood up. "Jimmy, I'll be gone for a while. Dutch will keep you company."

"Okay." The changeling understood part of the exchange. Dutch wanted to be alone with Jimmy. The way Nurse Deborah had.

After Grossbaum went out the front door, Dutch stared at the changeling for a long moment. "You don't remember what happened to you?"

"No." He returned her stare.

"How long ago was it?"

"One hundred eighty-three days."

"Do people who knew you before—your school-mates—do they come by to visit?"

"They . . . do. They did. No more." He looked at the ceiling. "Since sixty-two days."

"You're lonely." He shrugged. "I could be your friend, Jimmy."

"You could?"

She stood up and held out her hand. "Show me around the place? I want to see how the other half lives."

The changeling was confused. If she wanted the kind of union that Deborah had, she was going about it in an indirect way. It took her hand, though—she squeezed it, and the changeling returned the soft gesture—and followed her out of the breakfast nook. They walked around into the kitchen.

It was spotless and elegant. Tile and gleaming enamel everywhere; a constellation of stemware hanging over a bar, shining brass pots and pans on the wall. A Mexican cook, small and fat and timorous, cowering in the corner.

"*Buenos días,*" Dutch said. "*Jimmy me muestra la casa.*"

"*Bueno, bueno,*" she said, and turned her attention back to the clean pot she was scrubbing.

Through the kitchen into the dining room, heavy mahogany table under a glittering crystal chandelier, gas converted to electricity. Old paintings on the walls.

A new painting over the fireplace in the formal living room, of Mr. and Mrs. Berry standing on a lawn with a little boy and a Dalmatian. "Is that you?"

"No." The changeling thought. "Was who was me."

The furniture in this room was antique, very English, reupholstered in a lush red velvet. It didn't see much use.

"It's hard to believe there's a Depression on," she said. The changeling shrugged. It had only heard the word in its psychological sense.

The music room was cheerful, north light flooding through a picture window that looked down over a formal garden. There was a Steinway baby grand and a harp.

She plucked the deepest bass string. "Do you play these?"

"No." The harp was new; he'd never tried it.

"That's surprising. I should think they would make you take piano lessons, considering . . ."

The changeling sat down on the stool, uncovered the keys, and played the opening bars of "Appassionata."

Jimmy returned her stare. "I play this."

"I understand." It began to play soft chords in a strange rotation, not quite random. It didn't know the words for them, but they were alternating major and minor chords, wheeling on the flatted third. The effect was unearthly, not quite irritating.

She stood behind Jimmy and kneaded his well-muscled shoulders. "Could we . . . see your room?"

It stood up silently. This part it understood.

She walked demurely beside Jimmy, admiring his grace. "You get a lot of exercise?" He shrugged. "Swimming? Tennis?"

"I do those." Of course it could lie in bed all day and stay in perfect shape—or any shape it wanted. It was exactly the shape Jimmy had been when it dissected him.

They went through the library, yard after yard of books with uniform leather binding, into the main hall, parquet floor under a domed skylight of stained glass. Jimmy led her up wide curving steps to his floor, the third.

"Big place," she said. "Are you an only child?"

"Not a child." He opened the door to his bedroom.

"I suppose not." There was an incongruous hospital bed in one corner of the large room, and an elegant four-poster. It was still rumpled, the remains of breakfast on a serving tray. The wallpaper was beige silk. Double glass doors led to a balcony. She crossed the room and opened the doors and stood in the fresh breeze, salt air and flowers. Below her, two men were working on the formal gardens.

Behind her, Jimmy said, "Take off your clothes and put them on the dresser."

"We don't waste time, do we?" She stepped back into the room. "Why don't you take yours off first?" She went back to the door and locked it.

Jimmy pulled off his white cashmere sweater and the T-shirt beneath it, and stepped out of his sandals and white ducks. Hard muscles and a small penis, which evidently hadn't taken notice of her yet. He lay down on the bed.

She sat on the bed and ran a teasing finger down his chest and abdomen. When she touched his pubic hair, the penis sprang up like a tripped mousetrap.

"Oh my." It was a little larger than average, but not so big as to be intimidating. She held it, warm in her hand and rigid as a candle, and leaned over to lick it and take it in her mouth, very European.

"Take off your clothes," Jimmy said, "and put them on the dresser."

"Yes, sir." She smiled, realizing it was a stock phrase he must have learned from doctors examining him here. She undressed langorously, folding her clothes, carefully rolling her stockings. She turned her back to him when she stepped out of her knickers, discreetly applying saliva. She didn't expect the preliminaries to be elaborate.

She felt Jimmy's clasp on her waist and started to say something—and then there was a horrible stab of pain that forced the breath out of her. She gritted her teeth against screaming. "No, Jimmy! No! That's the wrong place!"

He withdrew obediently and she turned around, holding onto his penis, trying not to panic at the string of bloody mucus. "Let's wash this off and—"

He picked her up like a large doll and threw her onto the bed.

It was a good thing she'd left the glass doors open; the

gardeners heard her screams. Bad thing that she'd locked the door. By the time they had beaten it open, Jimmy was standing at the end of the bed, naked and unaroused, staring placidly at Dutch, who had crawled to the far corner of the large bed, cowering and whimpering and bleeding.

They knew better than to call the police. The one who spoke the best English called Mr. Berry at his law office while the others helped Jimmy dress and led him down to the pool. The Mexican cook and one of the male nurses tended to Dutch.

Mr. Berry showed up in ten minutes, bearing his most potent weapon, the checkbook. He listened to Dutch while she quieted her sobbing and haltingly described what had happened.

He was extremely sympathetic. Of course she was the victim here, but the law was complicated. Jimmy was, after all, a minor, and an unscrupulous lawyer might claim that she had seduced him.

She looked him in the eye, resolute through tears of pain. "I did start to seduce him. But then he raped me, two places. Should I go to the police?"

Mr. Berry asked the others to leave the room. In a half hour, an ambulance from a private hospital rolled up quietly to the service entrance, and Dutch was carried out over the gravel in Jimmy's old wheelchair.

The doctor who examined her had never seen a broken pubic bone before. He accepted her story about a bucking horse out of control, but suggested that during her confinement she might want to be examined for pregnancy, just in case.

- 9 -

apia, samoa, 2019

CNN runs a news special on 14 December 2019.

The camera pans along gentle surf, to rest on the artifact. It closes in during voice-over introduction:

MALLORY (VO)

Over the past several weeks, what began as a mystery has become an enigma. It started when a private marine research organization, Poseidon Projects, claimed salvage rights for an unclaimed wreck deep in the Tonga Trench a few hundred miles from this Samoan island.

With the help of Poseidon Projects, famous for having raised the *Titanic,* Atlantis used acres of floats to bring the "wreck" to within a few fathoms of the surface. They towed it with tugs to a holding location . . .

Archive footage of towing and parking the artifact.

MALLORY (VO, CONT.)

just offshore of Independent Samoa, where they had secured
a ninety-nine-year lease on a piece of undeveloped land,
which was being turned into a small research center . . .

Archive footage of the shrouded artifact being pulled
toward shore.

MALLORY (VO, CONT.)

built solely to investigate this *thing,* which was obviously
not the wreck of a ship.

Archive underwater footage: the shroud flaps teasingly,
to show the bright metal surface of the thing. A montage of
scenes while Poseidon engineers attach the towing collar
to the artifact, and start dragging it in.

MALLORY (VO, CONT.)

That cable is powered by this machine . . . capable of moving thousands of tons.
    But when this heavy thing—more massive than a Nau-
tilus submarine, but smaller than a delivery van—when it
came to the shoreline and dug into the sand . . .

Archive footage of the cable accident.

MALLORY (VO, CONT.)

it had met its match. One man was almost killed when the
cable broke.
    They had to find a way to move it the last hundred
yards, to the concrete pad that would become the floor of
their laboratory.

Screen fades to a live image of the thing with its rocket
attached.

MALLORY (VO, CONT.)

This is a self-contained Chinese booster rocket, normally used in the Glorious Wonder series, to carry up to a ton into low Earth orbit.

It's not going quite so far today.

Interior view: an improvised bunker a couple of hundred yards from the thing. You can see the artifact through a thick window. Mallory is sitting with two men, drinking coffee at a table made of a plank on stacked boxes.

MALLORY

We're going to watch this with Jack Halliburton and Russell Sutton, joint directors of Atlantis Associates.

I suppose this is going to be the shortest rocket trip in history.

JACK

There were some last century that only got an inch off the pad.

RUSS

This one's reliable as a Ford truck, though. Except . . .

MALLORY

What could go wrong?

JACK

We're not worried about the rocket. Just its attachment to the artifact.

RUSS

It's the irresistible force versus the immovable object.

JACK

We know the thing's mass; we know the properties of the
sand it's resting on. The rocket generates plenty enough
thrust to do the job.

RUSS

The only problem is the attachment between the rocket and
the artifact. If the collar that connects them breaks . . .
we'll need another approach.

MALLORY

And the rocket goes screaming into the center of town
there?

Telephoto zoom from the rocket's POV: straight into
Aggie Grey's.

JACK

No, there's an automatic shutoff if the rocket suddenly
feels no resistance. It might go fifty or a hundred feet.

MALLORY

But if it doesn't work?

JACK

Glorious Wonder carries a lot of insurance.

RUSS

A lot of people in Apia are off visiting relatives in the
country. I think I would be, too.

A loud whistle blows.

JACK

That's the ten-minute warning. You might want your cam-
eraman out of there.

Mallory stands up and looks through the glass.

MALLORY

They're gone. Just the camera attached to the booster.

RUSS

I hope it doesn't give you anything too interesting.

MALLORY

Have to agree, for once. . . . So this has to be some artifact from outer space.

RUSS

Well, you know as much about that as we do. It could possibly be the result of some natural process we've never encountered before.

JACK

Though its density makes that unlikely. Or inexplicable.

MALLORY

It's very ancient.

RUSS

The coral it was embedded in was old before there were any primates resembling humans.

MALLORY

So you don't think much of the "lost weapon" theory?

JACK

Bullshit.

RUSS

You do have to wonder how it got there, if it's an old Soviet or American device. If we'd just found it lying someplace, sure, that would be the first assumption. But it was *below* million-year-old coral.

MALLORY
So maybe they hid it there?

RUSS
You'd have to ask why. I'd want to hide it in my own country.

MALLORY
Have the Russians or Americans contacted you?

JACK
Sure.

RUSS
We don't want to talk about that. Yet.

Screen changes to an aerial view with countdown super-imposed. A 360-degree pan shows all the military helicopters watching. At ten seconds, it zooms in on the artifact. A laconic voice offscreen counts down.

VOICE (OFF)
Ten.

JACK
(Rising)
About time.

The three of them move to the window to watch. A split screen adds an aerial view. The voice counts down to zero.

The Chinese rocket ignites, its exhaust churning billows of steam in the sea behind it. For long seconds, as the noise increases to a banshee scream, it doesn't move. Then the artifact lurches and moves slowly, then faster, up the guide rails toward the metal cradle that will be its resting place. A camera by the cradle shows it fall into place with a jarring crash, just as the rocket goes silent.

RUSS

Textbook. Those Chinese are pretty damn good.

JACK

Glad they're on our side. For the time being.

san guillermo, california, 1932

The Berrys had to admit that Jimmy was unmanageable, and quietly had him committed to St. Anthony's, a private insane asylum.

It was a valuable change of venue. The drugs the changeling was compelled to take by mouth or injection were metabolically insignificant. The shock treatments, where they wrapped you in wet sheets and splashed you with buckets of ice water, were gently stimulating to a creature who could live on Mercury or Pluto.

But the changeling was surrounded by extremes of human behavior, in both the patients and their attendants, that it would never have seen at the mansion. It learned more in its first week than it had in months of cossetted coddling.

The guards were brutal and stupid. If the changeling did anything outside of a certain range of behaviors, they would wrap it in a straitjacket and throw it in the rubber room.

It came to understand coercion and confinement. It could have slipped out of the straitjacket, prefiguring Plasticman, and kicked down the door like Superman. But there would be no education in that. It submitted to beatings and rapes—rich pretty boy who can't tell on you. It learned something like sympathy for Dutch, though pain was just input to it, and humiliation was not yet in its emotional range.

It listened to the other patients when they had social time together. That it responded in monosyllables, sometimes bizarre, went unnoticed. In fact, it was getting a slow, and somewhat skewed, version of the learning process that a human child would go through. It "grew up" by observation and assimilation.

A large part of the puzzle was human linguistics, and the ultimately related problem of mimicking human thought processes. It took two years, but by the time "Jimmy" was twenty, no one was beating or raping him. He was moved into a clean, quiet part of St. Anthony's, and after awhile was allowed to have visitors.

His parents were so glad to see him acting "normal" that they overlooked the fact that he didn't act like Jimmy at all. He was released into their care.

The changeling had assimilated a wide range of behaviors, and a fairly sophisticated sense of which was appropriate at which time. To the Berrys, their son had become quiet and dignified and perhaps a little shy, which was a real advance over the brutal sodomist they'd tendered to St. Anthony's.

The changeling played piano for hours at a time, and it also spent a long time just watching the sea. It knew it was being observed and evaluated, this time by amateurs, and could deliver a nuanced performance.

It had learned how to simulate the behavior of a teenager who had been troubled, but now was on the road to recov-

ery. It had seen that that was the only way to get out of St.
Anthony's and move on to the next stage of development.

This was the most complex creature it had ever imitated. Its successes gave it a pleasure like joy.

apia, samoa, 2020

Once the artifact was seated on its pad, a gang of workers paid extra for speed and overtime began building the laboratory around it. The government moved in before the dry-wall was up.

Halliburton and Russell had come down from their hotel lunch to take a look at the building's progress. They crossed over the moat on a makeshift bamboo bridge and let a supervisor show them around the place. He claimed they could begin moving in equipment in four days; the trim and painting would be done in five. That was better than they'd contracted for.

When they started to go back, there was a man in a white tropical suit waiting on the other side of the moat, an uncomfortable-looking guard at his side.

"Mr. Halliburton, he—"

Halliburton cut him off with a gesture. "Who are you and who are you working for?"

"Dr. Franklin Nesbitt," he said, "chief of NASA Advanced Planning." He was a tanned muscular man with close-cropped white hair who stood absolutely still, except for offering his hand.

Russell took it. "We've had correspondence."

"Of a sort," Nesbitt said. "You basically said that whatever I was selling, you weren't buying."

"That's still true," Halliburton said. "You have no jurisdiction here."

"Nor claim any. But I have an offer you might find interesting."

"No, you don't. You've come a long way for nothing."

"Jack," Russell said, "we can at least be civil." To Nesbitt: "They're serving tea at the hotel. It would be nice to talk to somebody who isn't a reporter." He called ahead while they walked to the Jeep, and by the time they got to the hotel their private dining room was set with crisp linens and heavy silver.

An Irish woman brought in tea and trays of trimmed sandwiches and pastries.

"My indulgence," Russell said. "Jack is more like beer and potato chips."

"Total barbarian," Halliburton said, snagging a watercress sandwich as he sat down. "So what do you have that's so interesting? What do you have that's *interesting* at all?

The other two men waited while the woman poured tea and left. "General or specific?" Nesbitt said.

"General," Russell said.

He rubbed his forehead, and for a moment you could see the seven time zones of jet lag.

"Basically, and expecting initial rejection, I'm offering you our expertise for free."

"Right about that," Jack said. "The rejection."

"If we did seek outside help," Russ said, "why should it be you rather than the Europeans or Japanese?"

"We're older and larger—not in terms of money, true, but as a research organization."

"We are doing research here," Jack said, peering doubtfully into a sandwich, "but we're primarily a for-profit organization. One that doesn't have the faintest idea of what it will find. But we have a good chance that it will be earth-shaking.

"I've sunk most of a large fortune into this. I took on Dr. Sutton and his team because I felt I could trust them. In exchange for keeping their work secret, they are limited partners as well as salaried employees: if things go well, they all get a small percentage of what should be an astronomical return. If there's any leak, anything, they all get nothing."

"We're prepared to allow you to keep all financial returns from anything our people discover."

"People. That's the problem, Dr. Nesbitt. As an organization, NASA can promise anything it wants. But if one of your *people* stumbles on an antigravity machine, I think he or she might trade a job with NASA for limitless wealth."

Nesbitt nodded amicably, tasted his tea, and sifted some sugar into it. "Your investment is, what, about a third of a billion eurodollars?"

"Close enough."

"Then let me go from the general to the specific. We're prepared to match your funds. Wipe the slate clean."

"In exchange for?" Russ asked.

"A team of twelve researchers who would clear every publication with you, and also assign any present or future profits to you." He looked at Jack over the rim of his teacup and sipped. "Up in my room I have a long contract to that effect, which I'm told covers everything. Also, dossiers of the twelve."

"Including you?"

"I wish, but no. I'm just an administrator who loves science. I don't think you'd be impressed by my physics B.S. from Arkansas."

Jack smiled. "Maybe more by that than by your MBA

from Harvard." He tapped his hearing aid. "Wonderful machines, these."

Nesbitt didn't blink. "Is it tempting?"

"Of course it is," Jack said harshly.

"Jack, we agreed from the get-go. No government. No military applications."

"We'd be amenable to that. It's not what we're looking for."

"What *are* you looking for?"

"Half our team are exobiologists. It's not so much a 'what' . . . as a 'who.'"

woods hole, massachusetts, 1935

The Berrys were surprised when their son didn't want to go to Juilliard, which they certainly could have afforded. The changeling was interested in music, but its interest was not human, and it could be indulged anywhere. It could sit alone in the dark and play, in its mind, fantastic compositions that no human could play. With two extra imaginary hands, it could play a Bach fugue forward and backward at the same time. It often did things like that in the hours it had to feign sleep.

All it really knew of its origin was that it had come from the sea, and before taking human form it remembered having been for centuries a great white shark and a killer whale. There were other manifestations before that, and though the memories were vague, it seemed they had all been sea creatures of some sort.

Were there a lot of its kind? There was no way to tell. Others who had taken human form could pass for human indefinitely, appearing to age at a normal rate, "dying," and resuming life as someone else.

Its readings in psychology indicated that its transition, while it was learning the difference between killer whale behavior and human behavior, cannot have been common. There were tales of "feral children," supposedly raised by wolves or other animals, who might fit the pattern. He had plenty of time to investigate that.

There was no compelling reason for someone like it to become human. They could still be white sharks or killer whales—or coral reefs or rocks, if that made them content. The sea was a good hiding place.

So it decided that oceanography would be a reasonable place to start. If that didn't pan out, it could study some other discipline, switch identity and do it again and again. Time was of no importance.

The leading edge of oceanographic research was Woods Hole, a new, privately endowed institution. It was in Massachusetts, so the changeling applied to several places in that commonwealth. Turned down by both Harvard and MIT, possibly because most of its high school courses had been taught by home tutors, it wound up going to the University of Massachusetts, majoring in oceanography. Woods Hole did take graduate students from there as summer interns, and that was its eventual plan.

Its academic performance was predictably irregular; it aced anything that had to do with logic or memorization, but didn't do well in courses like literature or philosophy. It saw that many other students were that way, and most of them were shy loners, too.

After part of one semester of dormitory life, it moved out and got an apartment in town. That minimized the time and energy devoted to maintaining the Jimmy Berry façade, and gave it freedom to practice being other people, which it assumed would someday be a useful talent. After careful practice, it could become a different person of the same size in about ten minutes. Smaller or larger took twice as long or more, and was more painful and tiring. Once it became two children, though one had only average intelligence, and the other was dim-witted.

It had a cautious social life as Jimmy, going to a dance or the movies once or twice a month, always with a different girl. There was no shortage of dates for a handsome older California boy with money and family. There was no record of Jimmy's peculiar past in regard to the opposite sex, and in 1935, sex never became an issue on the first and only date.

(The changeling realized it would sooner or later have to learn sexual etiquette, but decided to put it off until later. There was almost no reliable information on the subject in America at that time; people in movies and books made obvious sexual overtures, but never followed through. It knew that "Take off your clothes and put them on the dresser" would only work under certain conditions. You did have to wind up alone and in a state of undress together, but how you got there from the passionate kiss or arched eyebrow was a mystery.)

So its course was set: four years of work that shined in science and mathematics and language, but little else, which was good protective coloration, and then a couple of years on a master's, then a doctorate and, eventually, Woods Hole.

It did get to work at Woods Hole for two summers, sailing the ketch *Atlantis* as a graduate intern. Every now and then, on days off, it would go to a deserted cove and spend an hour changing into a dolphin, to get back to the sea in a more personal, familiar way. These cold rich waters were another world from its Pacific home, and it learned a lot, some of which would direct its own research.

But before the doctorate came, war intervened.

The changeling saw people being drafted and assigned to whatever kind of job and place the military desired. But people who joined up were allowed to choose, within reason.

It wanted to study the Pacific, suspecting its origin must be somewhere out there. Danger wasn't a factor; as far as it knew, it couldn't die. So it joined the Marines, and asked for a Pacific assignment.

To most graduate students, it would be an annoyance and delay—not to mention the possibility of being shot or succumbing to some tropical disease. But to the changeling, time was just time, meaningless. Every new experience had been useful.

It didn't tell the Marine Corps about college, which probably would have led to a desk job. So instead of being a marine science Marine, it became a plain foot soldier, grunt, jarhead. Pearl Harbor was a year away.

13

EURASIA, PRE-CHRISTIAN ERA

The changeling wasn't alone on the planet. There was another creature, unrelated, who had lived on Earth longer than he could remember; who had lived thousands of lives, disappearing when he got too old, to reappear as a young man.

He was always a man, and usually a brute.

Call him the chameleon: an alpha male who never had sons, unless an adulterer cooperated. Unlike the changeling, he did have DNA, but it was alien; he could no more reproduce with a human than he could with a rock or a tree.

Also unlike the changeling, he seemed to be stuck in human form. It never occurred to him to wonder why this was so. But it didn't occur to him for tens of millennia—not until the Renaissance—that he might have come from another world. He assumed that he was some sort of demon or demigod, but early on realized that it was a mistake to advertise the fact. He couldn't be killed, not even by fire, but he did feel pain, and he felt it profoundly, in ways a human never could. At low levels it was pleasure, and he sought out varieties of that. But hanging and crucifixion were experiences he never wanted to do a second time. To be burned to ashes was agony beyond belief, and reconstructing yourself afterward was worse.

So after a few experiences that probably helped establish the myth of the vampire, the chameleon settled into routine existence, seriatim lives that were fairly ordinary.

He was usually a warrior, and of course a good one. Sometimes his career was cut short by being chopped in two or trampled or drawn and quartered. In the chaos of battle he could usually find a few minutes of darkness, to pull himself together, and then go off in search of another life. When his death and interment were witnessed by many, he had to fake a grave robbery or, reluctantly, a miracle.

In ancient times, he occasionally wound up being a warlord or even a king, by dint of superiority in battle and an instinct to advance. But that was always more trouble than it was worth, and made it almost impossible to arrange a private death and resurrection.

Like the changeling, he was a quick study, but he was a sensualist, indifferent to knowledge. All he needed to know in order to survive, his body already knew. The rest was just for maximizing pleasure and minimizing pain that was too great to enjoy.

He picked the right side in the Peloponnesian Wars, and went through several generations as a Spartan. Then he joined Alexander's army and wound up settling in Persia. He spent a century or so as a Parthian before he eased into the Roman sphere.

It was as a Parthian that he heard the story of Jesus Christ, which interested him. Killed in public and then resurrected, he was evidently a relative. He would keep an eye out for him.

The chameleon entered the history books only once,

and it was because of his interest in Christianity. In the third century, in Narbonne, he was a captain of the Praetorian Guard, and was a little too open in his curiosity about the fellow immortal. An enemy reported him, and Diocletian had him executed as a closet Christian, by archers. But his girlfriend, Irene, wouldn't leave him alone to die, and he "miraculously" recovered. Diocletian subsequently had him beaten to a pulp by soldiers with iron rods, whereupon Irene let him stay dead long enough to turn into a young soldier and escape, leaving behind the legend of Saint Sebastian.

He worked as a farmhand and soldier in Persia until 313, when the Edict of Milan made it safe to be a Christian. When he heard about that, he dropped his plow and walked to Italy, robbing people along the way, just enough to get by.

He didn't like being so close to authority, so he went back to France and shuffled between Gallia and Germania for awhile, keeping an eye out for other immortals. Things got ugly in the 542 plague, so he made his way over to England as part of the Saxon invasion.

England seemed more congenial than the Continent, as the Roman empire collapsed into chaos, and the chameleon lived many lifetimes there, first as soldier and farmer, but eventually learning a variety of trades: blacksmith, cobbler, butcher.

In 1096, he went back to soldiering, following the Crusades down to Jerusalem and beyond. He fought on both sides for a century or so, and eventually, as an Arab, went back to Egypt and started walking south along the Nile.

Making himself dark and tall, he became a Masai warrior, and it was the best life he'd yet encountered: lots of women and great food and, in exchange for a battle every now and then, sleep late in the morning and hunt for game with spears, which he enjoyed. He did that for several hundred years, still keeping an eye out for Christ or another relative, probably white.

But the first white people who showed up were bearing guns and chains. He could have resisted and conveniently "died," but he'd heard about the New World and was curious.

The ride over was about the worst thing he'd ever experienced—right up there with being boiled in oil or flayed to death. He lay in chains for weeks, stuffed in an airless hold with hundreds of others, many of whom died and lay rotting until someone got around to throwing them overboard.

It was a real chore. He thought about just bursting his chains, at night, and diving into the sea. He'd done that before, in Phoenicia, and swam dozens of leagues to shore. But Africa, after a few days under sail, would be months of swimming, so he'd just be trading one agony for another.

So he allowed himself to be carried to America, and in a way enjoyed being put up on the block—he was by far the healthiest specimen off the ship, since metabolism was irrelevant to him, other than as a source of pleasure. The Georgia man who bought him, though, was cruel. He liked to whip the new boys into submission, so at the first opportunity, the chameleon killed him, and then turned into a white man and walked away.

That was an amusing time. His version of English was almost a thousand years old, so he had to masquerade as an idiot while he learned how to communicate. He walked north, again robbing and murdering for sustenance, when he knew he wouldn't be caught.

He kept moving north until he got to Boston, and settled in there for a few hundred years.

"Little green men," Halliburton said, staring at Nesbitt. "You've been reading the tabloids."

"The thing is at least a million years old," Russell said.

Nesbitt nodded. "But it's obviously a *made* thing."

"Maybe not," Russell said. "It could be the product of some exotic natural force."

"Assume not, though. If some intelligence made it a million or some millions of years ago . . . well, we can't say anything about their motivation, but if they're like humans at all, there's a good chance the thing is inhabited in some sense."

"Still alive after a million years," Halliburton said, stacking up two little egg salad sandwiches.

"We're still alive after more than a million years."

"Speak for yourself, spaceman."

"I mean humanity, since we evolved from *Homo erectus.* We've been traveling through space in a closed environment, growing from a few individuals to seven billion."

"It's a point," Russ said. "That thing is a closed environment, in spades."

"Your eight billion little green men are going to be *tiny* green men."

"Well, it's probably not full of little hamsters in space suits," Nesbitt said. "It may not be inhabited in the sense of carrying individuals. It could have some equivalent of sperm and eggs, or spores—or it could be basically information, like a von Neumann machine."

"Oh, yeah. I sort of remember that," Russ said.

"I don't," Halliburton said. "German?"

"Hungarian, I think. It's an early nanotech idea. You send little spaceships out to various stars. Each one is a machine, programmed to seek out materials and build two duplicates of itself, which would take off for two other stars."

"Yeah," Russ said, "and after a few million years, every planet in the galaxy would have been visited by one of these machines. The fact that there obviously isn't one on Earth is offered as proof that there's no other space-faring life in this galaxy."

"That's a stretch."

Russ shrugged. "Well, the galaxy is thousands of millions of years old. The logic is that the project would be relatively simple to set up, and then would take care of itself."

"But you see the hole in that logic," Nesbitt said.

"Sure," Jack said. "I see where you're going. The argument assumes we would know the machine was here."

"It might well be hidden," Nesbitt said, "hidden in a place where it wouldn't be found except by other creatures with high technology."

Jack rubbed the stubble on his chin. "You're right there. No pearl diver's gonna find that thing and bring it up."

"And bringing it out of that environment into this one might be a signal that life on the planet has evolved sufficiently to initiate the next course of action."

"Make contact with us."

"Maybe. Or maybe eliminate us as rivals." He looked at both of them in turn. "What if a creature like Hitler had started the project? Genghis Khan? And they were at least *humans*. There are plenty of animals who simplify their existence by eliminating their *own* kind who threaten their primacy. We ourselves have destroyed whole species—smallpox and malaria—for our health."

"It's far-fetched," Halliburton said.

"But even if the probability was near zero, the stakes are so high that the problem should be addressed."

"Hm." Jack tapped his teacup with his spoon and the woman appeared. "Sun's over the yardarm, Colleen." She nodded and slipped away. "So how are your twelve people supposed to save humanity from alien invasion?"

"We discussed moving the whole operation to the lunar surface."

"Holy cow," Russ said.

"It would make the Apollo program look like a science fair project," Nesbitt said. "No one has a booster that can orbit one-tenth that thing's mass. And we couldn't send it up piecemeal."

Jack squinted, doing numbers. "I don't think it could be done at all. Mass of the booster goes up with the square of the mass of the payload. Strength of materials. Goddamn thing'd collapse."

"And you see the implications of that. Someone got that thing here from a lot farther away than the moon."

"That's still just an assumption," Russ said, "and I still lean toward a natural explanation. It probably was formed here on Earth, by some exotic process."

Nesbitt's temper rose for the first time. "Pretty damned exotic! Three times as dense as plutonium—and that's if it were the same stuff through and through! What if the goddamned thing's hollow? What's the shell made of?"

"Neutronium," Russ said. "Degenerate matter. That's my guess, if it's hollow."

"Baloney-um is what we called it in school," Jack said. "Make up the properties first; find the element later."

Colleen rolled in a cart with various glasses and bottles. "Gentlemen?" The NASA man stuck to tea, Russ took white wine, Jack a double Bloody Mary.

"So what does your dynamic dozen propose?" Jack asked as the woman left the room.

He leaned forward. "Isolation. More profound than extreme biohazard. The environment the military uses in developing . . ."

"Nanoweapons," Russ supplied. "Of course we're not *actually* developing them. Just learning how to defend ourselves against them, if somebody else does."

"Well, it's not just the military. Everybody developing nanotech uses similar safeguards to keep the little things isolated.

"We'd cover the lab building your crew is finishing now with an outside layer, sort of an exoskeleton. Basically a seamless metal room almost the same size as the lab. To enter, you have to go through an airlock. The atmospheric pressure inside is slightly lower than outside. The airlock's also a changing room; nobody ever wears street clothes into the work area."

"I don't think our people would enjoy working under those constraints," Russ said. "Feels like government interference."

"You could also see it as taking advantage of the government. We give you the functional equivalent of lunar isolation—air and water recycled, power sources independent of the outside."

"Plus getting back all the capital we've put in, to date?" Jack said, looking at Russ.

"That's right," Nesbitt said. Russ nodded almost imperceptibly.

Jack squeezed some more lime into his Bloody Mary. "I

guess we'll look into your contract. Have our lawyers look into it. Maybe make a counteroffer."

"Fair enough." Nesbitt stood. "I'll go up and fetch it. I think you'll find it clear and complete."

What they wouldn't find was a little detail about the "independent power source": As a public health measure for the planet, its plutonium load could be command-detonated from Washington, turning the whole island into radioactive slag.

amherst, massachusetts, february 1941

The changeling could have avoided the draft by simulating any number of maladies or deficiencies; one out of three American men were rejected. Like a lot of men, for various reasons, he avoided it by joining the Marines.

The Corps was not enthusiastic about recruits like Jimmy Berry, no matter how good they would look on a recruiting poster. He was tall, strong, handsome, healthy, and obviously from a rich family. He was probably lying about not having gone to college, to get out of being assigned to Officer Candidate School. He would be hard to break, which would make it that much harder to break the other shitbirds. And they had to be broken before they could be built anew as Marines.

They called him Pretty Boy and Richie Rich. But he was a little more of a problem than they'd anticipated. On their way to their first day in barracks, a big drill sergeant called him out of ranks—"You march like a fuckin' girl"—and made him do fifty push-ups, which he did without breaking a sweat. Then the sergeant sat on his back and said, "Fifty more." He did these with no obvious effort.

So the first night, the drill sergeant organized a "blanket party" for the annoying shitbird. He got three more big sergeants and three big corporals to throw a blanket over the sleeping Jimmy and beat some respect into him.

It was two in the morning and the changeling, mentally playing the piano with four hands, heard the seven tiptoeing down the aisle of the barracks, but dismissed the sound as unimportant. Nothing here could hurt it.

But when the blanket suddenly was wrapped tightly around it and someone struck it with a club, it did fight back for less than a second. Then it figured out the situation and was totally passive.

In less than a second, though, it had broken a wrist and two thumbs, and had kicked one man across the room, to get a concussion against the opposite wall.

One of the survivors kept swinging the club at Jimmy's inert form, until the others hustled him out. Then the recruits, by ones and twos, came over to see what damage had been done.

The changeling manufactured bruises and cuts and released an appropriate amount of blood. It was a ghastly sight in the dim light from the latrine. "We have to get him to the infirmary," someone said.

"No," the changeling said.

The overhead lights snapped on. "What the fuck is going on in here?" the drill sergeant roared. He was wearing clean pressed fatigues, but the shirt was only buttoned halfway, and his left hand hung useless at his side, the thumb turning purple and blue. "You shitbirds get back to your bunks."

Two noncoms sidled by him to the unconscious one lying by the wall. He moaned when they picked him up and hustled him away.

The drill sergeant stood in front of Jimmy, inspecting

his bruises and cuts and two black eyes. "What happened to you, recruit?"

"What do you think happened, Sergeant?"

"Looks to me like you fell out of your bunk."

"That must be it, Sergeant."

"Will you need medical help?"

"No, Sergeant."

"LOUDER!" he screamed.

"NO, SERGEANT!" The changeling matched his tone and accent perfectly.

"Good." He wheeled and marched back toward the door. "You shitbirds didn't see nothin'. Get to sleep. Formation at 0500." He snapped off the lights.

After a minute of silence, people started to whisper. The changeling sat upright in its bunk. Someone brought him aspirin and a cup of water.

"Where'd you learn to fight like that?"

"Fell out of bed," it said. "So did the sergeant."

That was repeated all over the camp, especially when the next morning they had a new drill sergeant, and the old one was nowhere to be seen. They gave the changeling the nickname "Joe Louis."

The new drill sergeant was not inclined to single out Joe Louis. But he didn't favor him, either. He had eight weeks to turn all these pathetic civilians into Marines.

For the first week they did little other than run, march, and suffer through calisthenics, from five in the morning until chow call at night—and sometimes a few more miles' run after dinner, just to settle their stomachs. The changeling found it all fairly restful, but observed other people's responses to the stress and did an exactly average amount of sweating and groaning. At the rifle range, it aimed to miss the bull's-eye most of the time, without being conspicuously bad.

It almost made a mistake at the gas-mask training "final exam." One at a time, the recruits were led into a darkened room where they had to wait until the gas-masked sergeant within asked you for your name, rank, and serial number. You gasped them out and then quickly put on your gas mask, saluted, and left.

The changeling walked into the dark room and took a breath, and was almost overcome with an inchoate rush of nostalgia. It had forgotten, after a million years, that its home planet's atmosphere was similar to this, about 10 percent chlorine. The smell was delightful.

The sergeant with the gas mask and clipboard let it wait for about two minutes. Then he turned a bright flashlight into its eyes. "Are you *breathing,* Private Berry?"

"No, sir."

"Don't call me 'sir'; I work for a living." He kept the flashlight steady for another minute. "I'll be goddamned. You swim a lot, Private Berry?"

"Yes, Sergeant."

"Underwater, I guess?"

"Yes, Sergeant."

He paused for another thirty seconds and shook his head. "*Dang!* Give me your name, rank, and serial number, and put the mask on." The changeling did. "Now get the hell outta here before you puke all over me."

The changeling went through the door where the EXIT sign glowed dim green, enjoying the last whiff of chlorine trapped inside the mask.

Outside, twenty men were sprawled around in various attitudes of misery, coughing and retching. There were spatters and pools of vomit everywhere. The changeling ordered his stomach to eject its contents.

A friend, Hugh, came over to where he was kneeling and pounded him on the back. "Geez Louise, Jimmy. You musta held your breath three minutes."

The changeling coughed in what it hoped was an appropriate way. "Swim a lot underwater," it said breathlessly. "God, don't that stuff smell awful?"

But the memory of nostalgia was strong. Where on Earth could it have lived, where chlorine was so concentrated in the air? Nowhere on the surface. That would be a good research project, after the war.

A lot of their training had a quality of improvisation, since much of the material of war had already left for the Pacific. So they learned how to work with tanks by advancing in formation behind a dumptruck carrying TANK signs wired to its front and rear. They carried World War I Springfield rifles and practiced with them on the range.

Hand-to-hand combat training was a ballet of restraint for the changeling, who had been a remorseless predator for most of its life. It allowed the other trainees to throw it around and simulate dangerous blows. When it was *its* turn to be aggressive, it spared everyone's lives, knowing it could rip off one person's leg and beat everybody else to death with it.

It was properly respectful to the sergeants, and studied their individual ways with the men. Those techniques were more interesting than the coercive strategies of college professors, who presumably had intellectualized the process. The sergeants instinctively reached back into primate behavior, becoming the dominant male by shoving and punching and screaming. Anyone who resisted them was punished—immediately and then again later, with assignments, "shit details," that were degrading and exhausting.

The changeling did its share of those—cleaning toilets with a toothbrush and pulling twenty-four-hour kitchen police—not, of course, because it had *actually* lost its temper or misread the sergeants' desires. Too much self-control would make it conspicuous. It had to play the game.

apia, samoa, 2020

Russ and Jack, especially, agonized over the contract, distrusting the government on principle, but unable to deny either the financial argument or the scientific one. They faxed it to their Chinese and stateside lawyers, and they agreed that it was what it claimed to be.

They signed it on Friday, and on Saturday morning their work crew was suddenly tripled, cargo helicopters thrumming in hourly with the prefabricated materials for their laboratory's exoskeleton.

The carpenters and painters who were putting the finishing touches on the lab were nonplussed, to say the least. The elegant heat exchange system was carved away and replaced with heavy-duty machinery. The carefully glazed windows that looked out on the ocean now had a view of plain steel plate.

The moat was filled with fast-setting plastic concrete that supported the footers for the new metal walls and roof.

NASA dug a new moat, wider and deeper and open to the sea: the lab became an artificial island fortress.

The twelve scientists, seven women and five men, were sensitive to turf. They never approached the artifact unaccompanied by the original team; they spent hours every day comparing notes with them, planning out approaches. It was a congenial, collegial mix, everyone linked by passionate curiosity.

None of the NASA scientists knew that the SNAP-30 reactor had been modified so that it could function as a bomb. Some of the mass that they thought was shielding was actually extra plutonium. Nesbitt had known, but his first allegiance was to the NSA, "No Such Agency," not NASA.

And he was no longer in the picture.

The NASA team was "all chiefs, no Indians," officially, but their nominal leader was Jan Dagmar, a white-haired exobiologist old enough to remember the first moon landing and young enough to go cave-diving for fun. She had advanced degrees in both physical and life sciences, on top of a B.A. in philosophy.

Her eleven compatriate scientists worked daily with the members of the original Poseidon team, and they worked together with them away from the site, too, comparing notes, planning out approaches. They all lived together in the Vaiala Beach Cottages, where number 7 was designated the common room, a big coffee urn always going, refrigerator and pantry full of food for thought.

Russell spent a lot of time in *fale* number 7, and had moved into number 5, leaving the fancy suite at Aggie Grey's, a ten-minute bicycle ride away. Jack stayed at his, saying he could think better in air-conditioning.

They all agreed, although Jack was characteristically impatient, to wait until the isolated environment was finished before starting their tests. So they had eight days of brainstorming their approaches. Equipment and supplies came in daily from Honolulu, Sydney, Tokyo.

The night before the first tests, Russ called Jan and they met at the rocks overlooking the site to share a bottle of the best champagne he could find in Samoa. The relationship that was developing between them was not exactly romantic in a conventional sense, but they had discovered in each other a kind of romantic reverence toward nature and science that went back to childhood. They had both wanted to be astronauts as children; Russell had actually been accepted as a mission specialist when the *Challenger* disaster put everything on hold, and he switched over to the doomed Mars missions.

They shared champagne and a pair of powerful binoculars, studying the crescent moon in the clear dark sky. The nightglass stabilizers hummed and clicked while he looked down the terminator edge and named the craters— Aristarchus, Messier, Globinus, Hell. "That's a deep one," he said.

She laughed. "I used to know some of the names. My dad had a telescope."

"You said they moved down to Florida to watch the moon rockets."

She nodded in the darkness. "And all the other ones, the shuttle and all. But the Apollo rockets were the biggies— Saturn V's. Deafening: you could feel the noise rattling your bones. And dazzling, the one they did at night."

"That was the first one?"

"No, the last. The first one was Apollo 11, in 1969."

"Oh, yeah. I slept through it, my mother said. I was not quite two."

"I was twelve," she said, refilling her glass. "The first time I ever tasted champagne. Still makes me think of it."

They stared out over the project into the night, in companionable silence. The dim yellow security lights at-

tracted bugs; small birds swooped out of the darkness.
"This may be even bigger," she said. "It almost certainly
will be."

"Even if it turns out to be homegrown," he said, "we'll
have to totally rethink physics and chemistry."

"Chemistry *is* physics," she said automatically. "Tell
you what. If this thing turns out to be terrestrial in origin,
I'll buy you the most expensive bottle of champagne in the
Honolulu duty-free."

They clicked glasses. "If not, I'll buy you two."

"What, you're that skeptical?"

"Hell, no; I agree with you. And I've got an expense
account."

A test area, about four inches square, was marked off by
tape on the artifact's side, about midway. An electron microscope and its positron equivalent could be easily
brought to bear on the area. They built a forced-draft hood
over it, to suck away and analyze poisonous vapors.

First they measured it passively. It had an albedo of exactly 1.0—it reflected all light that fell on it, in every wavelength. Optically, it presented a perfect curve, down to
1/200 of a wave of mercury light, a surface impossible for
a human optician to duplicate.

Although it looked like metal, it felt like silk; it wasn't
cold to the touch. It was not a conductor of heat, nor, as far
as passive testing could tell, of electricity.

Then they went to work, trying to dent it. Scrape it, cor-
rode it, chip it, burn it—do anything to make the artifact
acknowledge the existence of humanity.

When it was still underwater, Poseidon divers had tried
a diamond-tipped drill on it, to no effect. But now they
rolled in a huge mining drill: it used a 200-horsepower
electric motor to spin its diamond tip at 10,000 r.p.m., with
more than a ton of force behind it.

The scream it made was too much for the scientists' earplugs; they had to rig a remote control for it. At the maximum push, just before the diamond tip evaporated, it shattered all the useless windows and ruined the positron microscope beyond repair.

The electron microscope worked, though, and all it showed was a film of oxides from the metallic part of the ruined drill bit. When they cleaned that off, even at the highest magnification there was no difference between the test square and the undrilled surface next to it: a perfect mirror.

Many of Jimmy's boot camp compadres steamed across the Pacific with him, to join the Fourth Marine Regiment in Shanghai. They arrived in November 1941, and barely had time to get their land legs before they were ordered to sail again, this time for the Philippines, assigned to provide beach defense for Corregidor.

The naval command knew it was only a matter of time before Japan attacked American forces in the Pacific. America had severed trade ties with Japan in July, and frozen her assets in American banks. The Navy and the Army set about redistributing their meager forces to places that seemed most vulnerable to attack. That included the Philippines, which blocked Japanese access to the East Indies.

The Fourth Regiment set up shop in Corregidor and sent a detachment, including Jimmy, south to the small base at Bataan. They called it a "shit assignment," one step farther away from the amenities of Manila, but they didn't know how terminally bad it was going to become.

When the Japanese hit Pearl Harbor on the morning of the seventh (which was the eighth on Jimmy's side of the international date line), there was an immediate air raid alert in Manila and American fighters and bombers scrambled into the air to do battle. The timing was off, though; there were no Japanese in sight. They landed again, and when, a few hours later, the Japanese *did* come screaming out of the sun, there was no warning for the planes on the ground.

Bataan and Corregidor were constantly bombed and strafed, with little or no help from the air. Meanwhile, Japanese land forces were coming ashore to the north and south, in Luzon and Mindanao.

The original War Plan, before Pearl Harbor, had called for all American forces to go south to Bataan, and maintain a holding action there, delaying the Japanese advance into the East Indies. Instead, General MacArthur moved his forces up to meet the Japanese where they were landing.

MacArthur had at his disposal 120,000 Filipino troops, most of them reservists who had never fired a shot, and one-tenth that many Americans. They had the Japanese outnumbered but not outgunned, and the defensive move was an unmitigated disaster. He went back to the original plan on 27 December, and within a week all the northern Luzon forces were sharing Bataan's limited resources with Jimmy. They were soon joined by thousands of Filipino civilians, fleeing the invaders. In two weeks, everyone's food ration was cut in half; in February, they were reduced to a thousand calories per day, mostly from rice. They got a little tough meat from the slaughter of starving horses and mules.

Defeat inevitable, MacArthur and other top brass were evacuated to the safety of Australia, while the Japanese continued to pound the Bataan Peninsula.

In April, the Japanese ground troops moved down to take over. On the eighth, General Wainwright concentrated all his viable forces for a last-ditch effort on Corregidor, and on the nineteenth formally surrendered the starvelings left behind on Bataan.

The changeling had watched this all with interest. It had been killed twice by bombs, but in the chaos it was easy to reassemble at night and show up as a lucky survivor. It had mimicked the weight loss of the men around it, Jimmy going from a healthy 180 pounds to a haggard 130.

When they heard about the surrender, some of the men decided to chance it and try to swim across two miles of shark-infested water to Corregidor. The changeling could have done that with ease, of course, temporarily becoming one of the infesting sharks, but decided against it. Corregidor was doomed, too; why bother?

His friend Hugh, who had been with him since boot camp, told Jimmy that he was tempted to swim even though he knew he wouldn't make it; he couldn't swim two miles even if he were in good shape, and the water a placid swimming pool. "I got a feeling," he said, "that drownin' ain't nothin' compared to what the fuckin' Japs are gonna do to us."

That would turn out to be true for almost everyone but the changeling. They were about to begin a forced march from Bataan to a concentration camp some two weeks away, under broiling sun without food or water. The orders that the Japanese had been given in Manila said "any American captive who is unable to continue marching all the way to the concentration camp should be put to death." And they might be the lucky ones.

The changeling and Hugh and a dozen others were in a communications shack when the Japanese came. Five young soldiers with bayoneted rifles crowded into the small room and started screaming. They got louder and angrier, and the changeling realized that they expected their captives to speak Japanese. What else didn't they know?

By gestures they got across the idea that the men were

supposed to take off their clothes. One was too slow, and a soldier prodded him in the buttock with the bayonet, which caused an unusual amount of blood and hysterical laughter.

"Oh my God," Hugh whispered. "They're going to kill us all."

"Try to stay calm," the changeling said without opening its mouth. "They'll go after people who draw attention to themselves." As drill sergeants did.

They rummaged through the pile of clothing, and one of them found a Japanese coin. He held it up and started screaming at a man.

"That ain't mine," he said. "They told us to get rid of all that shit." A soldier behind him clubbed him with his rifle butt at the base of the skull, and he went down like a tree. The soldier clubbed him twice more, but stopped at a sharp command.

The one who seemed to be in charge screamed at the captives, repeatedly gesturing at their fallen comrade, who was bleeding from both ears and twitching. Then they left, as suddenly as they'd appeared.

A man kneeled by his friend and gently turned him over. Only the whites of his eyes showed. He drooled saliva and blood and something like water. "Cerebrospinal fluid," the changeling said.

"He gonna die?"

"It's very serious." The changeling sorted through the pile and found its fatigues and put them on. "Better get dressed," it said to the man holding his friend. "We want to all look the same to them."

"Jimmy's right," Hugh said, finding his own clothes. "They prob'ly gonna kill us all, but I ain't gonna go first."

While they were dressing, a new Japanese soldier stepped into the doorway. He had a clean uniform and no rifle. He pointed at the naked man on the floor. "Bury him," he said in English.

"He ain't dead," his friend protested.

"Oh." The officer unsnapped a holster and pulled out a Nambu pistol. He bent over and put the muzzle in the man's mouth and fired. The noise was loud in the small room. Blood and brains and chips of bone scattered across the concrete floor. "Bury him now." He holstered the pistol and walked out.

The man who had been holding his friend started after the officer. Two others tried to restrain him, but he broke free. At the door, though, he sagged and just stared out. "Bastards," he said. "Fucking Jap bastards."

o'swie cim, poland, 7 december 1941

While the changeling was enjoying the hospitality of the Japanese, the chameleon was helping to oversee the construction of Birkenau, a new extermination camp four kilometers from Auschwitz. He was about to meet his soulmate, Josef Mengele, for the second time.

The chameleon had a good instinct for the winds of war, and so had moved to Germany in 1937, and took the identity of a young right-wing doctor in Frankfurt. He was a perfect Aryan, blond and blue-eyed and athletic.

In 1938, he enlisted in the Nazi Schutzstaffel, the SS "Blackshirts," where he first met Mengele, also a young doctor. The randomness of war separated them, though; Mengele served as a medical officer in France and Russia, where he was wounded and decorated. The chameleon wanted to be in on the invasion of Poland, where he operated on a lot of people but saw no action to speak of.

In 1939 the chameleon found a position more amenable to his talents. He was deployed to Brandenburg for "Aktion

T4," the Nazi euthanasia project. People who had physical deformities, mental retardation, epilepsy, senile disorders, and a host of other conditions that made them inferior to the Aryan ideal were allowed "mercy killing." In other places, this was done by more or less painless injections. In Brandenburg, they pioneered the use of the gas chamber disguised as a shower room.

Hitler terminated Aktion T4 in August of 1941, because of public outcry after an influential bishop disclosed the truth of the project in a broadcast sermon. The chameleon was transferred to Auschwitz, where his expertise with gas chambers was valued, as well as his prior service in Poland.

He didn't like Poland at all. Brandenburg was a civilized university town, with sophisticated food and drink and vice. Auschwitz had nothing but subhumans destined for rightful extermination. Granted, the difference between human and subhuman was moot to him.

The chameleon was pleased when, in May 1943, his old acquaintance from Frankfurt was assigned—by Himmler, no less—to be chief women's doctor, and then was appointed chief doctor for both Auschwitz and Birkenau. The chameleon became one of Mengele's assistant surgeons.

By this time the Final Solution was in full swing, boxcars arriving regularly, crowded with miserable castouts: gypsies, communists, homosexuals, and, mostly, Jews. Himmler had ordered Birkenau built with a capacity for 100,000 prisoners, more than three times the size of Auschwitz proper; its gas chambers and crematoria could destroy 1,500 people in one day. It was all terror and chaos, and Mengele loved it.

One of the duties that doctors shared was to be "choosers," who stood in front of the doors when the boxcars were opened, and on the basis of visual inspection ordered people to go to the right, for the work camp, or the left, for extermination. A lot of the doctors detested this

detail, but Mengele loved it. He even showed up to watch
when it wasn't his turn, an arresting sight in his immacu-
late uniform, mirror-bright boots, white gloves, and riding
crop.

One reason he liked to observe the crowds staggering
out of the boxcars was to make sure that no twins were separated or sent to extermination before he could make use
of them. Twins comprised his main area of research, and
the chameleon helped him in this quest for knowledge.

Mengele's interest was twofold: he wondered whether
there might be some way to induce properly Aryan
women to have twins, so the Master Race could grow at
twice the usual rate, and he also did simple environmental
experiments that were a perversion of "nature versus nur-
ture"—he would leave one twin alone while he stressed
the other one to death with starvation, poison, asphyxiation, mutilation, or whatever occurred to him, and then,
after killing the control twin as well, usually with an injection of phenol to the heart, he and his assistants (including the chameleon) would conduct parallel autopsies,
noting internal changes that might be related to the cause
of death.

It was not exact science, and perhaps the motivation for
it had little to do with anything more exalted than taking
pleasure in control, torture, murder, and dissection. Mengele loved it, smiling and chatting all the while.

The chameleon was amazed. In tens of thousands of
years, he couldn't remember having met a human being so
similar to himself. Could Mengele be another one of whatever he was? When the time was right, he might find out by
killing him. Meanwhile, he just enjoyed his company.

Mengele appreciated the chameleon's skill in underwater autopsies, which others found unnerving. When they
killed people by asphyxiation, in the high-altitude simulation chamber, they put the corpses immediately underwater
for dissection. An observer watched for telltale bubbles, to

see which parts of the body retained the most air. There was a lot in the brain.

Most of Mengele's "scientific" records were destroyed as the Soviets advanced on Auschwitz in 1945. The high-altitude work survived, though, and eventually informed space research in both Russia and the United States.

When the Soviet soldiers marched through the gates of Birkenau, the chameleon was one of thousands of starving Jews. His pal Mengele escaped because, out of vanity, he had opted out of the SS practice of having your blood type tattooed on your arm.

The chameleon proceeded to track him down, keeping his Jewish identity and joining the Mossad under Issad Harel in the 1950s. He left the Israeli Secret Service after ten years, with a few tidbits lifted from the Mengele file, and met him just off a riverbank near Enseada de Bertioga, Brazil, on 7 February 1979.

He was a fit old man of sixty-eight, swimming. The chameleon changed back into his 1941 Nazi appearance when he waded out to say hello. The old murderer's eyes got very wide before his head vanished under the water. Mortal, after all.

19

APIA, SAMOA, 2020

Everything else having failed to impress the artifact, the NASA folks appealed to their opposite numbers in the American military.

For more than fifty years there had been an international agreement forbidding weapons of mass destruction in orbit. That didn't mean you couldn't build them on the Earth, of course, and wait for the law to change.

HESL, the High Energy Spalling Laser, was not technically a "weapon of mass destruction" anyhow. It was designed to vaporize a small target, like a tank or a ballistic missile or even a limo with the right person in it, from orbit. What kept it from being orbited, for the time being, was the powerful nuclear reactor that powered up its zap.

The machine had been designed to just fit inside the new space shuttle's cargo bay, which meant it was way too large for the protective shell around the artifact. It took six weeks to disassemble it and rebuild a structure large enough to house the weapon.

Inevitably, it caused some friction between Russ and Jan.

Russ sometimes reacted to stress by eating. He got to number 7 a half hour before their noon meeting, and while brewing tea orchestrated a huge sandwich. Ham and beef and salami slices alternating with goat and cheddar cheese, sliced pickle, and tomato and lettuce. They were out of pickled beet slices; he put them on the list. One slice of bread was slathered with mustard and mayonnaise, the other with peanut butter. He compressed the thing down to manageable proportions and sliced it in two diagonally.

"You're not going to eat all that by yourself, are you?" Jan was watching from the door.

"I'm willing to share." He put half of it on another plate and carried both to the table.

"Want tea?" She poured two mugs and brought them over.

She inspected the sandwich carefully and removed the pickle. "We've modified the thing so the first shot will be a tenth of the normal minimum power." She sliced a corner off the sandwich and nibbled on it. "Peanut butter?"

"So that would be about a thousand megajoules?"

"More like one and a half times that. We tried it out on a big block of stone down at the quarry."

"I'm surprised I didn't hear the explosion," he said around bites. "Peanut butter's the healthiest part of the sandwich."

"The engineers took precautions. It was swaddled in a ton of some kind of protective cloth. I mean, it *is* a spalling laser."

"So it spalled impressively?"

She nodded. "Blew it to flinders. Then blew out a piece of the quarry wall behind it, two hundred meters away."

"How long did it go?"

"Half a microsecond burst, they said."

He shook his head. "It's too big a leap. That must be a

thousand times the energy flux we've brought to bear on the thing."

"About eight hundred, I think. But that laser didn't even warm it up." That was true; they'd tried a twenty-million-joule industrial laser on it, and the thermal sensors hadn't budged. The thing seemed to be an infinite heat sink.

"What if we destroy it?"

"I think we'll be lucky to get enough ablation for an absorption spectrum."

"And if you don't, you crank it up to full power?"

"Only by degrees. We'll be cautious, Russ."

"Oh, I know you will." He took a big bite and concentrated on chewing it. "I'm mainly . . . I'm just worried about the first shot. If that doesn't affect it, it can handle another factor of ten."

"You anthropomorphize it. Brave little spaceship versus the monstrous military-industrial complex."

"You've been hanging around too much with Jack. Speaking of anthropomorphizing. He's angry with the thing."

"Well, it's resisting his advances." She looked at him steadily. "He doesn't like that."

Russ couldn't repress a smile. "He doesn't, eh?" Jack's attraction to the astrobiologist had been immediately obvious.

She rolled her eyes. "I'm a grandmother."

"But not very grandmotherly."

"Don't *you* start. I'm ten years older than you."

Eight or nine, Russ thought, but didn't press it. "You want something besides the sandwich?"

"Pepcid. I brought my own."

bataan, philippines, 28 march 1942

Thousands of American and Filipino captives were herded onto dusty fields outside of the town of Mariveles, and made to sit under the baking sun without provision of food, water, or latrines.

The changeling and Hugh had each managed two canteens, and they had a loaf of hard bread between them. The other fifty-some Marines were someplace else in the vast sea of suffering men. Some units had stayed together, which proved a significant advantage for individuals' survival; others, like the Marine detachment, were broken up.

Hugh carved an inch-thick slice of the bread with his mess-kit spoon, and they split it. The changeling could have done without, of course, but couldn't think of a reason to refuse. He took the smaller half.

"God, I'd kill for a burger," Hugh said quietly, eating the bread in pinches of crumbly dry crust.

"People will kill for bread soon enough," the changeling said, "unless they decide to feed us."

"Kill for water," Hugh said, taking a small sip.

People did die from water, starting that day. Dehydrated, they would greedily lap or suck from any source, and every source that wasn't purified was contaminated. Dysentery increased the foulness of the camp, and further dehydrated the dying men. The Japanese opened a tap that gave a trickle of brown water to people who were strong enough to stand in line for hours. Hugh had a tin of iodine tablets that made the water safe to drink, though the taste made most people gag.

The changeling thought the iodine was a delicious condiment. Like the chlorine it had enjoyed in boot camp, iodine was a halogen, toxic to most Earth creatures.

When night fell, the Japanese soldiers moved through the horde of collapsed captives, yelling and kicking at them. The ones who were dead, or not alive enough to respond, were buried by the ones who were able to hack a hole in the hard ground with entrenching tools.

Some were buried prematurely. If they struggled, a guard would help them along with rifle butt or bayonet.

At dawn, they started pulling people at random to form into marching ranks of forty to a hundred each. When he saw what they were doing, Hugh gave the changeling half the iodine tablets, folded into an old letter from home. That was a prescient as well as an altruistic act; minutes later they hauled him roughly away. They would not see each other again for a long time.

The changeling sat quietly for two more days, watching the crowd of strangers around it thin. From the lack of bread, it shrank imperceptibly, and tried to mimic the symptoms of starvation, to keep from standing out.

On the third morning, two soldiers hauled the changeling to its feet and pushed it to the road. It joined a motley crowd of Army and Navy men, some asleep on their feet, a couple being held up by others.

A Japanese yelled something like "March!" They straggled forward. Someone started to call cadence, but several others advised him to shut the fuck up.

At first they stayed in a fairly coherent group, but as the sun grew higher, the worst off began to fall back. The road was rough, torn up by tank treads and occasional torrential rains, and even a person who was totally in control of his faculties would have found it difficult to maintain a forced-march speed.

The only person in total control of its faculties was not even a person.

The Japanese hounded the stragglers, whipping them with ropes and punching them with gun butts, and prodding with bayonets the ones who still lagged behind. At first it was shallow jabs to the buttocks and back. After awhile they jabbed harder, and the ones who fell and couldn't proceed were shot where they lay.

All the time the soldiers kept up an indignant tirade against their captives. The changeling wondered whether they were actually so unworldly and ignorant as to suppose that everyone spoke their language. It began to work out a basic vocabulary, at least of imperative commands. It could see that there might come a time, soon, when it would be practical to change form for awhile; become Japanese.

For several days there was little variety, except when the blistering heat was punctuated by torrential downpour. That would leave rapidly shrinking mud puddles from which people could try to fill canteens, or just fall to the ground and lap, if the guards allowed it.

The changeling had altered its metabolism to do without food and water. It imitated the bone-weary stagger of the men around it, but still had its normal strength, which led to its murder.

A Japanese truck—a Chevrolet—full of soldiers rumbled by, and one of them did a trick he evidently had been practicing. He dropped a lasso around one of the marchers, intending to drag him along. But he chose the man who was next to the changeling. Crashing to his knees, he cried out, and the changeling automatically snatched at the rope and gave it a jerk, which pulled the Japanese cowboy suddenly off the truck. He hit the ground hard, and the others on the truck started yelling.

Everybody stopped for a few seconds while the soldiers checked their fallen cowboy comrade, whose face was a flag of blood when he shakily stood up. He pointed at the changeling and shouted, gesticulating.

An officer walked back to where it was standing. He was marginally neater and cleaner than the others, and carried a sword of rank.

He looked at the changeling's face for a long time, and said a few quiet words. Then he turned on his heel and walked off the road. Two guards took the changeling by the arms and followed. Others began yelling at the standing crowd, trying to get them moving again. There was some shouting from the Americans, but a rifle shot silenced them, and the changeling could hear the crowd shuffling on.

When they'd taken it a couple of hundred meters, they stopped, and one of the guards threw a shovel at the changeling's feet. "You must dig your grave," the officer said.

This was interesting. "No," the changeling said to him. "Make the one with the rope dig it."

The officer laughed, and said something in Japanese. The guards laughed, too, but then there was an awkward silence, and the officer whispered two syllables. The one with the bloody face began to dig, obviously stiff with pain. They tied the changeling's hands together.

It was a shallow grave, little more than a foot deep, and barely long enough for its six-foot frame.

"Kneel," the officer said, and someone kicked the changeling behind the knee. It heard the blade swishing down and felt a hard blow at the base of its neck, not as painful as changing bodies, and then another blow.

The world spun around, sky twice. The changeling's head came to ground face up, and it watched with interest as its upside-down body spouted blood, and then fell or was pushed into the grave. It couldn't see after that, but heard and felt the warm dusty soil being shoveled over it.

apia, samoa, 24 december 2020

Everybody wanted to be "there" when the laser was first used, but of course there wasn't room in the lab itself, which for this phase of the research didn't look much like a lab. The laser was basically a government-gray metal box the size of a pickup truck, squatting in the jury-rigged extension they'd welded on to the environmental containment vessel. Its barrel, a glass cylinder, was aligned with the taped-off four-by-four-inch square on the artifact's side, looking up at about a 30-degree angle. In the ceiling was an oval of optical glass that should be perfectly transparent to the laser's frequency. Better be. If it absorbed a hundredth of one percent it would melt.

The entrance side of the lab had been turned into a bunker, steel plate fronting concrete blocks. Three technicians were crowded in there, scrutinizing data feeds and watching the experiment over a video monitor.

Everybody else was watching a wide-screen monitor in *fale* 7, which was also crowded, with twenty-one people standing or sitting, attention riveted on the screen.

"Sixty seconds," the screen said, unnecessarily, the digital countdown rolling away in the lower right-hand corner.

Jan was seated between Russ and Jack, front row center. "Now we'll see," she said.

"Won't see a damn thing," Jack said.

"Bet you a beer," Russ said.

"On a measurable physical change? You're on."

Nobody said anything more as the countdown rolled to zero. Then the laser hummed, and there was a pale visible ray between the barrel and the target area, as its ferocious power ionized the air. The tape vanished in a puff of smoke.

Nothing obvious was happening to the artifact. "Should've held out for an imported beer," Jack said.

"Temperature's up," a technician said from the screen. "All over the artifact. Every sensor shows about a degree Celsius increase."

"I'll take a Valima," Russ said.

"How about the ambient temperature?" Jack asked the screen.

"Also up a degree, Dr. Halliburton. To twenty-one degrees."

"So no deal. It always matches the ambient temperature."

"Quibble, quibble," Russ said. "Still a measurable physical change."

"I think you should split a beer," Jan said, "and play nice."

Jack nodded absently. "Try full power?"

"Twenty percent," Russ said quickly. "We don't want full power with air in the room."

"Okay. Naomi," he said to the screen, "let's crank the laser up to twenty percent."

"Done." There was no visible change. After a minute she said, "Temperature's up another degree."

"Let's turn it off and examine the artifact," Russ said.

Jack was staring at the spot where the laser was concentrating enough power to melt through thick steel, hoping for a wisp of smoke, anything. "Oh . . . all right."

Naomi and Moishe Rosse, Jan's senior technician, went from the bunker into the slightly less confined "artifact room." They spent a couple of hours sending data back to the people in number 7: visual, electron, and positron. The air in the room showed an unsurprising increase in ozone and oxides of nitrogen.

Nothing important had changed.

"Let's go ahead and evacuate the room," Russ said, "and repeat the ten and twenty percent exposures. With no air in the room, any temperature increase in the artifact is going to be straight radiative transfer from the laser."

"We ought to crank it up to fifty percent," Jack said.

"If there's no change." Russ looked at Jan. "Okay?"

She nodded. "How long to evacuate the room?"

Greg Fulvia spoke up. "We figure about four hours to 0.1 millibar."

"We ought to check the laser periodically as the pressure goes down," Moishe said from the screen. "It's designed to work in a vacuum, but that's after sitting in orbit for a long time."

"What do you expect?" Russ asked.

"I don't know. I expect machines to malfunction when you change their operating environment."

"Do a system check every hour or so, then," Jack said. "The sensors, too, and microscopes. The positron's kind of a delicate puppy."

Russ looked at his watch; it was almost noon. "Let's all be back here at 1700. Who do you need, Greg?"

"It's all set up. I'll flick the switch and Tom and I can

take turns looking at the nanometer." He talked to the screen. "You guys let us know when you're battened down." Moishe said to give them ten minutes.

"Sails?" Russ said, a restaurant on the harbor. He and Jan rode bicycles over, and got drenched in a one-minute downpour. Jack was waiting for them at a balcony table.

"Nice cab ride?" Jan asked, rubbing a bandana through her ruff of white hair.

"Bumpy as hell." He pushed a bottle of red wine an inch in their direction. "I took the liberty."

"A glass, anyhow." She poured for herself and Russ, and they sat down heavily, simultaneously. "Not a cloud in the sky."

"Bicycling causes rain," Jack said. "Scientific fact."

"Glad there's *some* science today," Russ said. The waiter came up and they all ordered without looking at the menu.

"Every time we stress it without leaving a mark is a little science." She took a sip. "It's our technology versus theirs, or what theirs was a million years ago."

"And where are they now?" Russ said. "Either dead and gone or on their way home."

"Or they were us a million years ago," Jack said. "You read the *Times* thing yesterday?"

"Lori Timms," Russ said without inflection. She was a popular science writer.

"What was it?" Jan said.

"Just a new angle on the time capsule theory," Russ said. "She thinks our ancestors deliberately renounced technology, and carefully wiped out every trace of their civilization. Except the artifact, which they left as a warning, in case their descendants, us, started on their path as well.

"She handles the problem of the fossil record by postulating that they were as knowledgeable in life sciences as in

the physical ones. They repopulated the world with appropriate creatures."

Russ laughed. "And then what did they do with the fossil record that was already there? Carbon dating doesn't
lie."

"Maybe they cleaned 'em up. Had some way to find all
the fossils and get rid of 'em."

"That's a bit of a stretch."

"Well, think about it," Jan said. "What if the 'million-
year-old' part is wrong? What if *that* part of it was faked?
Any technology that could build the artifact could bury it
under an ancient coral reef. Then you only have to worry
about archeology."

"And the historical record," Russ said.

"'There were giants on the earth in those days,'" Jan
said, smiling.

"And fishburgers now," Jack said, as the waiter came
through the door.

bataan, philippines, 5 april 1942

The changeling waited until two groups of marchers had gone by, and there was no sound of nearby movement. It knew that the loose dirt of its grave would move around while it went through the hour of agony it took to change from one body to another.

It planned to leave the head behind, and become a foot shorter. Japanese.

"Agony" is really too human a word to describe what it went through. It was tearing its body apart and reassembling it from the center outwards, squeezing and ripping organs, crushing bones and forcing them to knife through flesh, but pain was just another sense to it, not a signal to modify its behavior. Besides, it was nothing new. It had been hundreds of people by now.

When it had become a Japanese private, complete with grimy uniform, it pushed up in a shower of dirt, to its knees, and then stood and brushed itself off. As it had calculated, the sun was well down, and it was pitch black.

Except for the flashlight.

Someone screamed and ran away. The changeling was at first impeded by the loose dirt, but then it sprang out, and in three long steps caught up with the fleeing intruder and pushed him lightly to the ground.

He was a Filipino child, cowering in terror, still clutching a canvas bag. Six or seven years old.

The changeling sorted through the few Japanese phrases it had accumulated, and decided none was appropriate. It used English: "Don't be afraid. I was just resting. We do it that way. It's cool in the dirt."

The boy probably didn't understand a word, but the tone of the changeling's voice calmed him. It helped him to his feet and handed him flashlight and bag, and made a shooing motion. "Now go! Get out of here!" The boy ran wildly away.

Perhaps it should have killed him. With a finger punch it could have simulated a bullet wound to the head. But what could he really do? He would run home and tell his parents, and they would interpret the event in terms of what they knew of reality, and be glad the boy had survived waking up a Japanese soldier. He would tell the other children, and they might believe him, but other adults would dismiss it as imagination.

(In fact, the changeling was wrong. The boy's parents *did* believe he had awakened a dead man, and told him to be quiet about it except to God, and pray thankfulness for the rest of his life, that God had chosen to spare him.)

The changeling widened its irises temporarily, so the starlit desolation was as bright as day, and started moving quietly but swiftly north. It took only a half hour to catch up with a group that had been allowed a few hours of rest. It had passed four Americans lying dead in the road.

It saw only one guard awake, leaning against the fender of a truck. It went behind the truck and forced itself to produce urine, and then casually walked forward, adjusting its clothes. *"Hai,"* it whispered to the guard, ready to kill him instantly if his reaction was wrong. He just grunted and spit.

It walked among the Americans, planning. The masquerade as a Japanese probably wouldn't pass muster during the day, among Japanese. So it would be best to change back into an American before dawn.

By starlight it examined every sleeping face. None of them was familiar, either from the Marine detachment or from the Mariveles camp. So it could become Jimmy again, and not have to fake a new history.

The people at the end of the group would be the ones nearest death, and probably least likely to be keeping track of who was around them. In fact, it found two that were dead, and quietly lay down between them in the pitch darkness.

It made as little noise as possible, changing the bones of its face back into Jimmy's starveling countenance. The uniform was trivially easy, and only made a normal rustling sound. It stretched the Japanese skeleton as much as was practical, with an occasional popped-knuckle noise, and got to within three inches of Jimmy's height.

What it wound up with was an even more famished version of Jimmy, which was fine. The weaker-looking, the better.

With the first light of dawn, the Japanese guards were working through their ranks, shouting and kicking. A sudden blue flash and rifle shot got them moving faster.

They left five behind, dead or so close as to make no difference. The sun sped up over the horizon, and in less than an hour, the morning cool had dissipated.

It had rained torrentially two days before, and although the road was dry and dusty, there were sometimes mud puddles at the edges of the fields. People would fall out of

ranks to go to them with their canteens, but the guards
would chase them off.

Finally there was a huge puddle, a wallow where two
water buffalo were cooling off. The water was green and
odoriferous, but there was lots of it, and a guard who was a
private made an ironic gesture inviting them over.

A man next to the changeling put his hand on its shoulder. "Wait," he croaked. "That's the asshole got us fucked
with yesterday."

Dozens of men staggered to the wallow and pushed the
scum aside to drink and fill canteens or cups. Some
splashed water over their heads and chests, cooling off like
the buffalo, which would prove a mistake.

An officer with a saber came running down the line
screaming at the ones in the water. They hustled back to re-
join the ranks.

The officer huddled the guards and then watched smiling while they moved through the crowd and pulled out
everyone with damp clothing.

They lined them up along the side of the road. The officer said one word and in a ragged volley they shot them all.

In the ringing silence after the shots, the man next to the
changeling said, "Shitty water woulda killed 'em anyhow."

The changeling nodded and, with the others, began
shuffling away from the execution scene. It was having difficulty trying to generalize about human nature.

Would Americans have done that, with the roles re-
versed? It seemed inconsistent with what it had observed,
except occasionally at the insane asylum, where there were
patients unable to see others as human beings.

After the war, it would have to look into this. That
wouldn't be very hard, since apparently the Japanese were
going to win, and everyone would have to learn their language, and be assimilated into their culture.

Unless they slaughtered all the Americans like animals,

as it had just witnessed. Well, it could become a Japanese who'd lost the power of speech. That had worked before.

They finally got to Balanga, the first town on their route of march. Filipinos lined the road, staring at the Americans, and began throwing food to them—sticks of sugar cane, rice balls, sugar cakes—until suddenly the Japanese started shooting.

The civilians scattered, running for cover. Two young men took off across a field, which apparently caught someone's attention. Three of the guards, clustered together, started firing at them, laughing. They kept missing them, either on purpose or from poor marksmanship, but they finally fell.

The three went out to inspect their handiwork, and evidently the two boys were still alive. They kicked them around and yelled at them, and finally shot them several times point-blank.

Most of the men watched this tableau in shocked silence. Someone behind the changeling growled "fucking Jap bastards," and someone else shushed him.

The changeling tried to interpret what was happening in terms of animal and human behavior, and the little it knew about Japanese culture. If they were trying to scare the Americans with a show of brutality, it wasn't working well; the ones susceptible to that were already nearly paralyzed with terror. Most of the prisoners by now assumed they were going to die, and were just concentrating on not being next. Each fresh horror seemed to increase the men's contempt for the Japanese "animals" (as if nonhuman animals ever behaved in such elaborate ways), and also increased their dissatisfaction with their own command, who had surrendered them. Though their defense of Bataan would have been unimpressive, without food, water, gasoline, or ammunition.

The Japanese behavior revealed vicious contempt, as if the individual Americans had decided to throw down their

arms rather than fight. That was an understandable simpli-
fication, for young men so unsophisticated they evidently
still thought, after all these days, that the Americans would
understand Japanese if they spoke it loudly enough.

The gulf between the two sides was so large it was as if
they were two different species. The changeling wished it
had had an opportunity to observe other cultures than
American without the complication of war. It resolved to
do that when the war was over.

The Japanese marched them into the middle of town,
into a dark hot warehouse building. It was already crowded
with prisoners, but the guards pushed them in tighter and
tighter, until it was literally impossible to sit or lie down;
the men were packed like sardines in a can.

They smelled worse than sardines, though, with no toilet other than their own clothing. The guards evidently
couldn't stand it after a half hour. They padlocked the door
and stood guard outside, while their charges steeped in
their own excrement. Many or most of them had some degree of dysentery, and had lost control of their bowel function. Urine baked on skin and the rags of uniforms, and if
someone fainted from the stench, or died, he remained
standing, just another sardine.

The changeling was near the padlocked door, and knew
it could break it down with little effort. That would probably earn a few people a minute of fresh air before they
were shot. If the men had been in a position to vote, they
probably would have said "go for it."

But it was content to wait and watch, the miasma no
more or less pleasant than the sea breeze outside. People
stopped talking and concentrated on living another minute,
hour, day.

In the morning, the Japanese opened the door and the
prisoners staggered or crawled out into the sudden light,
leaving twenty-five dead behind. They were beaten into
line and fed a small rice ball and a little tepid tea before

getting back on the road, which was already shimmering with heat.

Even with its superhuman metabolism, the changeling had lost five kilograms by the end of the march, on the morning of 15 April, at the San Fernando railway station.

The Japanese kicked and shouted the men awake and herded them into narrow-gauge boxcars, more than a hundred men per car. It was like a reprise of Balanga, packed shoulder to shoulder, with the added factor of the train's queasy rocking motion. A few people near the doors had actual air to breathe; the others had to make do with a hot stale atmosphere combining shit, piss, and vomit with carbon dioxide and dust.

One hundred and fifteen had been packed into the changeling's car. When they stumbled out five hours later, they left behind four corpses.

They were made to sit motionless in the hot sun at Capiz Tarlac for three hours, and then were marched across town to their final destination, Camp O'Donnell. There they confronted a nightmare several orders of magnitude larger than the march itself: twelve thousand prisoners were confined to a square of baking concrete one hundred yards on a side.

Most of the thousands of Americans and Filipinos were standing in a slow line waiting for the one water spigot. The old hands told them that it usually took about six hours—sometimes ten or twelve—to get to the spigot and fill your canteen. So after you filled it, you might as well just go back to the end of the line.

They were supposedly going to get food tomorrow. But the Japanese had been saying that for three days.

The changeling got into line, even though if it wanted water it could assimilate it directly from the air, or even break down carbohydrates for it. As the line inched along, the prisoners walking back toward the end would scrutinize faces, trying to identify old comrades through the masks of filth and exhaustion.

The inevitable happened. "Jimmy? My God—Jimmy?"

The changeling looked up. "Hugh."

"You're alive," he said.

"Just barely," the changeling said. "You, too."

"No! I mean . . . I mean . . . I saw you get your head chopped off! After you pulled the Jap off the truck."

"Must have been someone who looked like me."

One of the Japanese guards stepped over and seized Hugh by the shoulder. "Repeat what you just said," he said in almost perfect English.

Hugh cringed. "Thought he looked like somebody."

"Repeat!" The soldier shook him. "The truck!"

"He—he looked like someone who pulled a guard off a truck. But he's someone else."

The guard shoved Hugh away and clamped on to the changeling's shoulder and stared. "I buried you. I saw your face in the hole, looking up."

The changeling thought back and realized that he indeed was one of the guards on that detail. "Then how am I alive now?"

The man continued staring, the blood draining out of his face. Then he jerked the changeling out of the line and shoved him through the crowd toward a line of white buildings.

"Sit!" He pushed the changeling down on a step and shouted something in Japanese. Two young soldiers in clean uniforms scurried over to point their rifles at the changeling's head. It considered doing something to make them shoot, and simplify the situation by apparently dying. But it was curious.

The guard returned with another familiar face: the officer who had performed the execution.

He studied the changeling and laughed. "Do you have a twin?"

"They say everyone does, somewhere."

He stepped forward and fingered what was left of the insignia on Jimmy's uniform. "Not in the same Marine detachment, I think."

He said something in Japanese and the two soldiers prodded the changeling to its feet. "We'll see about you," the officer said. "What is your name?"

"Private First Class William Harrison, sir," it said, and made up a random serial number. The officer wrote it down painstakingly and barked an order at the privates. "Tomorrow," he added. By tomorrow, the changeling decided, it would be someone and somewhere else.

The privates pushed their prisoner through the door and down a dark corridor. A Filipino jailer, closely observed by a Japanese officer, unlocked a door of heavy iron bars. The changeling quickly memorized both of their faces. A basic plan would be to break out physically and kill one or both of them, and walk out as the officer's doppelganger.

The Filipino took the changeling to the last of six cells and locked the old cast-iron barred door. The changeling widened its irises in the darkness and memorized the shape of the key.

As the guard walked away, a hoarse voice in the adjacent cell asked, "What they get you for?"

"They haven't said. You?"

"Stole a can of sardines. Say they're going to let me starve."

"We're starving outside anyhow," the changeling said. "At least this is out of the sun."

The key rattled in the door and the Filipino let the Japanese officer in. He had a riding crop, and whipped the changeling's face and shoulders. "You quiet!" The changeling heard him do the same next door.

The cell had a board for a bed and a bucket for a toilet. The bucket was foul and buzzing with flies; maggots quietly rustled inside. There was a small open window about six inches square, up near the ceiling. Only a little light came through. It faced north and was evidently in the shadow of an eave.

The man who was sobbing next door was the only other prisoner who was conscious. The changeling could hear one near the jailer's station whose breath was so shallow and ragged he must be near death.

It could easily make itself slender enough to slip between the bars. It was also strong enough to bend the bars and widen that space, but that would make noise, and leave behind evidence of a prisoner who was not human. There was already too much curiosity about "William Harrison." Best to find a way to simply vanish. That could be explained away as bribery or carelessness.

There was a drain in the floor that would probably lead to a river. But it was only an inch in diameter. To form a shape that could slip through that would take hours; to keep enough mass to re-form into human shape would require a worm about a hundred feet long, and while it was turning into that grotesque creature, it would be conspicuous and vulnerable.

That gave it an idea, though. It heard the Japanese guard leave, and within an hour the Filipino was snoring.

It removed its right leg, with a sound like someone softly cracking his knuckles, then tearing clothes quietly. That drew no attention. The leg re-formed itself into a defensive creature that looked like a pile of rags but had teeth and claws like a saber-toothed tiger's.

The changeling began to re-form, not into a worm, but into a snake about the size and shape of a young reticulated python. It had a square cross-section slightly smaller than the high small window.

That took about an hour of vulnerability. It was the work of a minute, then, to merge with the saber-toothed section, which was also six inches in thickness.

It had hundreds of gecko-like legs, so scrabbling up the

wall was easy. It extended an eye through the opening and saw no one, though there were bright lights to the east. To the west there was a drainage ditch.

It slithered through the opening and down the wall, changing its color to match the dusty pink of the building. It stretched out along the length of the wall, as it had seen snakes do, and peered around the corner.

So far so good. To its right was the large square where the prisoners sleepily stepped along the undulating line to the water tap. There were plenty of guards, but they were standing or sitting with their backs to the drainage ditch.

Decisions. It would take too long to change back into a human form, and besides, the snake would probably be more efficient once in the water, assuming the ditch wasn't dry. If it were intercepted on the way . . . that would be awkward. It was a cross between a boa constrictor and a chainsaw, so there would be no question about the outcome of an encounter between it and one or several humans. But it would have more than ten thousand witnesses.

It looked around and thought. Electricity.

The power line that served the jail building went on to the prisoners' square. Seeing no potential witnesses, it slid up the wall and took one huge bite. Delicious taste of copper, dusty glass, and high voltage, and everything near went dark.

There were shouts and firing into the air, and then flashlight beams lancing, but all of the attention was directed inward, toward the prisoners. The changeling dropped to the ground and scurried on a thousand lizard legs to the ditch. Slid in and found a few inches of sewage, and slithered south.

It remembered from ordnance maps at the Bataan base that Manila Bay was about forty kilometers south, and there were plenty of rivers through the Panga and Bulacan Provinces. Once in Manila Bay, it was about sixty kilometers around the Bataan Peninsula to the South China Sea.

In the six hours that it took to get to the bay, there was only one witness, to its knowledge: a drunken man on a narrow wooden bridge. He screamed and fled. If anyone came out into the night to check his preposterous story, the changeling would be long gone.

Dawn was still hours away when the final ditch widened into a mud flat and the changeling wormed its way into the bay. It dove down to the bottom and began the process of changing into a fish.

A shark bit it in two, which was annoying. But it evidently didn't like the flavor, and left the two halves alone. The changeling crawled along the bottom, crunching up bivalves and crabs, and when it had enough mass, it took the familiar shape of a great white shark itself. By then it was in the South China Sea. It pointed itself east. Only ten thousand miles to California.

apia, samoa, 24 december 2020

The evacuation of the artifact room had taken a little longer than expected, but there were no leaks, and all of the data-gathering equipment seemed to be working fine. At five thirty, Naomi said through the monitor, "Okay. We can start the countdown."

Jack nodded. "Fire when ready, Gridley." No one else in the room knew who Gridley was.

After a few minutes, there was no temperature change at 10 percent. Naomi increased it to 20, and then to 30.

"Go to fifty," Jack said, and Russ and Jan nodded.

"Where's it all going?" Jan muttered, a question they'd all asked before. At least when there was air in the building, some of the energy had gone into heating the air. Now, the laser was putting out enough energy to run a small city into a hundred-square-centimeter area, and it was all disappearing—into the artifact, apparently.

"Go to a hundred?" Jack said.

"Seventy-five," Russ and Jan said simultaneously.

It never got there. The monitor went blank and a second later the people in cottage 7 heard the dull thump of an explosion.

Jan and Russ were the first ones there, with their bicycles. Half the building had collapsed, the big laser almost submerged in the water. Naomi and Moishe staggered out of the water, coughing and gagging.

Russ took Naomi's arm. "Are you all right?"

She ignored the question, and stared back at the wreck of the lab. "It moved."

"Moved?" Russ said.

"Floated up and crashed down."

"Holy shit."

"Merry Christmas."

Most of the equipment was wrecked, but a high-speed camera, which the manufacturer called "ruggedized," had been rugged enough to record the sequence of events before it lost power and fell into the water.

When the laser increased to 72 percent output, 300,000 watts, the artifact gently rose off its cradle, at a uniform velocity of 18.3 centimeters per second. When it cleared the laser's beam, the weapon punched a hole in the opposite wall, causing the slight explosion they had heard, as the building suddenly filled with air. The beam didn't do any other damage except to explode a coconut at the top of a tree on the Mulinu'a Peninsula, more than two kilometers away.

The artifact continued rising diagonally until it was poised over the laser's optical fiber gun-barrel. Then, whatever force had been holding it aloft quit. It fell, destroying the laser and collapsing that side of the building into the bay.

The camera didn't record what happened after that, but evidently the artifact floated back up and repositioned itself on the cradle in the now open-air artifact room. When the investigators got to it, a few minutes later, it was still beaded with salt water, and cool to the touch.

This would change the direction of their research.

grover city, california, 1948

The changeling enjoyed swimming for a few years as a great white shark—it had had that form for a thousand times as long as the human one.

For reasons it didn't understand, it circled for hours over the deep Tonga Trench, and dove as far as it could in comfort. But it was used to having its animal bodies do things out of obscure impulse, and after awhile moved on. When it got within a few hundred yards of the California coast, it dropped most of its mass and became a bottle-nosed dolphin.

At two in the morning, it swam into a protected cove, shallow enough to be safe from serious predators, and spent a painful hour turning back into a human being.

It used the familiar Jimmy template, but made itself a little shorter and gave itself dark hair with a touch of gray. It darkened its skin and created black pants and a black sweater—burglar gear.

It had to steal some money and information.

The lay of the land was similar to what it had faced the first time it had been human; it crossed a short beach and climbed some rocks to find a winding coastal road. It headed north at an easy lope.

Four times it hid from approaching headlights. After a few miles it came upon an isolated service station with a cottage out back.

Perfect for its petty theft. It could make dollar bills as easily as it made clothing, out of its own substance, but it didn't know whether currency might have changed, whether you still needed ration books—whether there might be some completely new wartime system. They might be using Japanese yen, if the war was over.

The placards in the service station window were in English, and none of them exhorted you to join the services— one did have an American eagle with the instruction to buy U.S. savings bonds, but not war bonds. Maybe the war was over and the Japanese hadn't won.

The door was locked, but it was a simple one. It turned a forefinger into a living skeleton key, and felt its way through the tumblers in less than a minute.

It wished for moonlight. Even with irises totally dilated, there was little detail.

One wall was shelves full of automobile supplies. It opened a quart of oil and drank it for energy and the interesting flavor, altering its metabolism for a few minutes to something it had used a few hundred thousand years before, lying alongside the vent of an undersea volcano.

It found a box of wooden matches and sucked the end off one, for the phosphorus, and then lit one, with a flare of light and a delicious sting of sulfur dioxide. It saw two things it needed: a 1947 World Almanac and a cash register.

After stuffing the almanac in its belt, it lit another match and studied the machine. Pushing down on the NO SALE key produced a loud chime, and the cash drawer slid out with a metallic hiss.

It studied a twenty-dollar bill in the match light. No obvious differences. American currency had changed in size three years before the changeling had become Jimmy, and people had still been complaining about it.

It gave a cursory check to the ten, five, and one, and put them back into the till. Then the lights went on with a loud snap.

An old white man stood in the doorway with a double-barrelled shotgun. "Finally," he said in a squeaking, trembling voice. "I finally got your ass."

Evidently someone had been robbing him. "I haven't—" the changeling started to say, but then there was a loud explosion and it couldn't finish the sentence, for lack of a mouth.

It ducked, and the second shot went high. Sensible of the impossibility it was creating by not falling down dead, it rushed past the man while he was fumbling to reload, forming a large temporary eye out of the gore of its face, and started sprinting down the road.

The old man fired two more shots into the darkness, but the changeling was out of range.

Once around the first bend, the changeling went off the road and sat in the darkness, working on an appearance less incriminating. Elderly farming woman, Caucasian with a deep tan. Faded seersucker dress.

In the moonless overcast night, the changeling moved swiftly inland. A few farm dogs howled at its passing. As the gray dawn approached, it hid in an abandoned truck in a wooded area outside of Grover City.

It made itself a purse and filled it with tens and twenties, and at dawn walked into town and sat on a bench outside the train station, reading the almanac.

There was a center section full of grainy black-and-white photographs, giving a history of World War II. There was even a picture of the Bataan Death March. Jimmy's was not among the drawn faces, the wasted bodies.

The Nazi death camps. Hiroshima and Nagasaki. D-Day and Midway and Stalingrad.

The nature of the world was fundamentally different. More interesting.

A boy pedaled up to the station on a squeaky bike, pulling a red wagon full of newspapers. The changeling tried to buy one, but of course the boy couldn't change a ten.

"You look like a nice boy," it said in what it hoped was a convincing little-old-lady voice. "You can bring me the change later."

He *was* a nice boy, in fact, though his face mirrored an obvious internal conflict. He refused the money and gave her a paper. "You just fold her back up after you finish; put her on this here stack by the station door."

It was the seventh of April, 1948. A British and a Russian plane had collided over Berlin, which was evidently split up among the countries that had defeated Germany. Arabs attacked three Jewish areas of Palestine. The House approved the establishment of a U.S. Air Force, and pledged a billion dollars to Latin America to fight communism. Airplane manufacturer Glenn L. Martin predicted that within months America would have bacteriological weapons, guided missiles, and a "radioactive cloud" much more deadly than the atomic bomb.

So the war wasn't really over. It had just entered a new phase. The changeling would stay out of this one.

An obvious game plan would be to go back to college. April was not too late to apply, but there was the problem of high school transcripts, letters of recommendation—the problem of establishing an actual identity with a verifiable past.

As soon as it defined the problem, the solution was obvious.

Four people had gathered. They didn't bother the old farm lady. A train approached, northbound. The changeling folded the paper carefully and replaced it on top of the pile, under the nickels people had left.

As the northbound train approached, the little old lady asked the four whether it was the train to San Francisco. They confirmed that it was, and she got on board.

The conductor changed her twenty with pursed lips but no comment. It continued to read the almanac, storing up information about how the world had changed while it swam around for six years.

Of course the war had changed the world's map, while leaving whole cities, and even countries, in ruins. The United States had been spared, and now seemed to be leading a coalition of "free" countries versus communist ones. Atomic bombs, supersonic jets, guided missiles, electronic brains, the transistor, and the zoot suit. Al Capone was dead and the changeling's namesake Joe Louis was still champ, which the changeling found gratifying.

At the San Francisco station, it picked up a copy of a women's magazine and stayed in a stall in the ladies' room for about ten minutes, then emerged as a woman of about twenty, dressed like a college student—two-tone loafers, bobby sox, plaid skirt (that had taken some effort), and a white blouse. It assimilated a chromed toilet-paper holder and recycled it as costume jewelry.

It took the bus to Berkeley and wandered around the campus all day, eavesdropping on people and getting the lay of the land. It tarried for quite a while in the Admissions office. College student was an obvious choice of occupation, but which major? It remembered all it had learned about oceanography, but of course would have to hide most of that, starting over. Physics or astronomy might be useful, and interesting, but if it were to track down others of its kind, anthropology or psychology—abnormal psychology—would be more useful.

Of course it had time for all of them.

It studied the posture, demeanor, and uniform of a janitor, and as darkness fell, let itself into an empty classroom and changed. There were still a few students hanging around in the halls, but a balding fifty-year-old man with a broom was invisible to them.

Around midnight, the changeling slipped into the Admissions office and locked the door. It moved swiftly and quietly, the room adequately lit, to its eyes, from the dim dappled light that filtered through a tree from a streetlight at the end of the block.

There were about fifty return letters from prospective students in the in-box of the young woman the changeling had earlier identified as the most junior secretary. It read through forty of the letters before finding exactly what it needed.

Stuart Tanner, a boy from North Liberty, Iowa, had sent in a letter thanking them for his acceptance, but saying that Princeton had offered him a scholarship, which of course he couldn't pass up. The changeling found his file in the "Acceptance" drawer and memorized it. He had an almost perfect academic record. No athletics other than swimming team, which was good. The photo was black-and-white, but he was a pale Nordic boy, blond and blue-eyed. The changeling took his face and noted that he'd have to assimilate about twenty pounds.

After making sure there was no one else on the floor, the changeling typed a letter of acceptance, noting that he was driving out to California immediately, for a summer job, so please change his address to General Delivery in Berkeley. It switched the letters and slipped out the door, a new man.

The most direct thing to do would be to go to North Liberty and quietly kill Stuart Tanner, and bring his wallet full of identification back to Berkeley. But that wouldn't be necessary. It would be sufficient to absorb enough of North Liberty to be able to pass for a native. Stuart grew up in

Iowa City, so he'd have to check that out, too. An Iowa driver's license would be easier to counterfeit than a twenty-dollar bill.

The changeling had seen enough killing in the Pacific to reserve it as a course of last resort.

The thought gave him pause. Until recently, killing a human had been no more complicated than eating or changing identity. He'd had no special feelings of mercy or compassion for his Japanese captors, at the time, but he did recognize having felt a special empathy with the other American soldiers during Bataan. Being a victim among victims may have done something.

Whatever it was, it was odd: something was changing the changeling. Something besides itself; something inside himself.

The change had been slow, actually. It started back in the asylum, when it came to understand the differences between individuals, and to prefer the company of one person over another. To like people.

Stuart Tanner had wanted to major in American literature. That would be an interesting challenge. Maybe the books, the novels, would help it understand what was happening to itself. "What is this thing called love?" the Dorsey song was always asking. Understanding friendship would be a start.

The changeling could read a book a day before September, and be ready for the literature major. It could minor in psychology and take an anthropology elective, that would grow into a second bachelor's degree. Then graduate work, searching for creatures like itself.

It wandered through Berkeley until it found an all-night café, where it sat down with a course catalog it had taken from the office, and mapped this out. Then it scanned the rest of the almanac, appearing to be flipping through it, looking for something. At first light, it walked back to the train station and booked passage through to Davenport, Iowa, which appeared to be the closest stop to North Liberty.

With three hours to go before the train left, it bought a suitcase at a pawn shop and packed it with used clothing from Next-2-New. At a used book store, it bought two thick anthologies of American literature and a half-dozen tattered novels.

It wouldn't do to be walking down the main street of North Liberty and run into Stuart Tanner or someone who knew him. In a stall in the busy men's room at the train station, he changed his hair to black and skin, swarthy. He flattened his nose and made his blue eyes brown.

The changeling had reserved a private compartment on the train, since it was only money. At five till eleven it went aboard and settled in.

It took most of the Rocky Mountains to read through the Joe Lee Davis Anthology, and before it got to the Mississippi it had read one book each by Poe, Hawthorne, Melville, Fitzgerald, Hemingway, and Faulkner. It had every word memorized, but knew from previous college experience that that wouldn't do the trick. Jimmy had been able to write well enough, just barely, to get a degree in oceanography, but his grades in English had been unimpressive. That would have to change.

Among Stuart's application materials was an eleven-page essay on why he wanted to major in American literature. The changeling had memorized not just the words, but also the handwriting. It copied the essay out twice, trying to understand why the writer had used this word rather than that; why it chose one sentence structure over another. Every time it finished a novel it wrote a few pages about it, trying to mimic Stuart's style and vocabulary; a plot outline and analysis of the author's intent, as it had done without great success in the required English and literature courses at UMass. By the time the train got to Davenport, it had worn its pencil to a nub, filling most of a thick tablet.

The Mississippi looked interesting. Maybe someday it would turn into a huge catfish and explore it.

It waited out a thunderstorm, since that's what a human would do, and then walked to the bus station. With a two-hour wait, it read two Iowa papers and reread, in its mind, *The Sun Also Rises,* which was clear but mysterious: why were these people so self-destructive? The war, it supposed; the previous one. Though it looked as if there might be just one World War, with breathing spaces for rearming, that would last until somebody won.

The ride to Iowa City was interesting; the bus rumbling past mile after mile of constant green, farmland occasionally punctuated by wild prairie or forest. There were individual farmhouses with barns, always red, but no towns until they pulled into Iowa City.

The bus was going on to Cedar Rapids, but the driver directed him to the train station, the Cedar Rapids and Iowa City Interurban Railway, which went up to North Liberty. The changeling walked through the university campus to get there, noting that students dressed about the same way they did in Berkeley. A little more casual, not as much obvious wealth. More pipe-smoking among the males, fewer women in slacks. Dresses to midcalf.

It had been listening carefully to conversations. There was a characteristic Iowa accent, but it had been more pronounced in the Davenport station. It would try to maneuver into a situation where it could overhear Stuart.

Stuart went to high school in Iowa City, the changeling knew from his records, so on a hunch it let two trolleys go by. Sure enough, when school was out, teenagers started arriving in groups of two and four.

Except Stuart, who walked alone, reading a book. He didn't talk to any of the others, and they ignored him.

The changeling maneuvered close to the boy and studied him surreptitiously while appearing to read its own book. He was slim and muscular, with a delicate manner.

The book he was so absorbed in was the twenty-year-old *Coming of Age in Samoa,* which the changeling had read as an undergraduate in 1939.

When the trolley came, the changeling got on behind Stuart and sat next to him. "Interesting book."

Stuart looked up sharply. "You've read this?"

"My father had a copy of it," the changeling improvised. "One of his textbooks in college."

"He let you read it?"

"No . . . I put the dust jacket from another book around it. He never noticed."

Stuart laughed. "My dad took it away from me. This one, I keep hidden when I'm home. But hell, I'm old enough."

The changeling nodded vigorously. "They're afraid you'll get ideas."

"As if that was bad." He looked at the changeling. "You're new?"

"Just passing through. Visiting relatives."

"What, in Liberty?"

The changeling thought fast. North Liberty only had a few hundred people; Stuart would know most of them. "No, Cedar Rapids."

"Where you from?"

"California. San Guillermo."

Stuart looked introspective. "Always wanted to go there. I was accepted at Berkeley. Didn't get a scholarship. Are you a student?"

"Taking some time off." It checked its watch. "Anything to do in North Liberty? I have a couple hours to kill."

"They would die," Stuart said. "Ice cream parlor, really just a soda fountain. Go out and look at the quarry."

"What do they mine?"

"Sandstone." He laughed and jerked a thumb back at Iowa City. "Did all the sandstone for the Capitol Building there. Then they moved the capital to Des Moines."

"And carelessly left the building behind," the changeling said in an attempt at humor. The boy gave him an odd look and laughed.

"You could kill an hour with a soda. Or go on to Cedar Rapids and get an actual beer."

"A soda sounds good. I like small towns."

"You could see all of Liberty in about ten minutes." They talked for awhile more, the changeling mostly listening or mining the memory of the day's papers.

They both got off at North Liberty, along with a couple of dozen students. Almost everyone went down the main street. When they went into the ice cream shop, a girl behind them said in a soft singsong, "Stew-ie's got a boy friend."

He turned pink at that. "Stupid girl," he muttered, as the screen door smacked shut behind them.

Interesting, the changeling thought. Could free-thinking Stuart be homosexual, attracted to the exotic out-of-towner? Dark and handsome, with a body almost a twin of Stuart's, defender of Margaret Mead.

They sat at a small round marble table by an oscillating fan. The changeling looked at the bill of fare, a small two-sided card. "How 'bout I buy us a banana split? I couldn't eat a whole one."

"I'll split it with you." He reached into his pocket.

"No, my treat. I'm researching the odd inhabitants of this island."

He snorted. "Margaret Mead wouldn't find much here."

"Oh, I bet she would. Probably about as many people here as on her island."

"Yeah, and we go around half-naked and screw anyone we want." They both laughed at that.

The soda jerk, a young redhead with a face full of acne, was approaching with his pad. He gave them an uncertain smile. "Where's that, Stu?"

He held up the book. "Samoa, Vince. We're gonna go there soon as school's out."

Vince gave the changeling a funny look. "Sure you are. Where the hell is Samoa?"

"Middle o' nowhere, in the Pacific."

"They fight there?"

"Don't know." He raised eyebrows at the changeling.

"Don't ask me." The changeling had passed the island group as a great white shark, on its way to California, and hadn't seen any naval presence. But the war still had a few years to go, then.

"So hi," he said. "I'm Vince Smithers. You're not from, uh . . ."

"Matt Baker," the changeling said, and shook his hand. "San Guillermo, California." This was interesting. The changeling had some difficulty reading subtle emotions, but jealousy isn't subtle. "We're gonna split a banana split, and I'll take a Coke."

He scribbled that down and looked at Stuart. "Vanilla Coke?" Stuart nodded and he went back to the fountain.

"You guys know each other?" the changeling said.

"Everybody knows everybody here. Vince and me used to go to school together, but his parents put him in a military academy. What was that shitty place, Vince?"

"God, I don't want to say the name. I left to pursue a career in banana-split-ology. Much to my father's delight."

They continued in a kind of uneasy banter, the changeling watching with an anthropologist's eye. They were less exotic to it than Polynesians, but no less interesting.

There was a conspiratorial edge to their exchange. They had done something forbidden together, something secret. Not necessarily sex, but that would be a good first guess. Did Stuart mean for his new companion to make that inference? The changeling's only experience with homosexuality had been in the asylum, and there had been no social aspect to it; he had just been a receptacle for two of the guards. There had been a third, who only came to him once, and had been more interesting than the two brutes:

he had quit after a couple of minutes and started weeping, and said how sorry he was, and evidently quit the job right after.

It was so much more complicated than it had to be, but the changeling had noted that this was true of every human biological function that wasn't involuntary.

Vince brought the split and Stuart's Coke. "You don't want some vanilla in yours?" he said to the changeling.

A complexity. "Sure. I'll try anything once." Vince nodded grimly. It was an obvious turning point.

They divided the confection meticulously, and pursued it from opposite ends. Stuart told the changeling about his scholarship to Princeton.

"Nice campus. Major in anthropology?"

"No, English and American lit. You've been there?"

"Once, visiting relatives." A semester, actually, studying invertebrate paleontology.

"You have relatives everywhere."

"Big family."

He made a face. "Mine are all in Iowa." He said it as "Io-way," with a downward inflection.

"You don't plan to come back and raise a bunch of Iowans yourself?"

"No and double no. Not that I don't *like* kids." He speared a piece of banana. "I *hate* them."

"Brothers and sisters?"

"Thank God, no. The kids at school are bad enough."

The changeling was absorbing all this avidly. They finished the split. "Well. Want to show me around fabulous North Liberty?"

"You got five minutes?" On the way out, the changeling gave Vince a dollar and airily waved off the change.

"Rolling in dough," Stuart said.

"Best crap shooter in San Guillermo."

"*Bull* shooter." They both laughed.

It actually took about ten minutes. From the center of town, Stuart led him down West Cherry Street.

"This is my house," he said. "Want to come in?"

"Sure. Meet your parents."

Stuart looked at his eyes, exactly level. "They're gone. They won't be home till tomorrow."

The changeling returned his gaze. "I don't have to be in Cedar Rapids till tomorrow. Missed my train."

The courting ritual was brief. Stuart raided his parents' liquor cabinet and fixed them bourbons that were much too large and strong. Just fuel to the changeling, of course, but if Stuart had been older, it might have killed his sexual desire.

It didn't, of course. He lurched up the stairs, dragging the changeling by the hand, into a bedroom that was not at all boyish. No models or posters, just hundreds of books in nailed-together bookcases.

The changeling had no idea of what the protocol was, still being ignorant of heterosexual protocol. So once in the bedroom it just did what Stuart did, one permutation after another. It narrowed the diameter of its penis for his comfort, remembering pain in the asylum.

Afterward, the boy slept in its arms, snoring drunkenly. It analyzed the genetic material he had left behind. He had a problem with cholesterol, and should take it easy on the banana splits. Also diabetes in his future. Maybe just as well he didn't want to reproduce.

There was no way they could have kept it secret. For one thing, a longboat crew had been practicing less than a kilometer away. They heard the explosion when the laser punched through the wall of the building full of vacuum. All thirty-four were still staring when the side of the building collapsed and there was a huge spray of water.

From their angle they couldn't see the artifact. But the building was continually monitored by an automatic extreme-telephoto camera that CNN had mounted on a hillside on Mount Vaia, overlooking the bay. It caught the building's collapse, and zoomed in on the artifact rising leisurely back up to its original position.

No one on Samoa knew that there was a hasty conference in Washington five minutes later, the president pulled out of a late-night poker game to help decide whether to vaporize their island. Somebody was disingenuous enough to point out that it really wouldn't be an act of war, since there were no hostilities between the two nations, and one of them would no longer exist after the explosion. The president's response to that was characteristically curt, and he went back to his game after demanding that a summary of events be on his table in the morning.

It would be one short page. Poseidon wasn't talking, and the NASA team abided by their agreement.

They ran the tape over and over, along with the sensor data, and on the hundredth viewing they knew little more than on the first. As the laser cranked up to 72 percent of full force, the temperature of the artifact began to increase, all over. When it was 1.2 degrees Centigrade above the ambient temperature, it rose diagonally off its cradle at 18.3 centimeters per second, travelling at a 45-degree angle until it was over the laser's output tube. Then it fell to the floor. It was like dropping an apartment building on a wineglass. The floor didn't resist.

The part under the cradle didn't collapse; it was independently supported. It probably *would* have crumbled if the artifact had fallen on it, too. But it seemed only interested in the laser. When it came back up, it settled into the cradle as gently as a feather.

The researchers had to study the CNN record of that part, their ruggedized camera lying ruggedly on the bottom of the bay, its backup power source sending a record of swirling silt. Exactly 1.55 seconds after the splash, the artifact rose back out of the water, still at a constant rate of 18.3 centimeters per second, and settled back into its cradle. The scene was unchanged when Russ and Jan pedaled up a couple of minutes later.

While a work crew nervously reconstructed the artifact room and its protective surround, a separate NASA crew—at least they wore identically new NASA coveralls—retrieved the drowned laser and power source and analyzed the damage. It was profound.

Jack Halliburton didn't normally walk into cottage 7 unannounced. The crowd of nine who were sitting around the table piled high with reports and lunch remains fell silent when he came through the door.

Russ was one of the most surprised. "Jack. You want a sandwich?"

He shook his head and sat down on the chair offered. "Get me the output curve for the laser just before the artifact fell on it."

Moishe Rosse, who had become their laser guy, picked up two cylindrical keyboards and started surfing, the big TV acting as a monitor.

"It's a simple step function," Russ said. "Turns off."

"I know. I want to know exactly when and why."

"Good luck with the why." The innards of the power source were deeply classified; they used it as a black box that always delivered what you asked.

"They told me a little something." A familiar graph appeared on the screen, the output of the laser slightly rising and then falling off abruptly. The abscissa of the graph was ticked off in microseconds.

"Give me a split screen and let's see what happens on the real-time tape a couple of microseconds before it turns off."

The artifact was slowly rising, two millimeters per microsecond. The image rolled around slowly—the slow-motion record of violent dislocation—when the laser beam slid under the artifact and punched through the opposite wall.

"Hold it. Stop it right there." The frame's time was 06:39:23.705. The graph showed the power shutting off at 06:39:23.810.

"More than a tenth of a second. So?" Russ gestured at the screen. "What did they tell you?" They had assumed that either the laser had shut off automatically, via some internal safety circuit, or the violence of the implosion had done the job. The feds weren't talking.

Jack was silent, staring, for a long moment. "What evidently happened," he said, "at 23.810, was that all the plutonium in that reactor turned to lead."

"Turned to lead?"

"Yeah. That's why it stopped working. You can't get blood out of a turnip."

"Good God," Moishe said. "Where did all that energy go?"

"At a first guess, inside our little friend."

"How many grams of plutonium?" Russ said.

"They're still not talking. But they acted nervous as hell. I don't think they have grams on their collective mind. I think it's tons, kilotons, megatons."

"TNT equivalent," Russ said.

Jack nodded. "They want to evacuate the island."

"Megatons?" Russ said, his eyes widening. "What have we been sitting on?"

"Like I say, they're not talking numbers. Besides, I have a suspicion that they're also not talking about the *thing* blowing up. I think they want to be free to nuke it to atoms if it looks dangerous."

"'If'!"

Jack looked around the room. "I suspect we'll lose some of our crew here, too. Can't say I'd blame anyone for leaving."

Moishe broke the silence. "What, when it's just getting interesting?"

They weren't going to move 200,000 Samoans just by saying "You're in danger; you have to leave." For one thing, the "independent" in Independent Samoa applied mostly to America. Anybody who wanted to live under Uncle Sam's thumb could take the ferry to American Samoa.

There was also the matter of where to put them. American Samoa was dismally crowded. New Zealand and Australia were virtually closed, having absorbed more than

100,000 Samoans over the past century—and that emigration of course siphoned off the ones who wanted to leave the traditional lifestyle.

The other islands in the group were mostly impenetrable jungle or volcanic waste. Savai'i had 60,000 people crowded into a necklace of towns along the inhabitable coast, and didn't want more.

Besides, most Samoans were deeply religious and somewhat fatalistic. If God chose to take them, He would. And it would be disrespectful to the point of sacrilege to leave their homes, with generations of ancestors buried in the front yards. Pollsters said that even if the United States completely paid for relocation, they'd only move about 20 percent of the population.

Samoans pointed out that it would be a lot simpler to move the artifact. The land didn't belong to Poseidon, let alone to the U.S. government; it was leased. The family that owned the land could evict them.

Jack applied his skills as a negotiator to that aspect of the problem. He had a meeting with the local village elders, the *fono,* and pointed out that evicting them, while a defensible act, had its negative side. It would be, in effect, capitulating to U.S. nuclear might. It would be a breach of agreement—an agreement that involved far more money and prestige than the village had ever known—and some would see that as a humiliation. Besides, if they cooperated, Jack would, in gratitude, renovate both schools and build a new church.

He never mentioned Poseidon. The deal had been with him.

It wound up costing the renovation of two more churches and the sponsorship of a celebratory feast. But honor won the day.

(The fact that the Samoan national government wanted the village to evict Poseidon had worked to Jack's advantage. The primacy of village law was written into the constitution, and there was no question that in matters of real estate—a touchy subject on the finite island—village law trumped the feds. The elders took pleasure in reaffirming this principle.)

The rebuilding was profound. The dome over the experimental area, besides providing environmental isolation, was to serve as a double blast confinement volume, a dome of titanium inside a dome of steel. Jack and Russ and Jan united in opposing the extra expense and complication. If the artifact decided to explode, the domes might as well be made of cardboard.

The government, still under the aegis of NASA but with much more money and clout than the agency possessed, agreed that they were probably right. The double dome was a just-in-case precaution.

Also "just in case" were the manacles that supposedly held the artifact down, attached to arm-thick cables that were deeply anchored in bedrock. They had calculated the amount of force it had taken to lift the artifact off its cradle; the manacles could hold down four to six times as much. No one who had seen the airy effortless grace with which the artifact had floated up would bet on the cables.

It was Jan's turn to run the show. Having scalded and frozen and zapped the thing, with no result other than disaster—maybe now it was time to talk to it.

berkeley, california, 1948

College was harder the second time around. Oceanography had been a natural pursuit for the changeling; English and literature were not, especially in the advanced classes mandated by Stuart's performance in high school. The changeling ground through one semester and changed its major to anthropology.

Anthro was a natural, too, since it had been objectively studying the human race for sixteen accelerated years. The only problem was limiting its class responses and papers to perceptions appropriate to a bright but unworldly lad from Iowa—who had never been in an insane asylum or boot camp, and had only read about Bataan in the newspapers.

The changeling changed. It would never be human, but it was human enough for something like empathy with its professors. They were trying to understand, and teach about, the human condition—but were themselves trapped in human bodies; stuck in human culture like ancient insects in amber.

The changeling had an advantage there. Whatever it was, it wasn't human. It began to suspect it wasn't even from Earth.

A few months before it had come up out of the sea onto California soil for the second time, a pilot named Kenneth Arnold had seen a formation of flying discs weaving through the Cascade Mountains of Washington State. People on the ground reported seeing them, too.

Then there was a lot of excitement over one of them crashing outside Roswell, New Mexico, though the Army Air Force investigators said it was just a weather balloon. Belief in the "flying saucer" explanation persisted, though.

During the changeling's first year at Berkeley, an Air National Guard pilot crashed while trying to intercept an Unidentified Flying Object, as they had come to be called. The Air Force (as *it* had come to be called) established Project Sign to investigate UFOs.

The changeling followed press reports avidly. As it turned out, though Project Sign's report rejected the idea of extraterrestrial origin, saying UFOs were misinterpretations of natural phenomena, an earlier top-secret "Estimate of the Situation" apparently thought otherwise. But that would stay top secret for a long time. Project Sign was changed to Project Grudge, and when it was terminated at the end of 1949, the Air Force explicitly denied the possibility of extraterrestrial origin, adding mass hysteria and "war nerves" to the natural-phenomenon explanation, and also said that many of the reports were cynical frauds by publicity-seekers or the hallucinations of psychologically disturbed people.

Most of the changeling's anthropology professors went along with the mass-hysteria/war-nerves explanation, but many of the students felt otherwise. They thought it was a government cover-up.

There were plenty of books and magazines to support that point of view, but the changeling found them unconvincing, even though it was pretty sure there was at least *one* being from another planet on Earth. By the time Project Blue Book supplanted Project Grudge, the changeling was looking elsewhere.

It searched both legend and science for shape-changers; for people suspected of being immortal, invulnerable. There was a lot more legend than science, all of it conveniently buried in history and hearsay.

It slipped away from Berkeley during vacation periods to search down and interview some suspects: two men who shed their skin every year, like snakes, and a woman who claimed to shed bones, just sliding them out through her skin. The woman was a fraud and the two men were apparently humans, but dermatalogical freaks. One of them had carefully peeled off a hand, outside in, over the course of weeks; he let the changeling put it on like a glove.

All human. But the changeling itself had instinctively hidden its true nature from the beginning, and had so far been successful. Others would probably do the same.

It briefly considered running ads in big-city newspapers—"Are you fundamentally different from the rest of humanity?"—but knew enough about human nature to predict the kind of response it would get.

It didn't think about the possibility of someone like the chameleon, who might track down the ad's creator with murderous intent. But then it didn't think it could die.

fort belvoir, virginia, 1951

The chameleon also took an interest in UFOs; unlike the changeling, it moved in on the source of information.

It had spent thousands of years in armies, and in fact had been a Nazi in World War II. The Korean War was kind of unappealing, but the chameleon knew enough about military red tape that it was only a matter of patience to make itself an E4 clerk on the Pentagon staff, Airman (a title only a month old) Fourth Class Patrick Lucas. Once there, it listened to scuttlebutt and managed to move itself into Project Blue Book.

Once there, it gave itself a promotion in an irregular way, which it had done before: when a new bachelor officer was assigned to the project, the chameleon studied his personnel file, befriended him the first day, got him alone in his apartment, and killed him.

In the bathtub it performed a rough-and-ready autopsy, thorough enough to ensure that the officer was indeed human—because something like the chameleon, if such existed, might also be drawn to Blue Book.

It wrote a suicide note for Airman Lucas, and at two in the morning traded uniforms and dogtags with the officer. Drained of blood, the officer looked like a pale, passed-out drunk. The chameleon carried his body quickly to its car, and drove to the end of a dirt road outside of Vienna, Virginia. It saturated the body and the front seat with gasoline, tossed in a match, and changed its appearance, almost instantly, to match the officer's. Then it ran through the woods back to civilization.

The short newspaper article only said that the body had been burned beyond recognition, but the car was registered to a Pentagon clerk. Investigators that morning found the suicide note, and the case was closed. Coworkers shook their heads; he always had been a loner.

The new lieutenant seemed to be a loner, too, and once the theory that he was a plant from the CIA was whispered around, people pretty much did leave him alone.

The chameleon-lieutenant's function for several months was to winnow through UFO reports, to find the 10 percent or so that warranted some follow-up. It ordered calendars back to 1948, and with the aid of an ephemeris, marked off the evenings and mornings when the planet Venus was particularly bright. That saved a lot of time.

It knew about Projects Sign and Grudge, and was not surprised to get the feeling that Blue Book was less interested in scientific evaluation of UFO reports than in public relations, mostly debunking. Some people saw evidence of a conspiracy there, but the chameleon just saw the conservative military mind at work. Project Blue Book was basically one officer and a few low-ranking clerks, with a couple of dozen other people, military and civilian, poking their noses in every now and then.

It seemed to spend as much time dealing with the press

and politicians as with UFOs. Whenever there was a slow news day, reporters would show up or phone, in search of copy. Politicians would demand to know why nothing had been done about some sightings in their districts.

With a typically military instinct for putting the right man in the right job, they put the chameleon in charge of the phone. Of course, it had had thousands of years' experience in dealing with people. But tact had never been its usual weapon of choice.

The chameleon observed its fellow investigators as keenly as it did the pilots and police and farmers who had reported the phenomena, reasoning that if there were something else like it in the world, it might gravitate to Fort Belvoir. But its counterpart was on the other coast, involved in the same pursuit in its own way, having given up on flying saucers.

After another year, the chameleon did, too. One day, instead of reporting for duty, it drove on into Washington and bought a wardrobe of work clothes from used-clothing stores, and by the time its superiors realized one of their investigators had gone AWOL, it was working on a dairy farm in western Maryland.

The idea of signaling alien intelligence with a message that didn't depend on language went back to 1820: the mathematical genius Carl Friedrich Gauss suggested clearing an immense section of Siberian forest, and then planting wheat in three squares that would diagram the Pythagorean theorem. An observer on Mars would be able to see it with a small telescope.

There were other schemes in the nineteenth and twentieth centuries, involving mirrors reflecting sunlight, huge fires demonstrating geometrical shapes, or cities blinking their lights on and off.

Around 1960, Mars no longer a compelling target, Frank Drake and others suggested an elaboration of this "Morse code" approach that would be visible from interstellar distances, using radio telescopes as transmitters rather than antennas, sending out a tight beam of digital information. The reasonable assumption was that any civilization advanced enough to receive the message would be able to understand binary arithmetic. So they sent, in essence, a series of dots and dashes that said "1+1=2," and went on from there.

The idea was to establish a matrix, a rectangle of boxes that would make an understandable picture if you made some of the boxes (corresponding to "1") black and left the others (corresponding to "0") white—like a crossword puzzle before it's filled out.

For it to make sense, you had to know the dimensions of the rectangle. The easiest way to do it would be to broadcast the information one line at a time, with pauses between the lines. Then a longer pause, and repeat the same thing over, for verification.

That does take a long time. Drake suggested that a single long string of ones and zeros would suffice, if there were some way to tell how many of them made up each line.

Prime numbers were the answer. Any pair of prime numbers, multiplied together, produces a number you can't arrive at with any other pair. The number thirty-five can only come from seven times five, so a sufficiently clever alien could look at this string of ones and zeros:

101010110100011110101101010010101

and come up with this rectangle:

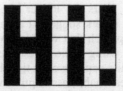

Of course a five-by-seven rectangle is just as likely, but gives this:

—which we would hope is not insulting in the alien's language.

With a large enough number of spaces, the difference between order and chaos is obvious. Drake's example was 551 characters, which made a map twenty-nine by nineteen spaces. Of course it didn't spell out an English word; in fact, it was meant to be an *incoming* signal: it showed a crude drawing of an alien creature and a diagram of its solar system, along with other shapes that indicated it was carbon-based life, that it was thirty-one wavelengths tall, and that there were seven billion individuals on its planet—and three thousand colonists on the next planet in, and eleven explorers on the next one.

The message Jan would send the artifact used the same technique, though it could be much more elaborate, since the receiver was inches away rather than light-years. Starting with the same arithmetic and mathematics, it went beyond a stick-figure-plus-DNA diagram to present digital representations of Einsteinian relativity, photographs of several different people, a Bach fugue, one of Hokusai's views of Fujiyama, and Vermeer's *Girl with a Pearl Earring* in black and white.

The signal took about fifteen minutes to transmit. Fo-

cusing on various parts of the artifact, they beamed it in
every frequency from microwave to X ray; they tapped it
out mechanically on the thing's surface. Of course there
was no way of predicting what its response would be.
Maybe it *was* responding in some way they couldn't de-
tect—saying "Shut up and give me some peace!" It was
reasonable, though, to expect that it would respond in a
way similar to the message: light or sound in a similar binary sequence.

Of course it might just be a dumb machine, capable of
moving itself out of harm's way, and nothing else.

After two weeks of no results, Jan was discouraged. She
asked Russ and Jack to meet her at the Sails for dinner and
strategy.

The two men showed up together just as the sundown
storm started. The setting sun was a dull red ball on the
horizon while sheets of rain marched sideways across the
harbor. No thunder or lightning; just an incessant downpour.

"Another wonderful day in paradise," she said.

"E.T. hasn't phoned home?" Jack said as he sat down.

"Got 'call waiting.'" The waiter appeared with the wine
list. Jack waved it away and ordered a bottle of Bin 43.

"So what do you think?" Russ said.

"Oh, I don't know." She refilled her coffee cup from a
silver thermos flask. "I guess it's time to move on to the
planetary environments phase. If it reacts to anything, I can
repeat the Drake algorithm then." She sipped the coffee.
"As you say, Russ, maybe it's asleep or in some dormant
mode. Maybe if we reproduce its home planet's conditions,
it will be more inclined to talk."

Jan winced as a shift of wind sent a fine spray over them.
"Waiter," Jack said, standing and pointing to a table just inside. He carried Jan's coffee flask in, and while a woman lit
candles, the waiter appeared with a bottle and three glasses.

"I'm willing to be patient," Jack said, going through the
tasting ritual.

"It's not a matter of patience." She put her hand over her wineglass. "I feel as if we've gone as far as we can in this direction."

"Well, we knew it was going to be all or nothing," Russ said. "Just one peep out of the thing and we'd be . . ." He rose an eyebrow and took a sip of wine.

"Yes, we would," she said. "But we're not. Let's move on."

"Starting at square one?" Jack said. "Mercury?"

"We could start anywhere," Russ said. "Mercury is going to cost out better. Just hot vacuum."

"So there's a decision?"

He looked at Jan. "Acoustic. We want to continue tapping out your message on the thing's surface. If it responds acoustically, we won't hear it in a vacuum."

"We can run a taut wire from it," Jack said, "like a tin-can telephone."

"Hard to get it through the wall without damping vibrations."

Jack shrugged. "So don't run it through." He spread out his napkin and clicked a pen open. He drew a square inside a square and attached the inner to the outer with springs. "See? You have your taut wire pulling on the back of *this*"—he tapped the inner square—"and it acts like an old-fashioned speaker. It's gonna vibrate in a way that mimics the artifact's vibrations."

"But we still can't hear it," Jan said.

"Ah, but we can *watch* it. Draw a grid on the square and put a camera on it."

"Fourier transforms," Russ said with approval.

"Duck soup," Jack said.

"We have no duck," the waiter said. He was standing behind Jack's shoulder. "We have clam chowder or chicken with mushrooms."

Russ looked at him and decided he wasn't joking. "I'll have the chowder and grilled masimasi."

"Me, too," Jan said.

"The usual," Jack said.

"Cholesterol with cholesterol sauce," Jan said.

"You will have a red wine with that?"

"Bin 88," Jack and Russ said simultaneously. "And I want it really *blue* this time," Jack said of his steak. "Cold in the center."

The waiter nodded and left. Russ imitated his accent: "Sir, we cannot guarantee that you will survive this meal. Samoan cattle have parasites for which there are no Western names."

Jack smiled and refilled both glasses of white wine. "Mercury, and then go on to Mars? Vacuum with a little carbon dioxide. Then Venus and the gasbags."

"Good name for a rock band," Russ said.

"Titan?" Jan said. "Europa?"

"Makes sense," Russ said. "And just outer space, 2.8 degrees above absolute zero. It probably spent a long time in that environment."

"Hold on," Jan said, and took an old computer out of her purse. She unrolled the keyboard and pulled out the antenna and typed a few words. "Let's be methodical here. Starting with the mercurian environment." They got halfway through the solar system before dinner came, and finished it over sherry and cheese, mapping out a rough schedule. They would spend five days with each environment, and one to four days in transition.

Hot Mercury, cool Mars, hellish Venus, cold poison Titan, arctic Europa, then the Jovian model: high-pressure liquid hydrogen and helium, flowing at about 150 meters per second, flavored with methane and ammonia.

Jan took a sip of sherry and scrolled through the schedule. "Something bothers me."

Jack nodded. "The pressure chamber's—"

"No. What if the thing misunderstands? What if it thinks we're attacking it?"

Russ laughed nervously. "I thought I was the anthropo-morphic one."

"If it does its little jump-off-the-pedestal trick while it's in the Jupiter simulation . . ."

"Be worse than a daisy-cutter bomb," Jack said. "Flatten everything out to here. They'll hear it in American Samoa."

"In Fiji," Russ said. "Honolulu."

cambridge, massachusetts, 1967

For a few months, the changeling and the chameleon were in the same city, doing more or less the same things.

The chameleon was at MIT, studying marine engineering. It had enjoyed Korea as a naval officer, and wanted to learn more about the design of warships.

It liked anything about killing.

The changeling had gotten its doctorate in anthropology in 1960. Combining its deep knowledge of Earth's biology with a broad knowledge of the cultures that crawled all over the planet convinced it that it had to be from somewhere else. So it went to Harvard with impeccably faked credentials (again a boy from California) and began the study of astronomy and astrophysics.

If they ever rode together on the Red Line or had a beer at the same time at the Plough and Stars, they were unaware of being in the company of a fellow extraterrestrial. They were both looking for other aliens; they were both too experienced to be found out.

Neither one was drafted for Vietnam. The changeling faked severe stomach ulcers. The chameleon finished its master's degree and joined Officer Candidate School.

So while the chameleon pointed eight-inch guns at unseen targets in the Vietnamese jungle, the changeling pointed huge telescopes at unseen targets outside the galaxy. It mostly counted photons and put the numbers into a BASIC program, which dispensed something like truth. Sometimes, unlike professional astronomers, the changeling unhooked the telescope from its photon counter and actually looked through it at the night sky.

It was fascinated with globular clusters, and eventually hunted down all of the hundred-some visible from Massachusetts. It saw its home, M22, as a fuzzy blob shot through with sparkles, and returned to it many times without knowing why.

The changeling had a master's in astronomy by 1974, but felt it had to know more about computers before continuing on, so it moved down to MIT for a couple of years, studying electrical engineering and computer science.

Two of its professors had taught an alien before.

It liked the area, and so returned to Harvard for its Ph.D. in astrophysics, where it had another coincidental encounter. As part of its graduate assistantship, it graded papers for an elementary astrophysics course, Atmospheres of the Sun and Stars. One of its students was Jan Dagmar, who it would meet more than forty years later, in Samoa.

Harvard followed the tradition of kicking its chicks out of the nest, so after its doctorate, the changeling had to look elsewhere for work. The natural place was the National Radio Observatory in Green Bank, West Virginia, where Frank Drake had started Project OZMA, which after twenty years had evolved into the SETI Project, the Search for Extraterrestrial Intelligence.

The changeling worked there, massaging data, for two years, and then took an indefinite leave of absence, and a

series of profound career shifts. It was an exotic dancer
and part-time prostitute in Baltimore for a while, then a
short-order cook back in Iowa City. As an old lady, it read
palms on the county-fair circuit in the Midwest, and
returned to California in its old Jimmy body to be a surf
bum for a couple of seasons.

Sacrificing half its mass, it became a juggling dwarf
with the Barnum & Bailey Circus, making contacts in the
freak world. It met some interesting people, but they all
seemed to be from Earth, no matter what they claimed.

It married the Bearded Lady, an even-tempered and sar-
donic hermaphrodite, and they lived together until 1996.
The changeling left behind a hundred ounces of gold and
no explanation, and became a student again.

After absorbing two stray dogs, it went back to the
Jimmy template, but took the body past California and
down to Australia. It studied marine science at Monash
University, aware that most of what it had studied a half
century before had been profoundly revised.

It had learned to trust certain feelings—memories
buried so deep they were no longer memories—and one of
those feelings was a special affinity for deep waters, and
the Pacific.

- 30 -

apia, samoa, 2021

They decided it would be prudent to build a blast wall between the laboratory and the island, before starting the planetary environment experiment. If the Jupiter simulation blew up, they might still hear it in Fiji, but at least it wouldn't level Apia.

The wall was three meters thick at its base, curving up to one meter thickness at the top, ten meters high. It was a semicircle 150 meters in diameter, open to the sea. Local artists were hired to paint bright murals on the land side, but it was still an eyesore. The local *fono* was appeased by a schoolbus and two stained-glass windows for the Methodist church.

In the event of an explosion, all the force that would have gone landward should be diverted straight up or expended on destroying the blast wall, which was made of a foamed concrete that would boil off rather than break.

But they were months away from Jupiter. The original plan had been to start with Mercury, but the technical staff argued for doing Mars first. Two of the techs, Naomi and Moishe, had gone to Florida and been fitted with modified NASA space suits, and spent a few weeks training with them. They could comfortably enter the Martian environment and check out the situation. Mercury was marginal; their suits' air-conditioning could only handle it for short periods. It was logical to start the experiment under conditions that allowed continuous direct human contact.

So for the first couple of days, Naomi and Moishe walked around on their tenth-acre of "Mars," checking the place for leaks from the outside world, running tests on all the sensors and communication devices in the relatively clement environment.

Only relatively: the atmospheric pressure was pumped down to about a hundredth that of sea level, and there was no oxygen in their brew, just carbon dioxide with traces of nitrogen and argon. It was refrigerated down to minus one hundred degrees Centigrade, and cycled up to a balmy twenty-six, simulating the Martian equator during the summer. The ambient light was dim and pink, heavy on the ultraviolet.

The environment caused no serious problems, so Jan essentially repeated the three-minute Drake message over and over, tapping it out and blinking it in various wavelengths, in a pattern they would repeat in every environment: radio waves to microwaves through visible light to ultraviolet. They didn't go up into gamma or X rays, which they felt could be perceived as aggression.

In the original back-of-the-menu plan, they started with radio waves at a wavelength of one meter, and then went to a tenth of a meter, and then microwaves at one centimeter, and so forth, the seventh and eighth iterations being ultraviolet. But Jack pointed out that there was nothing special about the number ten, except for creatures who have ten tentacles or fingers, so to be nonprovincial about it they used 9.8696, pi squared, as the divisor.

The artifact tolerated Mars but didn't remark on it, so they pumped out the thin gruel of its atmosphere and substituted the hot vacuum of Mercury. A blazing artificial sun crawled across the sky while Jan's message patiently tapped and bleeped and blinked through the inferno, 600 degrees K., hot enough to melt lead.

But Mercury was a picnic spot compared to Venus. They stayed on the safe side of the blast wall and pumped in hot carbon dioxide, ninety atmospheres of it at 737 degrees K. As had been true with Mercury, the artifact's temperature rose at exactly the same rate as the ambient temperature. Its response to Jan's message was the same silence. They slowly brought the temperature and pressure back down to Samoan ambience, warm for North Americans, if fatally frigid for Venusians.

Some wiring and components had been stressed too much, and it hadn't been easy on the human components, either. So they took a few days off while replacement parts were assembled and shipped from various countries, and everybody took a short vacation over on the more old-fashioned island Savai'i.

After you'd seen the famous blowholes, there wasn't a lot to do unless you were a surfer with a death wish, so they mostly walked around enjoying the peacefulness. Some of them watched or played cricket. Jan engaged an old woman to teach her how to paint the traditional *siapo* cloth, and she spent a couple of afternoons doing that, making souvenir placemats for her grandchildren while listening to the hypnotic ocean crash, sipping the local fruit juice, not thinking about much. Trying not to.

They stayed at the venerable Safua Hotel, which was actually just a bunch of cottages around a central *fale,* where a buffet feast was offered for supper and an automated bar served as a social focus.

There was no cube on the island, by law, so the evening entertainment was homemade. Russ and Naomi played chess while most of the others listened to a pickup band of local kids who alternated modern music with traditional Samoan. They tried to teach everybody how to dance Samoan style, with little success except, surprisingly, Jack. He mumbled something about Hawaii when he was in the service.

After three days they got word that all the replacement equipment had arrived, and installation would be complete the next morning. So they took a light plane back to Apia—the ferry over having been a little rough for most of them—and with binoculars could occasionally see rays and sharks in the transparent water.

Muese, one of the native Samoan techs who had stayed behind, had dug a deep fire pit on the beach between the blast wall and the laboratory, and was roasting a pig, buried wrapped in taro leaves. He made a shallow pit in the afternoon and wrapped yams and potatoes in foil, and put a rack over the coals to grill chicken and fish.

Jack provided tubs of ice with drinks and a keg of beer, and invited all forty-eight employees of the project to the luau. There was no special reason to have a party, but no reason not to have one, either. Work would resume in earnest the next day.

Just before sundown, Muese dug up the pig and spent a half hour carving it, while others tended to the chicken and slabs of tuna and masimasi. The automatic security flood-lights came on, less romantic than guttering torches, but good light to cook and eat by.

After the sumptuous meal, a group got together by the fire with guitars, a harmonica, a fiddle, and a tin whistle, and played improbable Irish and Welsh music, popular in the States. Russ and Jan sat apart with a bottle of cold white Burgundy wrapped in a wet towel.

"So what happens next," Russ said, "if we get out to Jupiter and still don't have anything?"

She shrugged. "More invasive procedures, I suppose. Jack must have ideas. He's not committing himself."

Russ finished off his glass but didn't pour another. "He has more than ideas. He has an offer. From China."

"He didn't say anything."

"Yeah. I only know because I was in the office when the machine decrypted it. He couldn't tell me not to watch."

"Let me guess. They want to bury the thing in chop suey."

"Not even close. Chop suey's American, anyhow."

"I know. What is it?"

"They'll cosponsor putting the artifact into orbit. Split the cost of a cluster of four Long March rockets."

"And once in orbit?"

"Take the big laser up with it, I guess. Try it at a hundred percent, safely off Earth."

She shook her head. "Remind me to be somewhere else when it's overhead."

"I think he can be talked out of it. It would mean taking government money." He refilled both of their glasses. "We have to come up with something else, though."

She stared at the containment dome. "We could just send it into the future."

"First we build a time machine."

"I mean one day at a time. Just put a fence around it and wait for science to catch up with it." She took a sip, still staring. "Suspend the project for ten, fifty, a hundred years."

"Jack would die first."

She nodded. "As would we all."

washington, d.c., 1974

The chameleon decided to stay in one place and make a fortune. It had been wealthy in the past, spoils of war, but it had never been a rich capitalist, which sounded interesting.

It kept the core identity of a man who went to the office every morning, did his administrative work like a good drone, and then went home to his bachelor apartment, presumably to watch TV and read. He seemed uninterested in women, and most of his coworkers thought he was gay.

What the chameleon actually did at night was become young and gay, in both senses of the word. It dropped ten or fifteen years and pounds, which it could do in a painless second, and exchanged the office uniform for something eye-catching but tasteful. Then it either went on a date or went trolling for a new source of money.

It had three wealthy men paying regular "gifts," for discretion as well as services rendered, and made even more per month by picking up men and robbing them after sex. If they fought, it would sometimes have to kill them, but usually the threat of exposure was enough. It preferred to leave them alive, so it could identify them months or years later for a repeat performance, with a different face and body. There was a gay "scene" in Washington in the seventies, and the chameleon moved through it like an invisible predator.

It didn't prefer gay sex to straight; one was much like the other. It made less money as a woman, though, and as a gay prostitute it ate at better restaurants, and the other man still picked up the bill.

The seventies and eighties were good for the stock market, at least for conservative investors, and all of the money the chameleon made from sex and extortion went straight to its broker. After the first million, it became a broker itself, handling its various identities under yet another false one.

It didn't have a plan, in the sense of ambition. It watched its various fortunes grow and shrink and grow again like a horticulturist tending a garden, fertilizing in one season and pruning in the next.

It slowly became the richest creature in the world, though the wealth was scattered among a hundred identities and a thousand accounts. It started two small wars, as experiments, and profited from both, though not as well as it did in drugs and dot-coms.

It left dot-coms a year before they tanked, but then, instead of pushing its advantage, left the money to marinate for a year or decade or two. Something would come along.

Maybe money could accomplish what research had not, finding another one like himself. Humans were no challenge to kill.

melbourne, australia, 1997

The changeling settled into the Gippsland campus of Monash University in 1997, and spent four years earning a double degree in marine biology and biotechnology. It enjoyed Melbourne, but often spent its free time in the water, being a subject as well as a student of marine biology, and enjoying fresher fish than any sushi chef could offer.

Its academic performance was flawless, Monash being no more difficult than Harvard or MIT, and it accepted a full scholarship to James Cook University in Queensland, where it spent four years getting its M.S. and Ph.D. in marine biology, specializing (naturally enough) in the behavior of marine animals.

It took its fresh doctorate to AIMS, the Australian Institute of Marine Science, where it began researching "wonky holes," the fisherman's name for muddy holes that foul trawling nets near reefs. Many kilometers offshore, they turned out to be fresh water percolating from subterranean streams—a natural process that was having an unnatural effect on the reefs, because the water carried nutrients from farms, which fed algae, attracting fish. Fishermen kept the locations of wonky holes secret, because they attracted schools of fish—an easy day's catch was worth the occasional fouled net.

Investigating this phenomenon gave the changeling its first opportunity to see itself as a great white shark. AIMS was using underwater videocams to monitor fish populations, and one weekend the changeling went out to visit a camera site. It grabbed the bait box, used to attract smaller fish, in its powerful jaws, and crunched it flat, thrashing around in a natural reaction to the strange metallic flavor. It made for some great footage, which had gone all over the oceanographers' world by the time the changeling had turned back into a human and returned to the lab.

"Ugly customer," it said when it saw the tape, to predictable response: "No, it's *beautiful,* can't you see? It's just being a shark." Actually, it was engaging in unsharklike behavior at the time, analyzing the difference in the ocean's flavor around the wonky holes: slightly acidic fresh water. Bad for coral in the long run, though in the short run it was like an all-you-can-eat buffet for the small creatures that fed on algae and plankton, and the larger ones that fed on them, and on up the food chain to the fisherfolk who cursed the wonky holes for mucking up their nets, but kept returning.

In the long run, though, the wonky holes were one of several interlocking factors that were destroying the offshore parts of the Great Barrier Reef, which was bad for tourism as well as fishing. The changeling made them his specialty, and being a part-time shark gave him a huge advantage over other researchers: he could smell out wonky holes in the early stages of development, before they had attracted enough fish to draw the attention of humans. So he did "productive" analysis in reverse: he found relationships between fishing patterns near the shore and the formation of wonky holes, and scientifically predicted where to find the small ones.

This eventually led to a selective reforestation program—the excess percolation of fresh water was indirectly caused by the absence of trees, which would normally store large quantities of water after a rainfall, to harmlessly evaporate back into the clouds.

By this time its identity, as James "Jimmy" Coleridge, had been well established, a Californian who had adopted Australia with enthusiasm. At twenty-seven, Jimmy was considered quite a prodigy in the small world he'd mastered. James Cook University offered "the Wonky Hole Man" a tenure-track professorship, and the changeling took it with some enthusiasm, seeing it as a good platform from which to observe the overall situation of marine science in the Pacific.

Somewhere out here was the answer.

Young Dr. Coleridge was popular with his students, both the undergraduates in the general oceanography courses and the graduate students who worked with him in Special Problems in Marine Ecologies. It wooed and married one of its graduate students, Marcia, a beautiful blonde from Tasmania.

She dropped out of course work to become a faculty wife, a position for which she was not particularly well suited. She drew a lot of the wrong kind of attention from the faculty husbands, and obviously enjoyed it, flirting with more and more energy as her marriage failed to provide her with children—a reasonable enough ambition, but hard to realize if your husband has no gender and is not really human.

Moody and volatile, she became Jimmy's Tasmanian Devil, and it was inevitable that other men would try to tame her.

When she became pregnant in the spring of 2008, a lot of people suspected what her husband knew for sure.

The changeling didn't relish the prospect of complicating its life with children, so it was happier than most husbands would be when it turned out that the newborn's father was obviously of a different race. (How different, only Jimmy knew.) Some people admired the calm way he took it, and his magnanimity on giving her a no-fault divorce and blessing her remarriage to the only black man in their circle of friends. Other people thought it was a shameful abdication of his rights as a man. Even in Queensland, they wouldn't say "white man," but that's what many of them were thinking.

The scandal might have retarded his advance at JCU, so when an offer came for a full professorship at the University of Hawaii, Jimmy snapped it up like the hungry shark he used to be, on weekends.

The changeling decided to stay in the Jimmy Coleridge persona for a while. Having studied and taught in Australia for thirteen years gave it a slightly exotic accent and manner, having honed its twenty-first-century social skills in the tropical north. Jimmy was popular with the male faculty and students as a hale-fellow-well-met, who never got more than pleasantly tipsy but could drink anyone under the table. Of course to the changeling gin was as harmless as rocket fuel or hydrochloric acid.

Coleridge carried a respectable class load, with two graduate courses and a seminar as well as the large lecture class in Introductory Oceanography, which had room for 150 students and was always oversubscribed. He turned out papers with gratifying regularity, as well; between his social life and academic life, some wondered when he had time to sleep.

He pretended to sleep, of course, sometimes in the arms of a graduate student or young professor, which didn't harm his reputation. He wrote most of his papers in that mode, eyes closed and mind in high gear.

In the tenth year of his tenure, 2019, everything changed. Like everyone else, he read and saw the news about the strange artifact that Poseidon Projects had brought up from the Tonga Trench. Unlike most people, the changeling felt a shock of recognition.

It immediately got in touch with the project, and hit an absolute wall: no hiring. Every position filled by people who'd been in it from the start. Thanks, but no thanks. You can read our published data and do your own work.

Of course the changeling knew they wouldn't publish all the data. They were in pursuit of profit, not knowledge.

For the first time in its life it considered revealing its true nature. Want a consultant who can *really* help you with aliens?

But not yet.

apia, samoa, 30 may 2021

Europa, under its ice surface, was not too difficult. They considered not trying it at all, since the environment—cold saline solution under pressure—wasn't all that different from the Tonga Trench, where it evidently had been since approximately the dawn of time. Of course that also was a good argument *for* doing it. The artifact might respond to the familiar.

It showed no gratitude for Old Home Week, though, sitting as passively as ever, mirroring the ambient temperature but not otherwise acknowledging their efforts. It was a good test for the containment dome's integrity, which was going to be challenged by Jupiter, but otherwise did nothing other than raise the blood pressure of the observers along with the water pressure inside.

After Jan had finished her familiar algorithm, they depressurized and drained the dome, and prepared it for Io, the innermost of the four large moons, the Galilean satellites.

Io's atmosphere is exotic and variable, but thin almost

to the point of being a vacuum. It can get up to about a hundred nanobars and down to one (the air on the top of Mount Everest is 330 million nanobars). The fact that it's a poisonous mixture of sulfur dioxide and sodium isn't relevant to human survival; a human would freeze solid in the middle of explosive decompression, not having time to notice that the air smelled bad.

Still, it was possible that Io's surface conditions were not unusual in the universe, so they went ahead with the model, a frigid near-vacuum with a scattering of frozen sulfur dioxide on the floor. They varied the temperature from 100 degrees K. to 130 degrees, enough for some of the sulfur dioxide to sublimate, and then fall back as snow.

The artifact faithfully mirrored the changes in temperature, but otherwise ignored the investigation.

It wasn't much of a change to simulate Pluto, just suck out the sulfur dioxide, lower the temperature to minus 233, and put in a dusting of snow: solidified nitrogen, methane, and carbon monoxide, with a squirt of ethane flavoring the nitrogen. To any Earth creature, it would be indistinguishable from Io, but conceivably might make all the difference in the world to you, if you were used to living on a snowball in Hell.

They used the space suits for the last time—that was a part of the deal, that they record the suits' performance in the various environments—and then sent them back to NASA. They would be no help for Jupiter.

For the other planets, they had simulated surface conditions. That wouldn't be possible on Jupiter. Theoretical models allowed the possibility of a rocky core, but you can't get there. As you descend through Jupiter's increasingly thick atmosphere, it becomes more like a star than a planet—the temperature coming to about thirty thousand degrees and the pressure about 100 million atmospheres. It's "liquid metallic hydrogen" there, and if anything could live under those conditions, it was unlikely to find Earth interesting.

Jan decided to try two Jovian regimes: the one deep enough into the atmosphere that it enjoyed the same air pressure as Earth at sea level, though the temperature was minus 100 degrees C., and the deeper one where the pressure was five atmospheres, but the temperature was an Earth-like zero degrees. In both cases the atmosphere was about 90 percent hydrogen, and the rest helium with a little spicing—methane, ammonia, ethane, acetylene.

In terms of temperature and pressure, it was a lot easier to handle than Venus. But carbon dioxide isn't flammable. She looked at the huge tanks of hydrogen waiting for the high-pressure phase and tried not to think of it as a fireball waiting to happen.

It was more than a thousand times the quantity of hydrogen that exploded in the Hindenburg disaster.

By now, most of the people, Jan included, had little hope that the artifact was going to respond to anything. When it did, they thought it was an experimental error.

The thing inside the artifact didn't think, not the way humans think. It didn't pose problems and solve them. It didn't wonder about its place in the universe. It felt no real need to communicate.

Its mandate was survival, and it had powerful tools to that end. If the life that decorated the surface of this planet seemed to be a threat, it could simplify the situation. It had patience, fortunately, beyond any human reckoning of the term. All this tapping and zapping and flashing—it could stop the annoyance with one exercise of will, fry the planet clean.

But a central part of it was still out there. It could wait for its return. Maybe, it finally decided, speed up the return by tapping back.

When the changeling got off the plane at the Apia airport, the place was crazy with celebration, even though it was three in the morning. A couple of dozen young men and women danced and clapped and sang in harmony; bunting and flags were everywhere.

When it had boarded in Hawaii, it couldn't help noticing that several of the Caucasian passengers were unusually old. When the singing stopped, while it was waiting for its luggage, it found out what the story was. It was the sixtieth anniversary of Samoa's independence, and these old guys were the last survivors of the American forces that had been stationed here in World War II.

Bataan came back in a rush of bad memory, while the mayor of Apia welcomed the old vets and told stories she'd heard from her father and grandfather. The changeling listened respectfully, its face revealing nothing.

It was a pretty face. The changeling had the form of a young attractive woman.

The ad it had answered on the net was looking for a laboratory technician who could operate this and that machine and had knowledge of marine biology and astronomy. It didn't call for doctorates in those subjects, but then the changeling could hardly advertise those. Its faked credentials were impressive enough; it only claimed "wide reading" in marine biology and a B.S. in astronomy. (The degree actually belonged to the woman whose appearance it had taken. Safely out of the job market herself, she was the mother of triplets in Pasadena.)

Putting together a fake identity was more complicated than it used to be. It was not particularly hard for the changeling to pretend to be the woman from Pasadena; it even had her fingerprints and tattoos and scent. But it had taken a bit of computer wizardry to erase the records of her husband and triplets and substitute an impressive job record. It had taken even more to temporarily make sure that computer, phone, and fax messages were routed through the changeling before Rae Archer got them.

The actual Rae Archer was beautiful, and took pains to look less than her thirty years. The changeling modified the details so that it was the same face, but merely pretty, and thirty.

It had done it all in less than a day, once the ad appeared on *Sky and Telescope*'s website. (It automatically monitored anything with the key words "Apia" or "Poseidon Projects.") As Rae, it had talked to Naomi and then Jan, who agreed to give Ms. Archer an interview if she were willing to gamble the airfare out to Samoa and back. The changeling thought it had done a good job of imitating an excited young woman trying to contain her enthusiasm.

The real gamble, of course, was background checking. The changeling had inserted files attesting to Rae Archer's job competence in every position she'd held. But if Naomi or Jan decided to call the States and ask for an actual person's recollection of the woman's work, the web of deception would evaporate.

Apia was muggy and buggy at three in the morning. Almost every cab in town was waiting outside the airport—the plane from Honolulu only came in twice a week—but the changeling asked directions and did the sensible thing, taking the bus into town. It was twenty miles of slow driving either way. For an extra three dollars, the bus went a block out of its way and delivered the changeling to its door, a bed-and-breakfast just a kilometer up the beach from the Poseidon site.

The proprietor was there, heavy-lidded but friendly, to

show the changeling to its room. It feigned a couple of
hours' sleep (while relaying four e-mails to the real Rae
Archer and monitoring a wrong number) and then went out
to watch the dawn come up over the mountains.

The changeling suspected there might be some slowdown in things because of the anniversary, but it didn't expect an absolute rejection.

"Come back day after tomorrow," the guard with the phone said. "It might even be a week before anyone can see you." She asked why and he shook his head, listening to the receiver. "We'll reimburse you for your extra expenses." Listening again. "There's too much happening now. Just enjoy the town."

The changeling, of course, could clearly hear the other side of the conversation. The excitement in the woman's voice—it knew she was Naomi from the Stateside calls—was palpable. It had obviously come one day too late. There had been some breakthrough.

It walked most of the mile into town, stopping at a souvenir store to buy some informal clothes and change out of its business attire. The clerk showed it how to tie a lavalava dress, and it chose a matching blue shirt that it would have called Hawaiian in any other context. Gaudy earrings and a necklace of shells completed its camouflage.

Samoa had actually gained its independence on January first, but since that was already a holiday, they sensibly moved the celebration up to June. The changeling walked on into town in a resigned, almost grim, mood. Enjoy, enjoy.

It found all kinds of dancing and singing, which might have been more interesting to an actual human. Feasting, similarly irrelevant. Canoe and outrigger races and horses prancing through dressage routines.

The changeling used its simulated Americanness and feminine charm to get close to a couple of the vets, both slightly over a hundred years old.

One was surprisingly clear-headed and articulate, especially about war: he was against it. After WWII, he had fought in Korea and had no sympathy for it or Vietnam or the dozen smaller wars and fake wars that followed.

(His WWII assignment to Samoa had been a stroke of luck. The Japanese high command had at the last minute decided not to invade and occupy the Samoan Islands; the only contact with them in the whole war had been a long-distance burst of machine-gun fire from a passing submarine, which hurt no one.)

He was unaware of the Poseidon project, though he well remembered the submarine disaster that had provided a pretext for its beginning. Never would have happened if the goddamned fat cats had kept their mitts off Indonesia, a not uncommon opinion which had not kept the United States out of the current conflict there. As part of the international peace-keeping force, that is, which was 88 percent American and was conspicuously not keeping the peace.

The changeling having practiced its "pretty American girl" routine on the old man got her a holovision news spot. That didn't hurt her job prospects, as it turned out, because it happened to be aired at the time when the exhausted research team broke for dinner, and Jan recognized her name. Russ probably decided right then that he was going to hire her, just to brighten up the place.

The changeling walked all day exploring Apia, aware that it was far from a typical day. No race could play so hard and expect to survive.

The next morning it was again rebuffed; everyone was too busy for interviews. It went back to the B-and-B and spent the rest of the day searching the web, building a mosaic of such information as Poseidon had parsimoniously released, along with a wealth of rumors and speculation.

Some of the speculation was extremely bizarre, ascribing to the project a CIA genesis, or even suggesting that they were all aliens, and had made up this ruse to slowly break the news to the human race.

The changeling was possibly the most intelligent reader who saw that one and wondered if it just might be true. In fact, though, it wasn't.

There were only two aliens on the island.

pago pago, american samoa, june 2021

Apia was too local and too small for a killing spree, and the chameleon was getting bored. He left work a few minutes early and took a cab to the little Fagali'i Airport outside of town, and got on the six o'clock puddle-jumper over to American Samoa. The twelve-passenger plane had sixteen passengers, but four of them were children sitting on their mothers' laps. The flight was only forty minutes long, but forty long bouncing minutes locked up with crying and puking children could turn even a normal man's thoughts to violence. The chameleon distracted himself conjuring images of infanticides past.

It was still blistering hot at the Pago Pago airport, but worse in town: it had been a "bad tuna day." Almost half of the people in American Samoa work in one of the two tuna canneries; the plants' malodorous waste goes into the harbor to compete with sewage for one's attention on hot still days.

Darkness brought a breeze, though. The chameleon

went down to the waterfront in search of trouble. The area east of the canneries, the Darkside, was where to find it. On his way down, he ducked into an alley and came out the other end looking like a rumpled Pakistani sailor.

The first couple of bars looked too quiet for fun, catering to the yachties who moored in the cesspool long enough to take on provisions—and perhaps avail themselves of the Darkside's cheap women and inexpensive drugs.

He heard a commotion and went into a dark dive called Goodbye Charlie's. Two tall and muscular Samoans were standing at the bar, yelling at each other in a couple of languages. The bartender watched them warily, evidently moving bottles and glasses out of reach. The other patrons were looking on with an air of detachment. It might be a regular evening diversion.

The chameleon took the only empty seat at the bar and waved an American twenty. The bartender sidled over, not taking his eyes off the two. "Yeah?"

"I would like a Budweiser and an ounce of whisky," he said with a pronounced Pakistani accent. The bartender gave him a look and snatched the twenty away.

He came back with no change, a warm bottle of Bud, and a tumbler that had been rinsed but not cleaned. He poured a generous inch of liquor into it from a bottle without a label.

"Are those gentlemen twinking?" the chameleon asked.

"Tweaking? I guess." American Samoa's drug of choice was methamphetamine, ice. People coming off it get into a dark mood, sometimes argumentative and combative, "tweaking." It could lead to violence.

The chameleon drank the whisky in two gulps and slid off the stool. He walked unsteadily over to stand in front of the two sailors. "I say." They ignored him. "I *say!* Will you quiet down?"

"Yeah, right, fuck with 'em," a drunk American said into the sudden silence. The two looked blearily down at the little Pakistani, a foot shorter than them. One leaned forward and swung at him, an open-handed slap.

The chameleon ducked under the blow and grabbed the man's wrist and twisted, bringing him to his knees. He twisted harder and pulled, and the man's shoulder joint popped like a chicken leg coming off. He rolled down on the floor, keening in pain. The chameleon silenced him with two vicious head kicks. Bar stools crashed all around as most people backed away from the action. The drunk American stayed seated and applauded slowly.

"Tough little Paki," the other Samoan said, and produced a box cutter from somewhere.

"Enough!" the bartender roared. "Take it outside!"

"Okay." The chameleon turned on his heel and walked toward the door.

Witnesses would later tell the police that whatever happened was too fast to follow. The Samoan touched the Pakistani on the shoulder, evidently, and he spun around.

The Pakistani handed the Samoan his box knife back and said, "Ta." The Samoan stood up straight and looked at the scarlet stain spreading on the abdomen of his T-shirt. Then loops of bluish blood-stained guts slid out, hanging to his knees, and he crumpled over dead.

No one saw the Pakistani leave. When they crowded out the door, there was no one there except an old man sitting on the pier, fishing with a handline.

In the morning, the police would find two prostitutes' bodies in a Dumpster. There were strangle signs on their necks, livid finger and thumb marks, but they'd died of cerebral hemorrhage, their heads beaten together.

When the sun rose higher, they smelled and found a dead Pakistani sailor in an alleyway, inexplicably naked. Case closed, anyhow.

The chameleon was gone by then, on the dawn flight back to Apia, in a much improved mood.

apia, samoa, june 2021

The third morning was clear and calm, so the changeling took mouthgill and gear down to the Palolo Deep Marine Preserve, less than a kilometer down the road. It had formed a bathing suit around its body, modest by American standards, but also wore the lavalava walking to the beach, so as not to offend the locals—who were all sleeping it off anyhow, except for the yawning young girl who took its money at the park entrance.

The tide was high. The changeling put on its unnecessary mask, mouthgill, and fins, and slipped into the familiar medium.

In the shallows between the shore and the reef, there was a scene of unearthly strangeness—a many-acre farm of giant clams, thousands of them, from a foot in diameter to the size of manhole covers and larger. There were smaller ones protected by enclosures of chicken wire; the changeling salivated at the thought of what they would taste like. It worked a small one out of its cage and, hardening its teeth, crunched down on it: delicious.

The reef was beautiful, a multicolor maze of living coral, but that wasn't the changeling's destination. It swam quickly beyond, out to where the waves crashed on the barrier reef that separated the island from the deeps. It cut through the strong swirling currents, found a jagged opening, and dove through.

It swam down through the cool stillness to the bottom, and stashed its equipment under a rock.

How fast could it change into a shark?

It took twelve pain-filled minutes, perhaps its fastest time. Halfway through, it was visited by a reef shark almost its size, which circled it a few times and nosed it, and apparently decided that whatever the strange thing was, you couldn't eat it or breed with it, and drifted away. Sea creatures did occasionally bite the changeling, but most of them immediately spit out the alien stuff.

It became a hammerhead for the good eyesight, and swam a couple of kilometers south, to visit the Poseidon site. It was easy to find, following a metallic taste that was quite different from anything it had experienced before. It found the source easily, warm water coming out of a discharge tube; it evidently cooled the nuclear reactor that powered the place.

After a minute's search, it found the intake tube as well. That could come in handy. If you plugged it up, how long would it be before the reactor started to heat up and shut down? Or melt down.

It inspected the parts of the blast shield that were in reasonably deep water, not wanting to attract attention. A nine-foot-long hammerhead would be pretty conspicuous in shallow water. It could hear children splashing and swimming on the village side of the shield, and was tempted to give them something to tell their playmates about—just swim up and smile—but no, best not to do anything unusual, unsharklike.

It might be on camera, anyhow. Better act like a confused fish who just wandered in too close to shore. Hammerheads are curious and incautious.

As if in response to the thought, it heard a powerful motor roar into life and begin heading its way. It swam quickly for the depths.

Fast boat. It caught up with the changeling before it got out of the relative shallows. There was a loud *bang!* and a harpoon spiked completely through the shark body, just below its head.

The motor immediately throttled down, and someone began to haul in his prize. The changeling let itself be pulled halfway to the boat and then flexed a sudden 180 degrees—hammerheads are agile—and swam away at top speed.

At the end of the line there was a sudden tug; then a scream and splash. Just for fun, the changeling flexed again and sped back to the boat, only a little hampered by the harpoon. The man was still halfway in the water when the shark bumped into his foot, the immediate change in the water's flavor a testimony to how much he enjoyed the experience.

Someone aboard the boat started firing a large pistol into the shark, two hits and two misses. The changeling twisted under the boat and took a healthy bite of fiberglass hull, and then headed at top speed for deep water. Once safely out of sight, it stopped the dramatic but unnecessary bleeding, and temporarily enlarged the first wound so that the harpoon could slide out easily. Then it swam north, staying comfortably deep.

It wondered whether the men had been motivated by fear or greed. Probably greed; with the harpoon and gun, they were set up for shark fishing. Its fins would make several thousand dollars' worth of soup, which was why there weren't many large sharks in the area, despite the abundance of food.

The mask, mouthgill, and fins were still safe under the rock. It took only ten minutes of pain to change back into the young woman, and another thirty seconds to secrete the bathing suit material. It was an imperceptible half-inch shorter because of the loss of material to the woundings. It would catch and absorb a couple of reef fish on the way back.

It was interrupted in that simple task. It had chased and caught a large snapper, and was enlarging an orifice to absorb it, when it heard a human voice.

The ticket-taking girl was about a hundred meters away, at the edge of the reef, shouting and gesticulating. It let the snapper go and relaxed the orifice to its usual size and let the bathing suit cover it. It swam toward her as a human might, relaxed on its back, with the mask pulled up to its forehead.

"You are Mrs. Rae?" the girl said.

"Rae Archer," the changeling said, standing up in the meter of water.

"Mr. Wade thought you were here." The man who owned the B-and-B. "He said the project people called for you and they want you to come at eleven. It's almost ten."

Time flies when you're having fun. "Thank you. I'd better hurry, then." The changeling kept its swimming speed down to that of an athletic human and then waded ashore with convincing clumsiness, in its fins. It could have taken them off, but it knew the pebbles were too sharp for human comfort. It retrieved lavalava and sandals and jogged back to the B-and-B.

It took a cold shower and shampooed quickly, though it could have done a better job on its skin surfaces and hair just by sitting alone for twenty seconds. It put on tropical office clothes and let Mr. Wade drive "her" to Poseidon, though she could have walked and been on time.

But if she had done that and shown up not sweaty and flushed, someone might wonder.

Outside the Poseidon gate, two men had a light fishing boat up on two sawhorses, showing a crowd of gawking kids the shark bite near the bow.

A large muscular woman, Naomi, met her at the door, but instead of going inside, led her back down the road to cottage 7. They left their shoes at the door, along with two other pair, and went into the air-conditioning.

At a wooden table, a man and woman in fit middle age. The woman looked familiar. Some pieces fell into place and the changeling remembered it had graded her papers at Harvard, back in 1980.

It shook his hand, Russell Sutton, and he introduced it to its former student, Dr. Jan Dagmar. They both looked hollow-eyed and wired, as if they'd done a couple of all-nighters on pills and coffee. They sat down heavily.

"Coffee?" Naomi asked, and the changeling said yes, black, and sat down across from Jan.

"First, tell us what you know about the project," Jan said.

"That would take a while," the changeling said. "I've done my homework." Jan shrugged in a friendly way.

It accepted the coffee. "Thanks. You stumbled onto this undersea artifact and salvaged it, and soon found that it was made of some substance too dense to find a place on the periodic table. Three times as dense as plutonium, but not radioactive."

"Three times if it's solid," he said. "It's probably hollow."

The changeling nodded. "If it's from Earth, it was made by some process we don't understand—putting it mildly! Likewise, if it was made on some other planet. You still don't know how it might have been made, but it's intellectually less uncomfortable to assume it came from some-where else."

"Which is what piqued your interest," Russ said.

"Me and seven billion others," it said. "Ever since your announcement, my computer opens up every morning with a search for new material with the word 'Poseidon.'"

It sipped its coffee. "You haven't been able to drill or file so much as a molecule off this thing. You tried to boil some off with a laser and . . . there was an accident."

"You know what happened then?"

"No. I saw the CNN pictures and read the popular press speculations. The thing can levitate?"

He raised an eyebrow. "We saw the pictures, too."

"But you haven't published anything about it."

"No." He looked at Jan and back at the young woman. "We can tell you a little more if you're hired and sign the nondisclosure form."

"But only a little more," Jan said. "There's not that much to tell."

"You got a bachelor's in astronomy," Russ said, "and then you quit?"

"Marriage," the changeling said, "and when it didn't work out, he left me with too much debt for me to go back to being a student." This was a part of its autobiography that would stand up to computer search, but not much beyond that. The "husband" had conveniently dropped off the map, and its state and federal tax forms were precisely hacked, as were employment records for the two low-level lab technician jobs.

It had gone to some trouble to find two Los Angeles firms that were so large and mobile that Rae might credibly not be remembered personally.

"I did some checking," Naomi said. "Your professors at Berkeley had a high opinion of you."

The changeling gave her a level gaze. "And they won-dered why I hadn't gone on."

"And why you became a lab tech."

"I had the training, from summer jobs. There aren't any jobs in astronomy."

"That's for sure," Jan said. "More than half the Ph.D.s are doing something unrelated to astronomy."

"I knew that when I chose the major," the changeling said. "My advisor advised me to learn how to flip hamburgers."

Jan laughed. "That's what my advisor told *me,* back in the eighties. So there's always hope."

"Do you plan to go back?" Russ asked. Under the circumstances, a question with no right answer.

"I keep up my reading at the library, *A.J.* and *Aph.J.,*" it said carefully. "My interest in astronomy is undiminished, especially globular clusters and star formation." It realized it was sounding too much like a college professor, but it had *been* a professor a lot longer than it had been a lab technician. Or a dwarf or a prostitute, for that matter. "But it would be hard to go back to being a student. I've been a working woman for too long." Thirty-one of the past ninety-four years, if being a female shark counted.

"The SETI aspect of working here fascinates me," it continued. "I never had any course work in it, except as part of radio astronomy. So it would be interesting as a learning experience, even if nothing ever comes of it."

He nodded and exchanged another look with Jan. "You know what we've been doing the past couple of months."

"The planetary environments thing. I saw the *Nova* show about Venus; that was incredible."

"Well . . ." Russ put his fingertips together and tapped twice. "This is secret. The whole world will know before long, but we're still sorting out what to say, the timing. You can keep a secret."

"Absolutely."

"We got a response from the artifact."

The changeling articulated a variety of physiological reflexes, that for a change reflected its actual state: pupils dilating, sweat popping, a sharp intake of breath: "During the Jupiter simulation?"

Jan nodded. "Jupiter. At first we thought it was just a glitch. You know we use pi squared as the factor from one frequency to the next?"

"Yes; that was interesting."

"What the artifact did was repeat the message, the first half of it, but at *ten* times the frequency."

The changeling nodded. "So it knows digits."

"It may know how many digits *we* have," Russ said.

"At first we thought it was a transmission mistake," Jan said. "It was the acoustic phase, tapping out the message. It's done automatically, with a small solenoid-driven hammer. The response, ten times faster, was in the middle of our stock message."

"It was recorded but initially ignored," Russ said. "One of the techs, Muese, was analyzing it as a kind of feedback noise—that's happened before—and then realized it had to have come from the artifact."

"We were up in the infrared by then," Jan said, indicating a distance with one hand over the other, "but we went back to the acoustic mode, returning the faster signal it had sent. It responded with a long burst, twelve minutes."

"Saying?"

Russ shook his head. "We don't have the faintest. Not a clue. But it's not random."

They seemed calm, but the changeling could hear their pulses. Jan spoke carefully. "You'd think an intelligent creature, an intelligence of some kind, would respond in the same code." She looked at the pretty woman with a studied casualness that said *this is a test.* "Why do you suppose it didn't?"

The changeling paused longer than it needed. "One, Occam's razor: it didn't understand that the first series was a code. It was just being like a mynah bird. But the second 'message' . . . the factor of ten is interesting, but maybe it, or whatever manufactured it, had ten appendages.

"I'll ask the obvious. Have you done Zipf analysis? Shannon entropy?"

Jan and Russ looked at each other, and Naomi chuckled.

"The Zipf slope is minus one," Russ said quietly, "so the message isn't just noise." Dolphin calls and human languages generate a slope of minus one; it can't occur by chance.

"The Shannon entropy is scary," Jan said. "It's twenty-sixth order."

"Wow," the changeling said, excitement growing. Human languages only had ninth-order complexity. Dolphins were fourth order. "So it didn't make up its own version of the Drake message?"

"We hoped for that," Russ said, "but it doesn't meet the first requirement: the two primes that would tell us the proportions of the information matrix."

"We did the obvious," Jan said, still testing.

The changeling stared at her. "Assumed the matrix would be the same size as yours, or the product of two other primes. But that didn't work."

"Not quite," Russell said. "We finally figured out that it's *three* primes multiplied together. That sort of ups the ante."

Jan nodded and leaned forward, elbows on the table. "You know, this organization is only weakly hierarchical. That is, Russ and Jack Halliburton call the shots; direct and define what the rest of us are going to do. At the working level, well, it's pretty chaotic. That's the way we want it.

"This isn't like some R&D enterprise, where you can assign duties and work to a timetable. We're all wandering in the dark, in a sense, going on intuition.

"Even old people like Russ and me know that education and experience can get in the way of intuition. When we hire people at your level, it's with the understanding that, although much of your work will be routine, there's always room for your input. The woman you may replace was always coming up with off-the-wall ideas, and sometimes they were helpful."

"Why did she leave?" the changeling asked.

"Illness in the family, her daughter. She might be back once things settle down, but it looks like a long watch."

"Meanwhile, we need someone like you," Russ said. "You're not likely to ... this is embarrassing. But the woman *she* replaced had to leave to have a baby. Likewise, we're about to lose our receptionist to motherhood."

"I can't have children," the changeling said, not adding *except by fission*. It reddened and touched its lips.

"We didn't mean to pry," Jan said, giving Russ a sharp look.

"Of course not, no." He looked like a man who desperately needed some papers to shuffle through. Instead, he studied the inside of his empty coffee cup.

"Oh, I'm not sensitive about it," the changeling said. "It's only biology. Simplifies my life.

"If I do get the job, what would the job be, at this stage? It doesn't sound like gas chromatography or spectroscopy are on the menu right now."

"Not now, not anymore." Russ took the cup over to the coffee urn and filled it. "Your CV mentioned cryptography."

"One course and some reading." A lot more, actually, in another life. When it had studied computer science at MIT, everyone was interested in it.

Jan tapped twice on her notebook and studied the screen. "It's not on your transcript."

"I just sat in. My advisor vetoed it as frivolous. She would've killed me if she'd known I was doing that rather than advanced differential equations."

"Been there," Jan said.

"Might have been a lucky choice," Russ said. "It's what you'll be doing for awhile, I think.

"With this pesky data string from the artifact, we're dividing into two groups. One, the one you'd be in, will try to decipher the message. The other's keeping after the artifact with a series of more complex messages, along the lines of the first one. That'll be Jan's group."

"You're keeping it in house? Keeping the government out?"

"Absolutely. We're a profit-making corporation, and there just might be an obscene profit in whatever this thing has to say. Better be, to justify what Jack's sunk into it."

"If we were in the States," Jan said, "the government might be able to step in on grounds of national security. But there's not much they can do here. Jack's even a Samoan citizen."

"You do have a NASA team," the changeling said.

"I'm on it," Jan said. "And we used NASA space suits, and they got us the use of the military laser that made things so interesting a couple of months ago. But our agreements with them are carefully drawn up, and the deal with the individual employees, well, it's kind of mercenary."

"It gives them all a cut of the profits if everyone behaves," Russ said, "and nobody gets anything if anyone leaks anything. Not to mention the pack of lawyers that will descend to worry the flesh off his bones and then crack the bones."

"Something like that will be in your nondisclosure statement, too. Jack is fair, I think, but not flexible." Jan tapped on her notebook again. "Obviously, I think you're hired. Have to pass it by Jack, who crashed a few hours ago and probably won't be making decisions until tomorrow morning. But the two of us and Naomi really do all the tech and administrative hires."

"So I just stay by the phone?"

Russ shook his head. "It's not that big an island. We'll find you."

"You can run, but you can't hide," Naomi said, and smiled.

apia, samoa, 13 june 2021

Trying to crack the artifact's code was the most interesting thing the changeling had ever done. If it could just be locked up in a room for awhile with the string of ones and zeros—and a data line to the outside—it could decipher the thing by itself. Whether that would take a week, a year, or a millennium, it didn't know. Or much care.

But the others were fighting the clock. Jack wanted the thing cracked while it was still news, and so if the lid stayed on it, they would announce the communications breakthrough one day, and the translation the next.

To help guard the secret, he upped the ante: there was a million-dollar bonus to the person or team who broke the code, as long as its existence stayed secret. Otherwise, the prize went down to a hundred thousand.

The changeling wondered what the man's logic was, or whether logic had anything to do with it. Why was he so sure there would be money in this? If the message just said, "Hi; here are some pretty pictures in return," and gave up

nothing more revolutionary than what had been given it—
which was what the changeling and most of its coworkers
expected—then how was Poseidon going to make a dime
off it? T-shirts and action figures?

When the changeling broached that question to Naomi,
she squinted and put a finger to her lips. "Ours is not to reason why," she whispered.

The number of ones and zeros was 31,433, which was
the product of a prime and a prime squared: 17×43×43. So
it might be seventeen squares, each forty-three dots and
dashes on a side, or forty-three rectangles, seventeen by
forty-three, arranged in various ways. Or just one line of
31,433 bits of information.

Their computers could marshal powerful decryption
tools, and no doubt if the government got into it, they
would have much more sophisticated ones. But the assumption had to be that this was not a *hidden* message, at
least not hidden on purpose.

This was where intuition came in, or maybe plain dumb
luck. Twenty people were working on it, and they had
twenty large flatscreens and five 1.5-meter cubes, for visu-
alizing in three dimensions. Find something that looks like
a coherent message, or at least part of one. The rooms they
worked in looked like crossword-puzzle nightmares, white
and black squares and cubes in constant chaotic dance.

The changeling "felt" something—it was not logic, certainly not numbers, but a sense that the thing really was
trying to be clear. It was just so inhuman that humans
couldn't get it.

Maybe the changeling had become too human itself, to
get it.

People hungry for the million were grinding themselves
down on coffee and speed and no sleep, so Russ declared a
"snow day." Everybody stay home and sleep or otherwise
relax. Jack had to go along with it. After five days, people
were getting a little crazy.

* * *

The changeling spent its snow day walking up the hill with Russ. They agreed not to talk about the project at all.

"Up the hill" was the steep four-kilometer hike to Vailima, the mansion where Robert Louis Stevenson had spent his last years. Russ had been there a couple of times, and so was "native guide" to Rae.

The changeling probably knew more about Robert Louis Stevenson's writing than everybody else on the project combined, by virtue of its English major some lives before. But it played dumb and let Russ educate it.

It decided that it had read *Treasure Island,* "Dr. Jekyll and Mr. Hyde," and nothing else by Stevenson. So as they trudged up the hill, Russ told her the stories of *Kidnapped* and *The Master of Ballantrae,* and some of the complex story of Stevenson's life on the island.

The changeling knew most of it, but was a good listener. How the great writer had come out here seeking relief from tuberculosis, and found not a cure, but a relaxed and relaxing style of life. He, or his wife, Fanny, imported a lot of things that made Vailima a transplanted corner of civilized Scotland: fine linens and china, a good piano that was rarely played, walls lined with books—even a fireplace, in case the Earth changed its orbit.

It would be a better story if Stevenson had written any of his classics here, but those were behind him. He did write five books, and threw great parties, for the Samoans as well as the Anglos and Europeans. He found people to love, a condition that Fanny may have been resigned to before they moved, and his last years were full of joy and ease.

The changeling was not seducing Russ; it was just being there. But that was sufficient. Russ had never been immune to attractive women, and he was at a stage in life that was like Stevenson's, minus wife and illness, plus good genes and all the benefits of twenty-first-century medicine. His body and mind were young enough that a liaison with a thirty-year-old woman was not ridiculous to either of them. As they pounded uphill together, sweating and laughing, stopping for a beer at a little joint, the difference in age became a novelty rather than a barrier.

They walked through Stevenson's mansion, shoes off, with a teenaged Samoan guide who hadn't read much of the author's work, but knew everything about daily life in the mansion, and talked as if Stevenson had just stepped out for awhile, perhaps riding down to Apia to see what the latest freighter had brought in, or joining the native workers in farm chores or clearing brush—she claimed that in spite of his physical problems, he took special pleasure in working to exhaustion, because afterward he could sit and look at the beauty of the forest and the distant sea, and truly enjoy it, his busy brain stilled. After the guide left, Russ said that he hoped it was true, but doubted it.

Not for the first time, the changeling wished it had discovered humans before 1932. It would have been interesting to watch the centuries go by; see how people changed.

After the tour, they climbed farther up the mountain, to where Stevenson and Fanny were buried. On his stone, the familiar inscription:

> *Under the wide and starry sky,*
> *Dig my grave and let me lie;*
> *Glad did I live and gladly die,*
> *And I lay me down with a will.*
> *This be the verse you grave for me;*
> *"Here he lies where he longed to be;*
> *Home is the sailor, home from the sea,*
> *And the hunter home from the hill."*

"I wonder if he really meant that," the changeling said. "'Gladly die.' Was he that ill? Or maybe he was talking about the natural order of things."

"He was gravely ill," Russ said, "but it wasn't in Samoa. He wrote it in California, a long time before he got here and his health improved."

The changeling took his hand and they looked at the stone for a few silent moments. "So what do you want to do for the rest of your snow day?" it said.

"I don't know. We could build a fort and have a snow-ball fight."

It laughed. "I have a better idea." About a kilometer back down the hill was a quaint twentieth-century hotel, where they spent a couple of hours under a ticking ceiling fan, making love and then quietly sharing their life stories. Russ did most of the talking, but then he thought he had lived a lot longer.

They got back to the project site just before dark, and for appearances' sake, went their separate ways, Russ going downtown for dinner and the changeling getting a sandwich at the beach concession.

The changeling assumed that their secret wouldn't be a secret for long; in fact, it was out before they left their hotel room, since the clerk had recognized Russ. On Samoa, gossip is a varsity sport, a high art. The clerk had a cousin who worked at the project, and every native employee knew some version of the story before Russ and Rae came down the hill. Everyone else would know in a day or two.

But they wouldn't know it all. Russell couldn't sleep that night. He liked women but was married to work; it had been almost thirty years since the last time he would have called himself "in love." But there was no other word for what he felt for Rae. He couldn't get her out of his mind. How lucky he was; how much this day had changed his life.

He didn't know the half of it.

los angeles, california, 25 june 2021

The fingerprints betrayed the changeling. The real Rae Archer had her driver's license renewed, and her fingerprints went into the Homeland Security database.

In a fraction of a second, a computer flagged them as identical to a set that was in a CIA database. The CIA thanked Homeland Security for the information and said they would take it from here.

Everybody working on the Poseidon project had unwittingly provided latent prints to a Samoan dishwasher who was employed by the CIA. When the CIA found that there were two Rae Archers with identical prints, one of them employed in a supersecret foreign scientific project, they went into high gear.

An apologetic man from the LAPD showed up at Rae Archer's place and said he had to do the driving exam fingerprints over; they'd been misplaced.

The real Rae Archer was pleasantly surprised that the state would come to her, rather than asking her to come back downtown, but wished they'd given her some warning; she looked a mess. The handsome officer didn't care, though, and neither did the woman in the car, behind the telephoto lens.

Back in Langley, in a bland building that had served the same function for sixty years, agents looked at the evidence and considered what was possible, what was legal, and what they would do.

They had several minutes of video of Rae Archer, somewhat harried mother of triplets, and six jpegs of Rae Archer, lab assistant in Samoa. They were at least superficially the same woman, a very attractive Japanese-American. That they shared features and figure was unusual; that they shared fingerprints and retinal patterns meant that the one in Samoa was a new kind of spy, perhaps a clone.

But who would bother to clone Rae Archer, and who could have done it, back in the nineties?

They asked around and confirmed that no, she was not one of ours, and no, the fingerprints and retinas were not in our bag of tricks. You could fake the retinal patterns by data substitution, but the fingerprints were pulled from a water glass the spy had handed to the dishwasher.

They desperately had to get her in a room and ask her some questions.

apia, samoa, 15 july 2021

The changeling was interested and amused by people's changing attitudes toward Rae. Some obviously thought she was a shameless manipulator, or maybe just a nympho-maniac. A lot of the men were happy for Russ, the old dog, or ruefully jealous. Rae didn't wear makeup and dressed severely, at least in the office, but the men said they had her pegged as a hot number from the beginning. The ones who had seen her swimming had seen part of the rising sun tat-tooed over her shapely butt.

Some of the men and most of the women could see there was more than sex going on, though. The way she looked at him and he looked at her; the way their voices changed when they talked to each other.

After the snow day, most people came back to work with renewed vigor. A few had not benefited from having a day to reflect on the lack of results—maybe it *was* time to bring the government in.

The government was coming in, but not for decryption.

Two CIA agents, masquerading as honeymooners, reserved the fancy Wing Room at Aggie Grey's for a week.
Four other agents rented the flanking rooms. They had
flown into American Samoa on military aircraft, and come
to Apia on the ferry, so there was no nonsense about luggage being searched.

A seventh agent, a white-haired old lady, got a room at
the bed-and-breakfast where Rae Archer was staying. An
hour after maid service the second day, Rae's room was
thoroughly bugged.

That surveillance did them no good. The changeling
was automatically cautious, mimicking human behavior. It
ate and drank and excreted at regular intervals, and lay
down in the dark for eight hours every night. That it was
analyzing 31,433 ones and zeros, instead of sleeping,
would not be obvious to any observer.

Three times she came in early in the morning, having
spent the night with her boss. That mitigated against the direct approach, going straight to Poseidon and showing
them what they knew about the mysterious employee. Besides the fact of her sexual relationship with the second in
command, perhaps a love affair, what they learned about
Jack Halliburton did not make them optimistic about his
cooperating with the American government, either. He had
cynically used the American Navy to put together a pool of
talented specialists, hired them away, and quit his commission in an acrimonious scene. He wasn't even an American
citizen anymore.

The other direct approach, just snatching the woman off
the street or from her room, had some merit—they didn't
know it would be easier to "kidnap" a Powell tank—but as
they had no legitimate jurisdiction here, they wanted to be
a little more subtle. They used a lure, an indirect one.

Russ had dropped his business card into a box for a
once-monthly drawing that awarded a weekend for two at
Aggie Grey's, at either the Wing Room or the Presidential

Suite. He won the Wing Room, the weekend after the honeymooners left.

They knew they would have to deal with Russ sooner or later. Best do it directly.

There were three possibilities: Russ would arrive first, or Rae, or they would come in together. The last was not likely, since they were still being discreet. But the CIA team was ready for any of the three, as well as the trivial case where neither showed up.

If Russ had come through the door first, they would have had to do some fast explanation. But it was the woman.

The changeling came into the sumptuous room and tossed its overnight bag on the bed, and went into the bathroom to check its hair. It heard a vague sound in the hall, which was a man shoving a wooden wedge between the door and frame, jamming it shut, and the plain sound of another door opening and closing.

It sped out of the bathroom and saw the man and woman who had just entered from the adjoining room.

"Don't make this difficult," the man said. "You know why we're here."

The changeling answered automatically while considering various options: "You tell me."

"You're not Rae Archer. But you match her so precisely that you must be a clone or something."

"I don't know what the hell you're talking about."

"We just talked to the real Rae Archer, in Pasadena. You're someone else."

"Who do you work for?" the changeling said.

The woman shrugged. "The United States intelligence community."

"So you have no jurisdiction here."

"We just want to ask you some questions."

The changeling picked up its overnight bag. "No." Halfway to the door it heard a rubber-band sound and felt a sting in the middle of its back. It reached back—revealing unusual suppleness—and pulled out a dart with plastic wings.

The man was holding what looked like a toy gun. "That won't hurt you. It will just make you a little groggy."

The changeling inspected the dart, sniffed it, and shook it next to its ear. "Seems to have a bit left."

"Doesn't take much—" The spy grunted, dropped the pistol, and fell to his knees. The dart was in his neck, deeply imbedded into the carotid artery. He managed to pull it out but his knees gave way and he fell over prone, arms and legs trembling and then twitching.

"You want to be careful where you inject that." The changeling tried the door, but it was stuck. It heard the soft sound of metal on leather, and in three leaping steps was on the woman before she could raise the automatic to fire. It jerked her gun hand sideways and heard finger or knuckle bones breaking just before the weapon discharged, almost silent, into the wall, and pulled it out of her hand.

She screamed in pain and a small man swung out of the door to the adjoining room, pointing a double-barreled shotgun. The changeling leaped sideways just as the first hammer went down, and the hot blast just missed its face. It reached for the weapon and the second blast blew off its left arm at the shoulder.

In the reverberating silence, blood pulsing from the ragged stump, the changeling raised the pistol to point between the man's eyes. "Bang," it said, and dropped the gun.

Two steps and it vaulted the couch and crashed through the glass balcony door. It hit the balcony railing and tumbled over, falling onto the awning over the hotel entrance.

Russ was a half block away, and had looked up at the sound of the shots. He saw someone slide off the hotel awning and hit the sidewalk hard, and come up running, bleeding from the stump of an arm.

It seemed to have no face, as if it had a stocking over its head. Russ rubbed his eyes.

It ran *over* the slow traffic, one step on the roof of a southbound car, the next on a northbound, then onto the opposite sidewalk, over the low fence into the harborside park, and while tourists and picnicking families gaped, it ran like an Olympic sprinter and was over the stone breakwater in a flat dive.

By the time anyone got to the breakwater, there was nothing but ripples. A siren threaded through the air.

The changeling sought shelter on the harbor bottom, under the shade of a tanker that was drawing half the depth of the water. It strained to become a fish as quickly as possible, bone into cartilege and denticles and teeth, muscle and guts into the streamlined swift form of a reef shark; bloody clothes left behind as a red herring.

The metamorphosis was just complete when it heard divers splash into the harbor back where it had dived in. It breathed a surge of warm salt water liberally flavored with diesel spill—delicious—and flexed the one huge muscle of itself toward the open sea.

A helicopter commandeered by the police made a search pattern low over the harbor, and with binoculars and sonar found nothing but the usual assortment of fish and discarded debris, from the surface to the bottom. A couple of large sharks, one evidently spooked by the helicopter.

Russ hadn't recognized the apparition as the woman he loved. Still trying to sort out what he had seen—there was a movie company shooting up in the hills; maybe they were using Aggie Grey's as a location for an action sequence—he stepped into the lobby of the hotel like a sleepwalker.

All the people at the registration desk were jabbering into phones. Two policemen with pistols drawn ran through the door and thundered up the stairs. While Russ was watching them, a man beside him said, "Russell Sutton?"

It was a short, stocky man who smelled odd. Gunsmoke? "Who are you?"

He held up identification. "Kenneth Swanwick. I'm a CIA investigator."

Russell shook his head. "I don't get it."

"Rae Archer is a spy. We—"

"Is this part of that movie?"

It was the agent's turn to be confused. "What movie?"

"The one they're shooting up by the waterfall."

He took a deep breath. "This is not a movie." He held up the ID again. "We used the raffle here as a ruse. We knew Rae Archer was a spy and wanted to catch her unawares."

"Come on. I *know* she couldn't be." But certain oddnesses began to crystalize.

"We picked her up to interrogate her and she killed one agent, injured another, and escaped by crashing through a glass door."

"That couldn't have been her. Maybe somebody who looked like her."

"That's exactly it," Swanwick said, "and we think we can prove it."

"Wait." Russell pointed out the door. "*That* was—"

"We don't know who that was. Claimed to be her. Looked like Rae Archer. Had her fingerprints."

"But—"

"But the real Rae Archer is still in California. We talked to her. She claims not to know anything about this, and I think we believe her."

They were joined by an attractive woman whose tense face was as pale as her ash-blonde hair. She was tightening a bandage around her right hand. "This is Mr. Sutton?"

"Yeah," Swanwick said. "He's a little confused."

"Like we aren't." She was the same height as Russell and fixed him with her large gray eyes. The pupils were pinpoints from medication. "My name is Angela Smith."

"And you're a spy?"

"An investigator."

He stared at her weird eyes. "And this is not a movie."

"I wish to God it was. We could strike the set and start over." To Swanwick: "You're going to have to go with the police in a minute. There should be a lawyer by the time you get to the station." She swiveled back to Russell. "You knew Rae Archer better than anybody else. You were intimate with her."

He nodded cautiously, and then shook his head. "Look, she couldn't do this. Not at all."

"So maybe it wasn't her," Swanwick said quickly. "Whoever it was is pretty damned dangerous, and on the loose."

"We have to talk but can't go up to the room," Angela Smith said. "Get in the way of the cops." She gestured toward the bar with her bandaged hand. "Uncle Sam will buy you a beer."

One of the few tables in the small bar was unoccupied. The bartender came over and took their order. The window that looked out over the park and the harbor showed a growing crowd of curious people, held back by two policemen in incongruous parade uniforms.

"Just for a minute, try to think of Rae as a spy," Swanwick said. "Did you ever get the feeling she was pumping you for information?"

That had an annoying alternate interpretation. "Not really," Russell said with some asperity. "We're both working on the same thing. We talked about it all the time. So does everyone else on the project."

"Think about it this way—ow!" Gesturing, she had bumped her bandaged knuckle. "She's supposed to be an astronomer. Did she seem like one to you?"

"No doubt about that. You'd have to ask Dr. Dagmar to be absolutely sure; she's our top astronomer. But Rae seems to really know her stuff, a lot more than me. I'm just a marine engineer, but I've been into astronomy all my life."

Swanwick nodded. "Did she show any special interest in defense or military applications of this thing? The artifact?"

He thought about that for a moment. "Defense? I can say no almost without exception, since that's an angle I'm not interested in. I'd remember if she tried to 'pump' me on that."

A policeman came into the bar, holding a sawed-off double-barreled shotgun in a heavy plastic bag. Swanwick stood up.

"Did you shoot that woman with this?"

"In self-defense. She was—"

"Ya, ya." He gestured to a big officer behind him, who came around quickly with handcuffs.

"That won't be necessary," Swanwick said, but the big man spun him around roughly and snapped them on. "She had a gun," he said.

"And you had this in your room for the little mice," the first policeman said. He turned to Russell. "Dr. Sutton, please wait here with your lady. A man will take your statement soon."

They watched the three of them leave. "He shot her . . . with *that?*"

"Hit her, too. Blew off her arm." There was a moment of dead silence. The people at the other tables were looking at them. She let a breath out in a puff. "Speaking of 'ladies'?"

He pointed. "Behind the gift counter, down the hall to the left."

She picked up her purse. "I'll be right back."

Unsurprisingly, he never saw her again.

faleolo, samoa, 15 july 2021

Once on the other side of the reef, the changeling stayed in the relatively deep water, plying west slowly toward the airport at Faleolo. There was a plane out the next day, to Honolulu.

It would take human form and come ashore after dark. Hide for awhile and then walk into the airport. Then go about the problem of getting a ticket, without passport or credit cards. It could create counterfeit cash, but even under normal circumstances, it would look suspicious to try to purchase an expensive ticket with cash. Maybe a Samoan could get away with it, but it didn't know the language well enough to pass among Samoans.

Eighty or ninety years ago, it would have just isolated someone, killed him, and used his identity and ticket. That was repugnant now. Maybe the man who shot Rae's arm off. The world might be a better place without him.

By the time it got to Faleolo, it had a better plan. Not without risk, but it could always escape into the water again. They'd eventually catch on to that. But it had escaped from a few jails in its time, too.

It went a half mile past Faleolo, to get away from the light. The moon, not yet first quarter, was no problem. The changeling sat in the shallows and changed.

About a pound of its substance became a plastic bag full of circulated fifty- and hundred-dollar bills. Another twelve pounds, a light knapsack with a change of dirty clothing and a wallet that had enough Samoan tala for a few cab rides and a night of drinking, with an American Universal ID and a California driver's license, matching the persona it painfully built. Newt Martin, a common type of denizen in this corner of the world. Young, restless; escaping from something. Money enough for food and drugs and a flop, and maybe a little more. Maybe a lot.

It made a passport that would pass visual inspection. The computer at passport control wouldn't be fooled.

At about eight thirty it crept ashore, squeezed the water out of its long blond hair, and walked down to the airport. It got into a cab and told the man to take him to the clock.

It was a simple plan of action. Find a young American desperate enough to temporarily "lose" his wallet and passport and ticket out, in exchange for a lot of money. The kid wouldn't find out until later that there was a little more than that involved.

"The clock" is an early-twentieth-century tower in the center of town, the main landmark. The changeling paid off the cab and walked down Beach Road toward the harbor. It knew there were some seedy-looking bars about halfway to Aggie Grey's, but it had never been inside one. "Rae Archer" wouldn't have done that. Newt Martin definitely would.

Bad Billy's looked promising. Smelled right even from the sidewalk, spilled beer and stale cigarette smoke. Loud rap music from twenty years ago. The changeling sidled in through a mass of people standing in the door, for the air, and went to the bar. There were only two other customers there, the rest of the clientele either shooting pool or sitting in clusters of folding chairs around small tables full of drinks, talking loudly in two languages. Its keen hearing picked up a third, a French couple away in a corner, whispering about the scene around them.

One of the English conversations was about the strange goings-on at Aggie's today. One of the Samoans had a friend in the police, and he said that he said it was an industrial espionage deal that had gone bad.

Right, somebody said—shotguns and old Jackie Chan superspies. It was just a publicity gag for the movie.

Wanting to draw attention, the changeling ordered a double martini. It had to explain what that meant, and wound up with a half-liter glass of cheap gin and ice with a quarter lime floating on top. (Having been a barmaid itself, it knew the smell of cheap gin. This stuff came in big plastic recycled soft-drink bottles from a distillery outside of town.)

The flavor was interesting, reminiscent of the underwater taste of bilge and oil spill.

An aromatic Samoan prostitute came over next to him. "What ya drinkin'?" She was still young but getting puffy.

Put an egg in your shoe and beat it, the changeling thought. Chase yourself, get lost—working up through the decades—bug off, fuck off, haul ass, twist a braid, give air. Instead it said, "Martini. Want one?"

"What I have to do for it?"

"You're not what I need."

She haunched up on the stool, short skirt casually revealing no underwear.

"I know some guys . . ."

"Not that." The changeling got the barmaid's attention; pointed a finger at its drink and then at the space in front of the girl. "You know where the drug action is?"

"Oh, man." She looked around. "Cops everywhere to-night. That thing at Aggie's."

The barmaid brought the drink and the changeling made a show of riffling through the thick wad of bills to find a twenty. "I've been out of town. You see it?"

"No, man, it was noon. I hadn't got up yet." She stared at the wallet until the mark put it away. "I could bring you anything you want. You shouldn't be on the street, man, cops're pickin' up any *palagi* they don't know." White man.

"Hold it here a minute." The changeling went back to the men's room, a single noisome stall, and sat in the dim light, changing slightly. It went back to the bar with the same features, but dark skin and black hair.

"Now that's somethin'." She rubbed its cheek with her fingertip and looked at it. "How long it last?"

"A day or two. So what happened at Aggie Grey's, do you think?"

"Say it looked like a stuntman thing. Some gunshots and then this guy crashes through a window, bounces off the whatcha-callit over the door—"

"Awning?"

"Yeah. Then runs like a bat outa hell across the street and the park and jumps in the harbor. Looks like he got his arm blown off, blood everywhere, but it don't slow him down, like special effects."

"The movie people say anything about it?"

"They say it's not them, but you know, bullshit."

"Yeah. Drink up and let's go."

"Where?"

"Dope. Dealers." The changeling drank off half the martini in one gulp. The girl tried, and went into a cough-ing fit. The barmaid brought some water and gave the changeling a sharp look.

"Maybe that's enough," it said when the girl quieted

down and was breathing more or less normally. "Don't know what they make this stuff out of, anyhow."

She sighed and nodded and slid off the stool unsteadily.

"There's a party. I take you there, you meet some guys, you take care of me?"

"What does that mean?"

"Like a hundred bucks?"

"We'll see." It took her shoulder and aimed her toward the door. "If I score, sure."

They walked along Beach Road a couple of blocks and then down an unmarked gravel alley. She stopped at a Toyota that had more rust than paint, and jerked the driver's-side door open with a shriek. "Here we go."

"You okay to drive?" The door on the changeling's side didn't open. She leaned across and pushed hard twice.

"Yeah, yeah. Get in." It smelled of mildew and marijuana.

On the third try the engine, older than the driver, sputtered to life, and they jerked on down the lane. She drove with a drunk's elaborate caution, weaving.

"You don't want me to drive?" It couldn't die, but it didn't want to attract attention from police by not doing so.

"Nah, this is fun." She found her way to the winding up-hill road that the changeling recognized as the one leading up to the Stevenson mansion. Traffic was light, fortunately. The girl didn't say anything. She was concentrating on staying near the center of the road.

They passed Vailima and came into a woodsy area with no homes near the road. "Look for a orange plastic ribbon on your side," she said, slowing to a walk. "Tied to a tree. 'Round a tree trunk."

"There it is," the changeling said, and then realized human eyes wouldn't see it yet.

"Where? I don't see." She peered over the steering wheel and the right wheels crunched into gravel. She overcorrected well into the oncoming lane, forcing a Vespa off the road. The rider yelled something in Samoan but rode on.

"Trust me. It's up there." After another couple of hundred yards the headlights caught the pale orange ribbon, sun-bleached emergency tape. She pulled into a dirt road just beyond it.

"You got some eyes." They could just see the road ahead, and the changeling held on. They splashed into potholes so deep the springs bottomed out with a clunk and the driver hit her head on the roof, laughing.

They came to a Western-style house, an incongruous rambler, a little light coming from behind drawn blinds, lots of cars parked in the circular gravel driveway. There were clapped-out hulks like the girl was driving, but also new cars, two taxis, and a shiny limousine.

Too many people, the changeling thought. Be careful.

They picked their way up a board walkway set on the muddy ground. Pine smell of construction; latex paint. The house was new. Business must be good.

She leaned on the doorbell and the front door opened a crack. A tall black man looked down at her. "Mo'o. You found some money somewhere?"

She jerked her thumb in the changeling's direction. "He's got plenty."

The black man looked into its eyes for a long moment. "Why should I trust you?"

"You shouldn't. I don't know anybody local. The slit said she'd take me where I could find some dealers."

"You buyin' or sellin'?"

"Right now I'm buying."

"Let me see some color." A flashlight snapped on. The changeling opened his wallet, fanning bills. The man murmured, then flashed the light in the changeling's face.

"We'll take a chance." He opened the door partway. "You know if you're a cop, your family dies, in front of you. And then you?"

The changeling shrugged. "Not a cop; no family." He passed through but the man stopped the girl.

"I got money," she protested. "*He's* got money for me."

"A hundred bucks," the changeling said, and took two fifties out of his wallet, and passed them back to her.

The black man let the money pass but still blocked the girl. "Go home, Mo'o. I don't need any more trouble from your *matai*."

"I'm over twenty-one and she's a bitch."

"You're drunk. Sleep it off in the car."

"Wait for me in the car," the changeling said, waving her away. "Give you another hundred if I get what I want." She walked away, mumbling and staggering.

Inside, it looked like the party was over but nobody'd gone home. There were about fifty people standing, sitting, or passed out. A table with food and bottles of wine and liquor was a picked-over mess. The air was gray with smoke. The changeling sorted out cigarettes, expensive as well as cheap cigars, the burnt-plastic smell of crack, and the heavy incense of hashish. No one was smoking heroin, but there were plenty of needles in evidence; on the buffet table three hypodermics stood point-down in a glass of clear liquid.

The room had an unfinished look, walls freshly painted with travel posters and Gauguin reproductions thumb-tacked here and there. New cheap furniture in a haphazard scatter.

"So what can I get for you?" the black man said.

"Hash, I guess." The changeling thought back to its circus days. "You have squiddy black?"

"Dream on. Most of these guys smokin' slate."

The changeling shook its head. "Nothing Moroccan. What you got Asian?"

"Red seal and gold seal. Cost you."

"Little bag of gold seal, how much?" He said $250 and the changeling got him down to $210.

It took the stuff and a glass bong to a folding chair in a corner where it could survey the room.

The hash had an interesting flavor. It burned hot, probably because of additives. A little asphalt.

The changeling was looking for someone who looked like he was used to having money, but was down on his luck. Preferably someone not native; about a third of the men qualified on that score.

An American would be preferable; one who resembled the changeling would make things easier to explain. There was one light-skinned black man who was fairly close to the changeling's current appearance, though a few inches taller and considerably heavier. He was sitting backward in a folding chair, chin resting on forearm, intently following a lazy argument two men were having, sitting cross-legged on the floor. Good clothes that needed dry-cleaning.

He was holding an empty bong. The changeling padded over and sat on the floor next to him, and relit the resin in its bong.

"So what do you think?" one of the arguers said to the newcomer. "How old is the universe?"

"Thirteen point seven billion years. I don't remember half that far back, though."

The other one shook his hand. "Close. Sixteen billion."

"He's using the Torah and general relativity," the black man said. "Smells good."

The changeling held out the packet to him. "Gold seal; have a hit." To the Torah guy: "I could spot you 2.3 billion. That's six really long days?"

He launched into an explanation about how small the universe had been back then. The other arguer stared at him with an expression like a spaniel trying to stay awake.

The black man broke off a little piece, rolled it into a ball, and sniffed it. He nodded and handed the bag back. "Thanks."

The changeling lit a wooden match and held it up for him. He breathed the smoke in deeply and held it. After a minute he exhaled slowly and nodded satisfaction. "So what are you after?"

"What, you don't believe in spontaneous acts of sharing?"

"You aren't fucked up enough to be spontaneous with gold seal."

"That's a good observation."

"So you want something, but it's not drugs. Must be sex or money." He shook his big head slowly back and forth. "Don't have either."

"There is one other thing." The changeling stood up, feigning difficulty. "Talk outside?"

He nodded but stayed put. He held up one finger and stared at it. "Oh, and I can't kill anybody. Don't want to go through that again." The two chronologists looked up at that, faces masks.

"Nothing like that. Come on." The man got up and walked with exaggerated care, perhaps more stoned than he looked or sounded. The changeling told their host they'd be right back.

Some animal scampered away when the door opened. Otherwise the dark forest was silent except for water dripping.

"This is the score. I have to be on the plane to America tomorrow. But I don't have a ticket or a passport."

The man squinted at him in the faint light from the shaded windows. "Okay?"

"So do you have a passport?"

"Course. But no way you could pass for me."

"That's not a problem. I've done this before."

"But then I'm stuck here. What do I do about *that*?"

"Nothin' to it. I'll mail it back to you, overnight, from L.A. But you don't have to trust me. If you don't get it, wait a few days and you go to the embassy and report it lost. They'll check you out and issue a temporary; you can replace it when you get back to the States."

"I'd have to think about it. How much?"

"Five thousand up front, plus the cost of a ticket. They probably just have first class open; that'll be a thousand.

"But I'll give you five thousand more if I get to L.A. with no problem. Send it in a package with your passport."

"For that part I just have to trust you? A total stranger I met in a hash house?"

"Think of it as my insurance policy. It's not in my interest to have you report your passport stolen."

He was lost in thought, sorting that out. The changeling took the opportunity to stare into his dark-dilated eyes and duplicate his retinal pattern, in case.

"You throw in two bags of gold seal and you've got a deal." They shook on it, the changeling getting his fingerprints in the process. Then it wrote down an address for the cash and passport return.

It had him wait on the doorstep and went back in to score the hash. The man said four hundred dollars and stayed with it; no deeper discounts unless you want a lot more. Ten bags would only be fifteen hundred. The changeling declined and left with the two.

His partner in crime wanted them right away, but the changeling said no; not until it had the ticket in hand. They crunched down the driveway to the rusty Toyota. The young prostitute had reclined in the driver's seat and was deeply asleep, snoring softly. The changeling gently transferred her to the back seat and took the keys from her pocket.

The black man also slept while the changeling drove back into town. It wanted to avoid Beach Road and downtown; the police probably would recognize the car, and might wonder why he was driving it. It didn't know the back roads, and so proceeded by dead reckoning, bearing roughly west and south until it came to Fugalei Street, which it knew would have the Maketi Fou—central market—on the right and nothing but swamp on the left. Then it hit the beach at the flea market on the edge of town and turned onto the airport road.

It was a half hour of slow driving, the changeling easy on the speed bumps, to keep its crew asleep. The airport was brightly lit, and there were lots of cars and cabs waiting. The airplane that it would take out tomorrow would be landing in about an hour. It remembered that, the late hour notwithstanding, the ticket office had been open when it had arrived the month before.

The black man rubbed his eyes and yawned; no room to stretch. "So. You give me the money. I go in and get myself a ticket to L.A.; bring it back and collect my hash."

"Close." The changeling handed him a roll of bills secured by a rubber band. "But I'm going to keep you company. The hash stays here, in case they have dogs or sniffers. We come back here. You give me the ticket and passport; you keep the change and the hash. I drive you back into town." The changeling pulled into a space close to the waiting area.

"Okay up to the driving. I take a cab back."

"What, you don't trust me?"

He snorted. "Once you have the ticket and passport, I'm more use to you dead than alive."

"I hadn't thought of that," the changeling said honestly. "You must know the criminal mind better than I do."

"'Ask the man who owns one,'" he said. They got out and walked into the building. It was open-air, no walls on the ground floor.

There were dozens of people sitting around on plastic chairs, reading or watching television. A group of teenaged boys and girls in traditional garb chattered happily. They would be the song-and-dance welcome for the flight from the States.

The changeling went upstairs to the bar while his accomplice approached the ticket counter. There was no line and only a single agent, making no effort to appear happy or alert.

It got a beer and sat near the stairway, where it could watch the transaction. It could imagine what would happen Stateside, if you walked up after midnight and tried to buy an international ticket with fifties and hundreds from a thick roll, no luggage.

The young woman treated it as if he were buying a loaf of bread, though she looked at his passport.

Back at the car, the changeling checked the passport and ticket, and handed the black man the keys. "You okay to drive?"

"If I go as slowly as you did, yeah. You staying here until the flight?"

The changeling reached over to the back seat and stuffed a bill into the girl's shirt pocket. "Go back to the hash house and don't tell anybody where you've been."

"I might just go back and get my car, and head home. Enough excitement for one night. What if the girl wakes up?"

The changeling considered. "Best just tell her you dropped me off at a house in town. And . . . don't come back to the airport tomorrow. That could be awkward."

"Yeah. I already figured that out." He started the car, then shook his head. "This is crazy."

"Just keep an eye on the mailbox." They exchanged stares for a moment, and the man drove off.

The changeling had a few things to do, but there was no rush; the gate didn't open till twelve. It went back inside and left passport and wallet in a storage locker, and then set out to find twenty pounds of flesh.

In the daytime it would have been easy: just go into a supermarket and buy twenty pounds of meat. It didn't want to chance taking someone's dog or piglet, so it had to be the sea.

It walked back to the road and headed away from town. Everyone had gone to bed and clouds covered the stars; between headlights the world was black as pitch. The changeling came to a path that led to a stone beach, and slipped quietly into the water.

There was no need to masquerade as a fish. It just stretched its feet into something resembling swim fins, unhinged its jaws, and made its mouth and throat wide enough to accept a large fish. It glided out to the reef and looked around with nose and skin more than its large eyes—like a shark, it could sense the change in electric potential that meant a large fish in trouble.

That was the meal ticket—it felt the slight tingling and went straight toward it, and came to a reef shark wrestling with a skipjack tuna half its size. The changeling killed the shark with a big bite, severing the notochord, and easily chased down the crippled tuna and ingested it in one gulp. Then it went back and consumed the shark.

The two of them had provided plenty of mass. It swam back to the shore, grew feet inside shoes, and walked back toward the airport, a large white American, and took a cab into town.

Bad Billy's was still open—it advertised being the last bar to close in the Western Hemisphere—but the changeling didn't want to attract attention, so it had the cab stop at the first vacant motel, the Klub Lodge, where it took a small room and lay thinking for some hours.

It hated leaving the artifact, hated leaving Russ, and considered just presenting itself for what it was: obviously from another planet, and possibly related to that impossible machine. But it didn't want to wind up a specimen to be examined, and they could probably infer enough about its abilities to build a cage from which it couldn't escape.

Would Russ protect it? If it returned as Rae? No; he knew by now that Rae wasn't really a woman, and had tricked him.

And could trick him again. After a cooling-off period, the changeling could show up as another woman, and win his love again. It wouldn't even be acting.

But it wouldn't be smart to hang around Samoa. The island would be thick with U.S. government agents in another day or two, once they figured out what they had almost caught. Even if they didn't figure it out, and thought the changeling was some sort of augmented human or spy machine, they'd still be all over the island trying to track it down. It hoped they were looking for a one-armed woman.

It waited until almost ten to walk into town; the sidewalk was crowded enough that it didn't stand out particularly, just another sunburnt tourist. It had earlier, as Rae, found a church charity store; it went straight there and bought a suitcase and a few changes of clothing. At a more touristy place, it bought a couple of bright shirts and a souvenir lavalava. An assortment of toiletries from a convenience store, and a couple of gift bottles of Robert Louis Stevenson liqueur. In a coffeehouse rest room it disposed of some of the toothpaste and shaving gel, so they wouldn't look just-bought, and caught a cab to the airport.

There were three uniformed policemen on duty, and one Samoan woman in a business suit pretty obviously surveying the crowd. It occurred to the changeling that its choice of identity might have been disastrous, if Scott Windsor Daniel, African-American hash hound, was known to the police.

Best done quickly. The changeling went into a crowded men's room and waited for a stall. Once behind the door, it went through the uncomfortable business of changing its face and hands to match Daniel's. It also changed shirts, putting on a souvenir one that, under the circumstances, acted as protective coloration.

The whole business took fifteen minutes. If anyone noticed that a white man had gone in and a black man had come out, they didn't say anything.

The first test was passport control. A native woman checked documents and retinal scan, and collected departure tax, but the woman sitting behind her in the booth, right arm in a sling, was the one from "the United States intelligence community," who had almost put a bullet into Rae the day before.

Neither of them paid any special attention to Scott Windsor Daniel, so maybe they actually were looking for a woman. A small white one with a missing arm? They did do a fingerprint check, though, as well as the usual retinal scan. The spy woman put on a jeweler's loupe and, glancing, clumsy with one hand, compared the thumbprint to one on a card.

Security was likewise easy, which was encouraging. It hadn't occurred to them that they were looking for a shape-changer. They sorted through Daniel's unremarkable luggage, wanded him, and sent the suitcase down a chute and him through an optical baffle into the multilingual murmur of the waiting room.

It sat at the bar and nursed something they claimed was chardonnay, leafing through the Samoa *Observer*. The disturbance at Aggie Grey's was the front-page story, with an interesting twist—the movie people were "not at liberty to say" whether it was part of the thriller they were filming. Presumably someone had coached them; they *were* an American company, and the government could hassle them if they didn't cooperate. Though it could be that they came up with the evasiveness on their own, latching onto free publicity.

Interviews with Aggie Grey people and the police were not much more informative. Some tourists agreed that the "man" who ran across the park and dived into the harbor appeared to be one-armed. Their consensus was movie.

Hard to plan with so little information. The flight switched to Delta in Honolulu, and there was a six-hour layover. It might be prudent to switch identity again there, in case they'd picked up the trail to Daniel. If they had, there would be a greeting party at LAX. If Mr. Daniel didn't show up there, they would no doubt smoke the real one out in Samoa.

Or they might be waiting in Honolulu. What would it do? The airport wasn't too far from the sea, but harder to emergency-exit from than the Wing Room at Aggie Grey's. They would presumably be expecting someone with unusual powers—depending on who "they" were. The spies might not have told the police everything. So one scenario was "police looking for a drug dealer with Mr. Daniel's passport," which wouldn't be that hard to step around.

It set that problem aside, and returned to its usual mental occupation, analyzing 31,433 bits of information. Or noise. It continued its methodical way through those gazillion permutations as it filed through early boarding, took its seat in first class, and selected a random movie on its monitor. It nodded for champagne and made rote responses to the attendant's rote queries.

If it spent one second on each possible combination of the 31,433 digits, it would take about as long as the Roman Empire had lasted. The changeling did have the time, but it was hoping that some sort of pattern would emerge long before that.

It had no seating companion, so the time went quickly, in a blur of ones and zeros. It came out of its five-hour reverie when the landing gear hit the tarmac in Hawaii.

First class exited democratically, allowing one hoi polloi interleaved between each of the elite, and the changeling entered the airport with a neutral expression, looking around with no particular interest, just a guy changing planes, who had to go through the inconvenience of passport check and baggage transfer.

There was nothing unusual at first. But then he saw that every U.S. CITIZEN checkpoint was protected by a large policeman, standing between passport control and the luggage check.

Maybe they were always there. He didn't remember them from earlier flights, when he was going back and forth between Australia and the States. It would be better not to take the chance.

There were two bathrooms, for the convenience of people who were willing to take a later place in line, in exchange for comfort. The changeling angled toward the men's. Its timing was good.

As it entered the privacy baffle between the corridor and the men's room, an attendent with a cart was backing out of a utility room. After a glance confirming that there were no witnesses, it covered the man's mouth and nose and shoved him back into the room.

It punched him on the chin just hard enough to daze him, and slapped on the light. It was a room about the size of a walk-in closet, with racks of supplies. It plucked a roll of wide duct tape and carefully pressed a piece of it over the man's mouth, and squares over each eye, after capturing his retinal pattern. Then it undressed him and put on his uniform, and bound him tightly with tape.

It took his fingerprints, studied him for a moment, and then turned out the light and concentrated on becoming him. It wasn't too painful, skin color and facial structure. Then it pushed its way out behind the cart, leaving the door locked.

How much time did it have? If those cops were waiting for Mr. Daniel, it was only minutes.

It hesitated by a door that said AUTHORIZED PERSONNEL ONLY, trying to imagine what might be behind the sign. It could be the place where janitors went to catch a smoke. Or it might be full of nervous security types.

Turning the cart around, it headed back toward Customs. There were six lanes open for U.S. citizens, and three for foreigners—and one marked "employees."

It got halfway through the short lane, and somebody shouted, "Hey! Asshole!"

It stopped and turned around. A fat cop said something angry. It was in Hawaiian, unfortunately.

It shrugged, hoping that not everyone who looked Hawaiian spoke Hawaiian. "You know the drill," he said. "Where the hell you goin'?"

"Just out to the car," the changeling said. "My dinner is in the cooler."

"Yeah, *liquid* dinner. Just leave the goddamn cart on this side, okay?" The changeling trudged back and parked it out of the way.

Once outside, of course, the uniform made its wearer stand out rather than blend in. It would be conspicuous to hail a cab or get on a bus. Bad planning, not to carry along Daniel's clothes.

It would take about twenty minutes to "grow" inconspicuous clothes, and discard the janitor's. Too long. Taking a chance, it ducked into a souvenir shop and bought fairly modest tourist clothes—Hawaiian shirt, Bermuda shorts, and flip-flops. It changed in the men's room—also changing its skin to pale white—and carried the uniform out in the shop's paper bags.

In the line at the cab stand, it started mapping out its strategy. It told the cab to take it to the downtown Hilton, but paid attention for the last mile, looking for a more seedy place. The Crossed Palms looked suitably run-down.

It paid off the cab with an unremarkable tip, and walked straight through the Hilton lobby. On the way back to the Crossed Palms, it threw the janitor's uniform into a Dumpster.

The chain-smoking woman at the desk was glad to give "James Baker" a room for three days, paid in advance with cash, no ID or luggage.

The room was musty and dark, and definitely not worth $150 a night. But the changeling was finally able to relax, for the first time since the side door to the Wing Room had opened to admit the unwelcome spies.

This couldn't be rushed, it told itself; the identity it took back to Apia had to be absolutely bulletproof. It could go back to California and re-create its college-boy surfer dude, but why not just stay in Hawaii? Closer to Samoa, and so a more likely point of origin for a job-seeker.

There would be a job opening soon. Michelle, the project's receptionist, was seven months pregnant. She was looking forward to quitting and becoming a full-time mother.

The changeling had perhaps a month to construct a perfect replacement and establish her in Samoa.

Receptionist would be good. It didn't dare try lab technician again, but it did want to be someone Russ would notice, and fall for.

It had evidently been caught because it had masqueraded as a real person, and was snagged by some routine security procedure. "We talked to the real Rae Archer" was all the changeling knew or needed to know. Using an actual human had been lazy. This time it would create a woman from the ground up.

The changeling knew pretty exactly what Russ liked in a woman. But it probably wouldn't be too smart to make a woman perfectly built to order—even if it didn't make Russ suspicious, someone else might notice.

So she wouldn't be a modest slender Oriental woman with a degree in astronomy. A normally plump blonde Caucasian who had studied marine biology. It would be smart if her first impression (especially to Jan, but also to Russ) was not too sexy. She could work on Russ slowly, in time-honored ways.

It bothered her to be sneaky with him. She loved him more than she had any other man or woman on Earth. But she had to find a way to the artifact, either through trust or stealth, and Russ was the obvious candidate for either.

What is this thing called love? that song asked when she had come out of the water the second time—back when those ex-Marine centenarians at the anniversary celebration had been horny young men. Could the changeling really know the answer, even eighty years later; even all those books and plays, poems and songs later?

It thought so. The answer was Russ.

If she couldn't have him as Rae, conjure up a second best love. Someday she would amaze him with the story. First, though, she had to seduce him again.

The changeling wanted to be about thirty years old, married once briefly and widowed, no children, no ties. It had to be in complete control of the woman's fictional paper trail, starting with birth.

It took most of a beautiful morning, walking through Kalaepohaku Cemetery, before the changeling found the perfect burial plot: Sharon Valida, born in 1990, died in '91. Her parents were buried beside her, both dead in 2010.

A short computer search in the library showed her parents had died together in an auto accident. Sharon, just to complicate things, had been born in Maui, and died there. She was cremated and her ashes brought back here. But her death certificate was presumably in Maui, and had to be pulled from the system there.

Best to do things in proper order. The changeling flew over to Maui, still the pasty-faced tourist guy, and easily found the office where birth and death records were kept.

It spent a night in a closet, listening, making sure the place would be empty the next night. There was one complication: although there was no night watchman, there were video cameras covering every hall.

The changeling didn't like to take the form of objects rather than living things; it was difficult and painful and time-consuming. But there didn't seem to be any alternative in this case.

It became a sheet of grimy linoleum. The floors of

every hall were the same dirt-colored plastic. So it was able to slide out through the millimeter clearance between door and floor and slowly undulate down the hall to Vital Statistics. There were no cameras in the office, so it rolled up into a cylinder and turned into a sort of cartoon human for convenience, or at least a roll of linoleum with feet and two two-fingered hands, keeping the drab linoleum color and texture.

The file drawers weren't locked, so it was easy to pull the paper death certificate. The electronic record was another matter. Even if it knew which machine to use, there would be passwords and protocols. It would have to solve that problem from outside the system, as Sharon Valida.

It found Sharon's birth certificate, and memorized the handprint and footprint on it. No retinal scans in 1990.

It gave itself a 2007 driver's license, still no retinal scan. It had to take a chance on the Social Security number, changing a few digits from one that belonged to a person born in Maui the same year as Sharon.

Her parents' driver's licenses were still on file, with pictures; they'd lived in Maui until 2009, the year before they died. Her mother had been a strikingly beautiful blonde, which was convenient. The changeling generated a teenaged version for Sharon, with a 2007 hairstyle, nothing extreme. No facial tattoo or ritual scars. For "Scars or identifying marks," it gave Sharon a small hummingbird tattoo on the left breast.

Russell would like that. Dipping into the nipple.

It found a map with school districts, but of course they'd have been much different in 2007. Guessing would be dangerous; some damned computer was liable to do a routine systems check and flag an anomaly. It took a little searching, but there was a file called "HS District Archives"; it found the one closest to her parents' address and enrolled her.

It gave her a science track with APS; she aced all her

science and math but didn't do too well in humanities and arts. She also aced business and keyboard, which might count for more than her college degree. That would be the next day's work.

Checking against other students' yearbook entries, it gave her Chess Club and volleyball. Religious preference, none. Then it worked back through middle school and grade school records, which were mostly routine stuff. Her fourth-grade teacher noted that she did her work "with ease and dispatch," a compliment she had given to about half the class. She skipped fifth grade, making it possible for her to finish college the year her parents died.

It was not quite dawn when the changeling turned back into linear linoleum and slid down a corridor to a location that wasn't covered by the cameras, a stairwell that led to a musty basement. It took its janitor form, remembered from Berkeley, and waited until ten to walk upstairs and pass through the crowd, out onto the street.

It turned back into the tourist in a public library rest room stall, and used the library computer system to outline Sharon Valida's academic career at the University of Hawaii, a more reasonable destination for an ambitious girl than the community college on Maui. She would study business with a concentration in oceanography—in fact, she would take an introductory oceanography course from herself, as the charismatic professor Jimmy Coleridge. The changeling used its intimate knowledge of the university's academic and bureaucratic structure to give Sharon a respectable-but-not-brilliant four years of study. Inserting the paper and computer records verifying her existence there would be even easier than the past night's work in Maui.

(The changeling had not just dropped everything when it changed from Professor Coleridge into Rae Archer. The timing had been perfect; the *Sky and Telescope* ad appearing right at the end of the term. So the professor turned in his grades and told everyone he was taking the summer off for a diving vacation in Polynesia, which was not completely a lie.)

There was one thing left to do before going back to Honolulu. The changeling went to a mall and bought a recent wardrobe for Sharon, and then went back to the Crossed Palms and spent a painful half hour changing into her. She rented another room for the night and went back to the Vital Statistics office at four thirty, a half hour before closing.

"May I help you?" The woman at the window, about forty, had a bright fixed stare as if she'd been caffeine-loading to stay awake till five, and seemed less than sincere in her desire to help.

"I can't find my birth certificate," the changeling said. "I need a certified copy to get a passport."

"Photo ID," the woman said, and the changeling handed over the fresh, though worn, driver's license.

The woman sat down at a console and typed in Valida's name. She stared at the screen, cleared it, and typed it in again. "This says you died in '91."

"What, *died?*"

"One year old." She looked up suspiciously.

"Well, duh. I didn't."

"Wait here a moment." She hustled off in the direction of the room where the changeling had spent the night.

She came back shaking her head. "Computer error," she said, and deleted the record with a couple of strokes. Wordlessly, she made a copy of the birth certificate and notarized it. She went down the hall to have another clerk witness it. The changeling walked out with its new existence certified.

In a way, it was simpler for Sharon to get a college degree than it had been to go through grades 1 to 12, since the changeling could work from inside. It changed its retinal pattern to match that of Professor Jimmy Coleridge, to get into his front door, and took a cab from the Honolulu airport to his apartment off the Manoa campus.

The changeling didn't think anyone saw Sharon entering the apartment, but if they did, it wouldn't be that uncommon a sight.

The next morning, it took a half hour to change back into Jimmy, who fortunately didn't weigh much more than Sharon. It put on teaching clothes and walked over to Coleridge's office at the School of Ocean & Earth Science & Technology.

The departmental secretary was surprised to see him. "Back from Samoa already? I thought you were gone till August!"

"Just for a couple of days. I've got an open ticket on Polynesian Airways. Thought I'd catch up on some stuff and get a few decent meals."

"What do they eat in Samoa? Each other?"

"Just for variety. Usually McDonald's."

"What about the space alien? Were you there?"

"Yeah—they think it's some Hollywood stunt."

"I hope they're wrong. That would be so maze."

"Would be." There was a double handful of mail waiting. The changeling took it to Coleridge's office, dumped it in a drawer, and held the desk's identifier cable up to his eye. The console pinged to life and it started typing.

It wanted to give Sharon a bachelor's in business administration, with a minor in oceanography. It only took twenty minutes to map out her course of study, and then another hour to verify which courses had been offered in which year.

The oceanography minor was easy—she took OCN 320, Aquatic Pollution, as well as "Science of the Sea," from Professor Coleridge, and got an A. The business major was harder. It had taken some business courses as protective coloration in 1992 and 1993, while it was being a California surfer, but things had changed a lot in the past thirty years. Majors had to have calculus and advanced statistics.

It wouldn't be smart to try to generate actual class records; nothing on computer. But it could fake a paper copy of her transcript, and sneak it into the proper file at Business Administration, which was also at the Manoa campus. It was unlikely that anyone would ask for her transcript, but if they did, maybe the scam with the birth certificate could work again.

The changeling gave itself, as Sharon, glowing job references from two dead professors and Coleridge, who of course was off diving but could be reached at jimmyc@uhw.edu.

apia, samoa, 16 july 2021

"She wasn't human," Jack Halliburton said. "No human could have an arm blown off and then outdo a Hollywood stuntman in falling, running, swimming. What was she?"

Jack and Jan had Russell alone in Jack's suite at Aggie Grey's. "You loved her?" Jan said.

"This is so confusing," Russell said.

"You had sex with her," Jack said.

"Jesus, Jack." Russell winced and turned away.

"No, listen. You've had sex with other women; lots of them."

Russell looked toward Jan for support and got a blank stare. "I wouldn't say 'lots.'"

"So was there anything about her anatomy that seemed strange? Anything about her psychology?"

"I did love her," he said to Jan. "I fell for her like dropping off a cliff."

"But *think!*" Jack persisted. "Anything that wasn't human?"

"She was a hell of a lot more human than *you*, Jack. She was funny and sweet and interested in everything."

"That's scary," Jan said.

"I know it is." Russell sank back into the big soft easy chair. "More scary to me than anybody."

Jack levered himself up off the couch and stalked across the room to a table with three crystal liquor decanters. He poured himself a splash of whisky and dropped an ice cube into it. "Do you think she could have been some kind of construct, sent to spy on us?"

"Yeah, sure," Russell said. "A robot. That accounts for the metallic sound when you rapped your knuckles on her."

"I mean biological."

"Of course. You think anybody in the world is capable of 'constructing' a superhuman?"

"She came from somewhere." The phone rang and Jack snatched it up. He listened for about a minute, giving monosyllabic responses, and then said, "I don't know what to say. We'll get back to you. Thanks." He set the phone softly back on the cradle.

"Who was that?" Jan said.

He twirled the ice around in his glass. "Woman named Peterson, Doctor Peterson. Forensic pathologist. Local." He shook his head. "They sent a flesh sample from the arm over to Pago Pago for analysis, DNA identification."

"They identified her?"

"It's not a 'her.'" He took a small sip. "It's not even human—not even animal. It doesn't have DNA."

"Holy Christ," Russell said.

Jack sat down. "Russ . . . you were fucking an alien from another planet. That's probably illegal in Samoa."

honolulu, hawaii, 18 july 2021

The changeling had winced when it saw the headline SPACE ALIEN DISCOVERED IN SAMOA. It bought a paper and learned that it had murdered a "high-level American intelligence operative" by "injecting a mysterious substance."

An editorial urged tolerance rather than fear. The alien would come forward if it knew it would not be harmed. The American government could be reasonable.

That was tempting. The electric chair would be a stimulating experience.

The story explained that scientists knew it was an alien because a tissue sample had no DNA. Was there any way to fake that?

The changeling had several degrees in biology, but didn't know much about its own. It didn't know what mechanisms were involved in changing from one creature—one *thing*—to another. It was as natural as breathing or photosynthesis were to organisms on Earth, and no more amenable to auto-analysis: if you were the only creature around that breathed, you could hardly dissect your-self and learn about lungs.

Of course the changeling *could* dissect itself, and did on a regular basis, but that didn't teach it anything on the molecular level. Besides, the only science it knew was human science, and whatever it did when it changed into a shark or a roll of linoleum wasn't covered by Organic Chemistry 101.

It did absorb DNA when it ate, naturally, and human DNA sometimes when it had sex with a male human. But whatever passed for metabolism in its body didn't retain the stuff. It could absorb a school of albacore tuna and somehow change their substance into a Volkswagen.

Poseidon was probably going to be on the lookout for their alien returning, and would test job applicants for the presence of human DNA. What procedure could Sharon Valida expect?

A little research showed it that DNA testing for pur-poses of identification was usually done with buccal swabs, just wiping a few cells off the inside of the cheek, noninvasive and less personal than a blood or sperm sam-ple. All it had to do was contrive to have a mouthful of human flesh before it sat down to apply for work.

Biting somebody, alive or dead, on the way to an inter-view didn't seem practical. You could buy live portable DNA in the form of blood or sperm, but both posed practi-cal problems, when it came to opening one's mouth for the doctor or police officer.

Pure DNA was sold for research purposes, but only in microscopic quantities, hardly a mouthful. Besides, they might even decide to *be* invasive—want a job? We'll have to take a little blood.

If it were only Russell involved, the changeling would just come out and tell him. Show up one night as Rae to get his attention, and explain. But there were all those tiresome people with guns—and Jack was ultimately in charge, not

Russell. Jack felt dangerous, almost feral in his greedy intensity, and he could infer the changeling's abilities from what had happened at Aggie Grey's. There probably wouldn't be a window facing the sea if Jack had anything to do with the conditions of their meeting.

On the other hand, the changeling knew enough about the Poseidon labs to know they couldn't test for DNA inhouse. The samples would go to Pago Pago, or even back here to Honolulu. That would buy some time, and also might afford an opportunity for substitution.

Perhaps the smartest thing would be to wait, to go join the circus again for a couple of decades; let things cool down. Jack and Russell would die, and new people would be in charge of the artifact.

But there were factors arguing against that, not the least of which being its feelings for Russ; it wanted him, above all others, to know what was really going on. Also, in twenty years—or five, or one—it was likely that the artifact would wind up in a vault in Washington, or Langley, impossible to approach.

There was something deeper, too, that the changeling couldn't quite put a name to. Something in that pattern of ones and zeros was coming together—not logic, not numbers, but some sort of message.

Jan and Russ and the rest of Poseidon were analyzing the digits by looking for an analogue to the Drake message. But maybe the message was not for them. Maybe it was not for any human.

They decided to set a trap for the alien.

"Rae wanted to get to the artifact, but was playing it cool. She asked me about getting around the security protocols so she could actually be in the same room with it; touch it." Russell was doodling while he talked, drawing precise geometrical figures. He and Jack and Jan were outside Jack's suite at Aggie Grey's, talking quietly on the balcony. Jack had belatedly realized the spooks could have had his room bugged. It was less likely with the wrought-iron patio furniture, exposed to the elements.

"You told her you could arrange it?" Jan said.

"Put her off. I said security'd probably be relaxed soon, if the artifact stayed calm."

"Leading her on," Jack said.

"Maybe so. But I had no reason to think it was anything other than normal curiosity. Who wouldn't want to go take a look at the thing?"

"Especially someone who'd come all this way to take a

low-paying job, out of curiosity about it," Jan said. "We tested her enthusiasm, remember, by having her pay her own way out for the interview."

"Which we can do again, for the trap," Jack said. "But maybe we should be more subtle."

Russell nodded. "Whatever Rae is, she knows human nature well. She's either going to be very careful or direct. She might just phone us and set up a meeting, one where she can control the conditions."

"I wonder how old she is," Jack said.

"Thirty-some."

"Try thirty thousand. She can't be killed—at least not by a point-blank shotgun blast, or by drowning—and she can masquerade as another person down to the fingerprints and retinas. Who was she before Rae Archer? Before that? She might go all the way back through human history and prehistory.

"She might have come to this planet even before humans evolved. Wandering around as a saber-toothed tiger. As a dinosaur before that."

"No," Jan said, "I don't think she's an alien at all. Just a different kind of human. They probably evolved along-side us and learned to keep their nature secret—or some-what secret. There are legends about shape-changers and immortals."

Jack rubbed his beard. "If so, there can't be many of them. They'd just take over."

"Maybe they have," Russ said. "We ought to check every world leader for DNA." He and Jan laughed nervously.

"The CIA is probably having this same conversation," Jack said.

In fact, by the time Jack said this, every employee of the CIA had donated a few cheek cells to the agency, as had employees of NSA and Homeland Security. A "suggestion" had come down from the White House that all of the country's leaders be tested.

Laboratories that did DNA testing were initially overwhelmed, but then their usual work was not just testing for the presence of DNA, but rather analyzing a sample to link it to a particular microorganism or person. This called for time-consuming processes like electrophoresis or mass spectrometry. But of course in those cases they already knew that a sample contained DNA; the question was pinning down its origin.

It turned out that a DNA/no DNA test was a lot simpler. You took the buccal swab and swirled it around in a test tube containing a solution that turns acid in the presence of even a microgram of DNA, then added a drop of phenol red. If it turned yellow, voila, the scraping was from a human cheek, or at least it came from something that had DNA of some description. It couldn't discriminate between onion DNA and human, but in this case it didn't matter. Samples of the "flesh" and "blood" in the arm that resided in a freezer in the Apia police station had been sent all over the world for analysis. The samples had the right proportions of carbon, hydrogen, oxygen, phosphorus, sulfur, and nitrogen to have come from the amino acids that make up human (or animal) protein, but their chemistry was not human. It was not even organic chemistry.

The thing it came from had not been alive, in the sense that a human is alive.

The tests proved that every member of the American intelligence community was human, at least in a nominal sense, and so were all prominent politicians, including the president, which surprised a few people.

apia, samoa, 22 july 2021

Just a week after it had been blasted with a shotgun and swam to the airport, the changeling returned. Sharon Valida had a brand-new passport, a six-month work permit, and a suitcase full of light business outfits. Over the internet, she'd landed a job with a bank in Apia looking for a customer representative who could speak German and French.

She also had packed a nice bikini and cute jogging outfit; a dinner dress and a bottle of Sudafed unlike any other in the world. Each capsule had been carefully opened and emptied and refilled with a couple of hundred dollars' worth of reference DNA stolen from a teaching laboratory at the University of Hawaii. She had bitten down on one every few hours from the Honolulu airport to the Apia one, where a uniformed man apologetically stuck a swab in her mouth and stroked the inside of both cheeks. He did something under the counter and then waved her through.

The changeling was in a quiet race against time. It had

to establish a convincing identity as a working woman in Apia before Michelle Watson, the Poseidon receptionist, retired to have her baby. It knew that Michelle's husband was a pleasant but unemployed beach bum, and she wanted to work as long as she could waddle down to the bank with her paycheck, which was okay with Poseidon.

Some time in the next six weeks they would advertise for a replacement. The ad wouldn't ask for a pretty young woman with a degree in business and minor in oceanography, but that was what they'd get.

The changeling rented an apartment on Beach Street, a few blocks from the project site, and began a routine that included jogging at dawn and dusk, which was when Russell was out riding his bike. He said he used the time to think, but he probably wouldn't be thinking so hard that he would ignore a pretty blonde in a tight silver jogging outfit with PROPERTY OF NOBODY stenciled on the back.

Its bank job was not difficult, and was moderately interesting when they actually needed Sharon as a translator. The rest of the time they had it out front, being pretty and a teller, both of which the changeling could do without thinking about anything but ones and zeros.

Three of the men at the bank asked Sharon out, and she dated them in strict rotation, without becoming "involved." It had been a woman often enough to know that men would accept a lack of sexual activity for a long time, if you were attractive and kept them talking about themselves. They were British, American, and Samoan; reserved, brash, and shy, respectively. The Samoan was the most interesting, taking his *palagi* woman to native places where no one else was Caucasian, and doing physical things like sailing and swimming. More traditional physical behavior, she was reserving for Russell.

Russell pedaled by her almost every morning, either approaching with a conventional I'm-not-looking-at-your-breasts smile and nod, or slowing down and coasting as he closed on her from behind.

The changeling contrived an incident the second week. Hearing the familiar bicycle about a block away, it stumbled and fell, skinning a knee.

Russell raced up and dropped his bike with a clatter. Sharon was looking at the minor wound and tentatively picking gravel out of it. The changeling manufactured enough histamine to make itself on the verge of tears.

"Are you all right?" He was a little out of breath.

"It's nothing," the changeling said. "I'm such a klutz."

"Wait." Russell stepped back to his bicycle and got the water bottle. He unscrewed the top and, steadying her with a light touch to the calf, poured cool water on the abrasion.

"Ooh." There was no pain, actually, but the changeling made itself flinch. "No, it's all right."

It was more than all right, actually. His familiar touch and the smell of his sweat. If the changeling had been slightly more human, she would have grabbed him and held him tight.

"We have a first-aid kit back at the office," he said, nodding in the direction of the project, about a block ahead. "We ought to clean that and wrap it up. Wounds get infected so fast here."

"Thank you, I . . . I don't want to be any trouble. . . ."

"Nonsense." He gave her an arm and helped her up. The changeling shivered slightly at his touch on its waist.

It limped a little, hand on his shoulder for support. "Your bike?"

"Nobody'll take it. It's a junker; I don't even carry a lock."

"People are different here, aren't they? Back home, someone would steal it whether it was worth anything or not."

"Where's home?"

"Honolulu; Maui originally."

He nodded. "You're not a tourist, are you? I've seen you around."

"Work at a bank downtown, translator."

"You speak Samoan?"

"No." She shook her head and brushed away her hair in a graceful gesture that was not Rae's. "French and German, some Japanese. I'm studying Samoan, but it's hard."

"Don't I know. I've been here two years and can't even say 'pass the disgusting vegetables.'"

"Aumai sau fuala'au fai mea'ai ma," the changeling said. "I haven't learned 'disgusting' yet." It hadn't given Samoan a thought since starting on the ones and zeros, actually, but remembered some from the first few days of that incarnation.

"Pretty impressive, actually. Languages come easy to you?"

Job interview? "They did when I was younger. I learned Japanese and some Mandarin."

"Hawaiian, of course?"

"No," it said quickly, remembering that Jack did speak some. "Funny thing, you don't really need it socially, and no one expects someone who looks like me to speak it." It shrugged. "Probably a class or race element, too. My mother and father wouldn't have been thrilled."

"Know what you mean." He waved at the guard in his little kiosk and unlocked the door to the main building. "We lived in California, and my dad wasn't happy about my taking Spanish. Even though it was the most useful second language." The changeling knew that, of course.

They went into the familiar reception room. He sat the changeling down in Michelle's chair, the one it hoped to be occupying soon, and began opening and closing drawers. "First-aid kit, first-aid kit." He pulled out a white plastic box. "Ah."

The changeling had a sudden thought. "Would you mind . . . I feel a little faint. Could I get something to drink?"

"Sure. Coke?"

"Fine." She unzipped the little wallet on her wrist.

He waved a hand. "Free with my card." It knew that, and knew the machine was out of sight down the corridor.

When he turned the corner, it slowly spun the chair around 90 degrees, so its back was to the camera behind Michelle's desk, and plucked a Sudafed capsule from the wallet. Broke it between thumb and forefinger and sprinkled DNA into the wound. It got some on the fingers of both hands, too, slipped the empty capsule back into the wallet, and returned to its original position before Russell got back, feeling a little silly for being so thorough. But Russ wouldn't be Russ if he hadn't thought it through enough to suspect any new woman who came into his life.

"Thanks." It took the Coke and drank an appropriate amount, and looked around. "So this is the place."

He pressed an antiseptic pad against the knee. "This is the place, all right. Welcome to the madhouse."

"Mad island," it said. "Creature from outer space and its UFO."

He shook his head and tossed the pad into Michelle's trash can. "There are other explanations. But they're no less bizarre." He shook a can of bandage spray—"Cold"— and sprayed the knee liberally.

"What explanation do you like?"

"It's as good as any." He tapped the knee around the wound, checking the spray. "What do the people at the bank think?"

"Most of them are UFO. One guy's convinced it's all a movie gimmick, and you'll all look like fools when they reveal it."

He stood up. "I'd take bets against that. I talked to the movie people. They're exploiting it for all they're worth, but they were obviously as surprised as anyone else."

"That's what I told him. They would've had someone around who happened to have a camera. Else why spend the money?"

"Yeah, no-brainer. Can you flex the knee okay?"

It swung her foot carefully. "I think it's fine." She took his arm and stood up. "Thanks."

"Are you doing anything for lunch?" He laughed nervously and kneaded his brow.

"I'm tied up today," the changeling said, not to appear too eager. "Tomorrow's free." Putting out her hand: "Sharon Valida."

"Russell Sutton. Noon at the Rainforest?"

"I'd be delighted." It smiled at him, wondering if her dimples were too cute. "My knight in shining armor."

"Bicyclist with a water bottle." He escorted her out. "'Bye." He watched her jog away, slightly favoring the injured knee, and then walked back to retrieve his bike.

Could it be? he wondered. She didn't look anything like Rae, but the assumption was that she could look like anyone.

He leaned the bike up next to the entrance and went back inside. In the bio corner of the lab he got a latex glove and a plastic bag. Back at the reception desk, he picked the bloodstained pad out of the trash can and put it into the bag. He emptied the Coke can out in the men's room and put it in the bag, too, gingerly holding it by the rim, and printed SHARON VALIDA on the bag with a Magic Marker.

Trying to outthink an alien intelligence, they'd figured that one obvious avenue back to the artifact was Russell's weakness for pretty women—for women in general, actually. If Sharon had been a small attractive Asian, he would be more suspicious.

One part of him wanted the samples to have no DNA, so they could close the trap. A smaller part hoped she was just a sexy blonde with a sense of humor and a nonalien intelligence.

He put the bag on the bio desk with a short note to Naomi. Then he went back to the bike and checked the cyclometer. Only four miles; one more to go.

He pedaled off in the direction Sharon had gone, but didn't see her. Went home to shower before work, perhaps, or maybe to check the oil in her *other* flying saucer.

Russell was lost in reverie, staring at the monitor without seeing it, and was startled when Naomi set the bag down next to him, with a clink of Coke can.

"Your Sharon has plenty of DNA, I'm afraid. Next move is up to you."

"What? Oh, lunch."

"Hope she tastes good," Naomi said with a lecherous wink. Russell balled up a piece of paper and threw it at her.

Back to the secret message. He was putting together a one-page website that only Rae would completely understand. It was called "A Rae in the Darkness" and was headed with three photos—Russell and Rae flanking a snap of Stevenson's gravestone verse he'd taken the hour before she'd led him down the hill to the hotel.

He'd skimmed through a book of Stevenson's poetry, and didn't like much of it, but this one quatrain was not far off, and he typed it in:

LOVE, WHAT IS LOVE?

LOVE—what is love? A great and aching heart;
Wrung hands; and silence; and a long despair.
Life—what is life? Upon a moorland bare
To see love coming and see love depart.

—Robert Louis Stevenson

Then he pasted in thirty characters of the artifact's message:

11010010110100101110100100101

And then his own message:

> *Rae, when I did see you depart, literally, I didn't know it*
> *was you, and it deepened the mystery.*
>
> *If you have to disappear, that's your decision. But you*
> *know that if there's anyone on this world you can trust,*
> *it's me.*
>
> *I know I don't know you, but I love you. Come back in*
> *whatever guise.*
>
> —*Russ*

There was a box for "affinities," words that would draw a searcher, or surfer, to the site. He typed in "Poseidon," "Apia," "artifact," "alien," and so forth, ending with "Rae Archer" and "Russell Sutton." He knew that the first people drawn to the site would probably be the CIA and their ilk, but there was no way to get around that. He assumed that Rae would be canny enough to anticipate them, too.

The Rainforest Café was nostalgic nineties funk in a jungle setting. Bamboo and palms and elephant ears under blue lights and mist nozzles, quaintly angry rap whispering in the background.

Russell felt a little underdressed in cutoffs and an island shirt. It was the weekend, but Sharon had come from work, wearing suit and tie. She loosened the tie and patted her brow with a tissue, prettily.

"I should have suggested an air-conditioned place."

"Glad you didn't. I was freezing in the office." She shrugged out of her jacket.

"You've always lived in the tropics?"

"In the heat, anyhow. You?"

"As soon as I could choose." Russell told her about growing up in the Dakotas. He'd gone to college in Florida, and never had to live through another winter. "Most of my experience with being cold now is underwater, working in a wetsuit."

"Been there." She covered her mouth, laughing. "When you don't have enough pee to warm it up."

He poured her some iced tea. "You dive a lot?"

"When I was in school, a little. Now I mostly snorkel. A guy at work took me out to the reef at Palolo last week—all those giant clams, I couldn't believe my eyes!"

"They're something." He served himself. "Was it your major, marine science?"

"No, I did business administration. Minor in oceanography—that was my real cold-water experience. A summer course diving in the Peru current." She'd actually been there as professor, not student, but the university records would confirm she'd taken the course and made an A.

"We used to be out there," he said. "My company, Poseidon. We did marine engineering out of Baja California."

"Until you found the alien thingie."

"Well, we didn't know what it was, at the time." He broke open a roll and buttered one half carefully with healthy spread. "We pinged it with sonar and registered it for later salvage. It was a while before we actually went down and took a look." He gestured down the road with the roll. "Then this happened."

"It must be exciting."

"Exciting and frustrating in about equal measures. We're not getting anywhere." He drew a shape on the table-cloth with his fingernail. "What do *you* do for excitement? Or frustration."

"I don't know. Come out here, run, fall down." They laughed. "I've been kind of drifting. Both my parents died when I was in college, like ten years ago, eleven."

"I'm sorry. . . ."

She dipped her head. "Yeah. They left me some money, and I sort of wandered around Europe, then Japan. Now that the money's gone, I wish I'd stayed in school. Not much you can do with a BBA."

"You're still young. You could go back."

"I guess thirty-one's young." She stared into her tea. "Maybe not to graduate school admission committees."

"You'd go back to business?"

She shook her head. "Maybe macroeconomics. Pacific Rim economics. But I've been thinking more oceanography. I could get a B.S. in a year, maybe three semesters." She smiled. "Come out here and work for you."

"Not with a bachelor's," he said seriously. "Take a couple of years and get a doctorate. The artifact's not going anywhere."

"But you don't know that," she said. "It might decide to go back to Alpha Centauri."

Their sandwiches came. Russell discarded the top piece of bread and carefully sliced the remainder into one-inch strips, then rotated the plate 90 degrees and cut the strips into thirds. The changeling remembered the habit and smiled.

"Saves me a hundred calories," he said. "The media all think the thing's from another star. That's the easiest explanation. We're trying to come up with something less obvious."

"Like what? Secret government project?"

"Or that it's always been here. You know what hell this has been for physicists and chemists."

"I can imagine."

He took a bite and then salted everything, as the changeling expected. "*That's* no different whether the thing is local or from another galaxy. It means there are very basic laws we don't understand about . . . the nature of matter." He speared a square of sandwich and gestured with it. "It's chaos. Nothing we know is true anymore."

"Can you really say that?" the changeling said, carving its own sandwich into quarters. "Like we learned in school, Galileo's physics was an approximation of Newton's;

Newton got swallowed by Einstein; then Einstein by Holling."

"Hawking, then Holling, to be technical. But this is different. It's like everything worked, down to eight decimal places, and then somebody says, 'Hold it. You forgot about magic.' That's what this damned thing is." He laughed. "I love it! But then I'm not a physicist."

"They must be going crazy." She picked up one quarter and nibbled on it.

"You should see my e-mail. Actually, *I* should see my e-mail. This indispensible woman, Michelle, throws out nine-tenths of it before I come to work."

"She knows physics?"

"Well, like you—she's an accountant with some course work in various sciences. But she reads everything, knows more about general science than I do."

"She doesn't really throw them away," the changeling asked. "You at least glance at them?"

"Oh, yeah. At least the ones that have some entertainment value—we call them the X-files. I get together with Jan, our space scientist, every Friday to run through them. Kind of fun, actually." He speared another square. "Pleasant nutlike flavor."

"Did you ever get anything useful?"

"Not yet." He turned serious. "The whole game is going to change soon. We're going public with . . . an aspect we've kept secret. Wish I could tell you."

The changeling was glad he couldn't. Knowing about the message gave it an edge for Michelle's job. Those credits in Math 471 and 472, advanced statistics. "Oh, come on. Pretty please?"

He smiled. "Your womanly wiles will get you nowhere. I'll tell you on Monday, though, if you'd like to have lunch again."

"Okay. Can I bring my pal from the *Weekly World News*?"

"He might already be down at the office. We're making the announcement at nine o'clock."

"You really think you'll be free for lunch, then?"

"I'm telling you too much." He looked left and right. "That's why we chose Monday. No planes till Tuesday morning. Gives us, what, some measure of spin control."

He did look a little worried. The changeling reached over and patted his hand. "Mum's the word."

"'Mum's the word'?" He chuckled. "I haven't heard that since I was a kid."

Oops. "My mother used to say it. Where does it come from?"

"Where do any of them?" He relaxed. "How are things at the bank working out?"

"They're nice enough people," it said, quickly. "No real challenge, though. A few times a day I haul out a language to calm down a customer. Walk him through a document or just help with numbers. The job description said 'international relations,' and I suppose that's technically true."

"Apia's smaller than you thought it would be?"

It shrugged. "I read up on it. No real surprises . . . except you guys. I expected a bigger deal."

"Well, it's only fifty people. We had a pretty low profile until a couple of weeks ago."

"Your space alien. That made the front page in Honolulu. You found her?" It closed its eyes and shook its head. "Sorry. Mustn't pry."

"No; I wish we had. Love to spring that on the tabloids."

"You don't believe it's in a secret wing in the Air Force hospital in Pago Pago?"

"No, it's locked up in Roswell, New Mexico." He laughed. "Before your time." The changeling had been there twice, actually, as a juggling dwarf and an anthropology graduate student.

So Monday they were going to reveal the artifact's coded response—or at least the fact that it had responded.

The changeling wondered how that would change its situation, and what it could do before then to help its chances for the job.

Russell offered a possibility. "You work tomorrow?"

"No, everybody goes to church. Except me."

"I'm off, too. You want to bike somewhere for a picnic?"

"God, I haven't ridden a bike since college. Give it a try, though. I guess I could rent one someplace."

"Oh, I have a spare." He scratched his chin. "I usually go out to Fatumes Pool or Fagaloa Bay on Sunday, but that's a little far if you're not used to it. We ought to just tool around, see some local sights, wind up at Palolo or the project for a picnic and a swim."

"Does the reef go over that far?"

"No, it's just a white-sand swimming beach. The local kids like it. We even set out a shark barrier last week."

"You get a lot of sharks?"

"Just takes one. A big hammerhead attacked a boat in the shallows—bit a hole in the hull!—and so the family, the *aiga* that technically owns the land the project's on, asked whether we'd cooperate in putting a barrier up to protect swimmers. Just a wide-mesh net"—he sketched a six-inch square with his fingers—"to keep out really big fish. We bought it and they provided the manpower."

An interesting challenge, the changeling thought. A hammerhead could pretend it was a dolphin and jump over it. "That sounds good. They have picnic tables and all?"

He nodded. "A grill. Let's be American—I know a place with fairly convincing hot dogs. I'll pick some up this afternoon and put them in the office fridge."

They made arrangements to meet at the Vaiala Beach Cottages in the morning, bring a bathing suit, and she went back to her air-conditioned bank.

As he pedaled off toward the butcher shop, Russell thought about what he was getting into. He couldn't afford an actual girlfriend; he had to be "available" for the Rae-alien's return. That was one element of their plans to trap the creature, because when it returned it was likely to repeat the previous strategy, and try to seduce Russell. Or maybe Jack or Jan. Anybody new who came into their lives would have to pass the DNA test.

He toyed with the idea of arguing to the others that maybe the alien had figured out a way to manufacture DNA, so he should continue to pursue Sharon even though she'd passed the test—all in the name of science, of course.

apia, samoa, july 2021

Russell knew he wasn't the only one in passionate pursuit of the alien. But he didn't know that his competition was more formidable than the CIA agents who were just now becoming interested in Sharon.

The chameleon had been in and out of Apia ever since he knew they had a vehicle from another planet. If there was anybody else like him on Earth, he would be drawn here, too.

The changeling also had spent much of its human life looking for another changeling. It saw the meeting as a kind of reunion—"together again for the first time." They could sit down and talk, and perhaps together solve the mystery of their origin.

The chameleon, on the other hand, was not interested in mysteries. He was interested in eliminating competition.

He wasn't stupid. Over the millennia he had often attained his culture's highest degree of education. He knew that his desire to destroy the competition was not rational.

But it was programmed into every cell of his body; it was what he had instead of the urge to reproduce. And sexual desire was a pale flame beside his passion to destroy, to protect himself.

On his own terms it was easy to rationalize: if the creature was like him, their first meeting would be short and brutal. Best strike first. No human could kill him, but no human knew how profoundly damaged he would have to be in order to actually die.

He did know and had to presume his competitor would as well.

apia, samoa, 24 july 2021

The changeling regretted the impulse that had made it say it hadn't ridden a bike in years. It had been riding since before Russell was born, and simulating clumsiness on a single-speed Schwinn was an Oscar-level performance.

"How you doing up there?" She was leading them up Logan Road, not too hilly and no traffic, Sunday morning.

"I'm getting the hang of it." She stood up to crest the hills, and felt the gentle pressure of eyetracks on her butt. Maybe it shouldn't have worn the form-fitting jogging outfit, which got some disapproving stares from people on their way to church. But it certainly kept Russell's attention.

"All downhill from here. Just keep bearing to your left."

"Yeah, I've run this way. The project's down after the second light, V-something Road."

"*Vaiala-vini*. We'll make you a Samoan yet."

"As long as I don't have to like breadfruit."

"*Fuata*. We'll start out with hot dogs and move our way

down the food chain. After turkey tails and mutton flaps, you'll be begging for *fuata*."

"Oh, I've got a freezer full of turkey tails. Deep-fried, you can't beat 'em." They laughed together, but there was an edge to it. They both knew the Samoan diet had been transformed by Western intrusion, all for the worse. Turkey tails and Big Macs, mutton flaps and corned beef— there weren't many natives over thirty who were lean and heart-healthy.

Russell waved at the guard as they went through the project gate. They dropped the bikes, no locks, in front of the main building, and raided his office fridge for hot dogs and beer, and put them in a foam cooler. He found charcoal in a utility locker and went out to start the fire while Sharon changed.

She studied her body in the ladies' room mirror and made a few minor adjustments here and there. She knew she had Russell hooked. The question was whether to reel him in. It might be better to play a waiting game, and let Michelle get closer to delivery.

Or maybe force the issue. Get Russ in bed, and see what comes up.

It was a nice bright red thong bikini. The changeling pulled out a few pinches of excess pubic hair and ate them. It arranged the top so it just showed the wing tips of the hummingbird tattoo. It slightly deepened its lumbar dimples, a feature she remembered Russell noticing in her Rae incarnation.

It closed in for the kill, first wrapping a lavalava around its waist. It could wear the revealing suit as long as at least its toes were in the water, but Samoans weren't happy about insensitive tourists flaunting their charms on the way there.

Russell was wearing the same blue-jean cutoffs he'd bicycled in, changing it into a swimsuit by taking off his shirt and shoes. The changeling smiled at his familiar body, a little pudgy in spite of athletic legs and arms, skin almost milk white—he never went out into the sun without total sunblock; both his parents had had skin cancer. His body hair was a silky down of black and white mixed, no gray, and his only tattoo, not visible now, was a small DO NOT OPEN TILL CHRISTMAS tag attached to a big scar he'd gotten from an emergency appendectomy by a village doctor in the Cook Islands. How many other women had giggled at that the first time he undressed in front of them?

He noticed her own tattoo immediately. "Bird?"

"Hummingbird." She pulled the top of her bra down almost to the aureole. Her breasts were small, which he liked.

"Very nice." He smiled and turned his attention back to the grill, splashing the charcoal with 100 percent isopropyl alcohol from a lab bottle. He snapped a sparker at it and it ignited with a blue puff.

"How much longer?" the changeling said. "I'm famished."

"At least twenty minutes." He gestured at the small cooler on the picnic table. "Beer? Or swim."

"Swim first. I'm all sticky." She turned her back toward him to step out of the lavalava, which under other circumstances might have been a modest posture. She snatched her face mask, fins, and mouthgill off the table and ran for the water. "Last one in has to cook the hot dogs." He stood and watched her run, with a growing smile. Then he jogged after her. She was already sitting in the shallows, only her head showing, when he splashed in.

"Oh well. I was going to cook them anyway."

She got the fins on, then spit into her mask and rubbed the saliva around. "Any reefs out here?"

"None close in. Some outside the shark net."

"Want to live dangerously?"

"Sure. I always wanted to see a fourteen-foot hammerhead up close."

I was only nine feet. "That's what bit the boat?"

"Not to worry. They harpooned it and shot it in shallow water. It attacked out of pain and confusion, most likely." He splashed water in his mask. "I've seen lots of sharks and never had a problem."

"Me, too. Maybe we never met a really hungry one."

"Maybe." He pointed. "There's some reef out that way. I'll hold up the net and you can swim under."

"Okay." They bit down on their mouthgills, and swam the hundred yards out to the net. They wriggled under it without any problem and proceeded out to the reef, the changeling naturally taking Russell's hand when it was offered. They swam in easy unison, moving fast with powerful surges from the fins.

The reef wasn't too impressive, compared to the dramatic one past the giant clam farm at Palolo, but it did have lots of brightly colored fish and a small moray eel, watching their intrusion with its customary sour expression. Russell found an octopus the size of his hand, and they passed it back and forth until it tired of the game and shot away.

Russ pantomimed eating and Sharon nodded. They headed back to the net, with a short detour to chase after a medium-sized ray, hand in hand.

"That was nice," the changeling said, taking off her fins in knee-deep water, quite aware that when the suit was wet it left nothing to the imagination. "Especially the octopus."

"That was lucky. 'The soft intelligence,' someone called them."

"Jacques Cousteau." His eyebrows went up. "My oceanography prof had his old book."

As they waded ashore, Russell waved at a boy of six or seven who was sitting at their table with a bucket.

The bucket was half full of ice, with a large bowl of *oka,* the Samoan version of ceviche, fish marinated in lime juice and served with coconut cream and hot peppers. "Caught this morning, Dr. Russell."

He peered into the bowl. "Skipjack?"

He shrugged. "Ten tala."

"I don't have any money with me."

"I've got some." The boy was staring at her crotch, transfixed. She wrapped the lavalava around her waist and pulled a few bills out of a pocket, and handed him a ten.

"*Fa'afetai*," he said, giving her the bowl and backing away shyly. "Thank."

"*Afio mai*," she said, and he turned and ran with the money.

They watched him go and Russell laughed quietly. "They're funny. Casual about nudity but conservative about clothing."

She nodded. "I'll never understand religion. Or fashion, for that matter." She set the bowl on the table and fished through the grocery bag for a couple of plastic forks. "Appetizer?"

"Thanks. Let me put on the dogs first." He smoothed the white pile of coals with a stick and got four hot dogs from the cooler.

The fish was cold and firm and spicy. "I could get used to this," the changeling said. "How long have you lived here?"

"Got here last summer, when I came out with Jack Halliburton to set up the lab." He arranged the hot dogs in a precise row. "I commuted for a couple of months, finishing up old business in Baja. Pretty much stuck here since the lab was finished and the artifact was in place."

"You don't like it?"

"As a *place* it's okay. Vacation spot. Hard to do science here, though." He sat down next to her and speared a piece of *oka*. "Even with modern communications, virtual conference room and all, it's really isolated. You can break a fifty-cent part and be shut down for two days, waiting for the plane. And you miss . . . it sounds snobbish, it *is* snobbish, but I miss the company of like-minded people, people you don't work with—scientists, artists, whatever."

"I would have taken you for a loner."

"Well, I am, or was. The place in Baja was miles from nowhere, and that's one reason I leased it. But I could be in L.A. in an hour, and had an apartment just off the UCLA campus."

"Where you seduced college girls. I know your type."

He laughed and blushed. "Back when I had hair." He got up to check the dogs. "I do miss the college-town atmosphere. Bookstores, coffeeshops, bars. The libraries on campus. The girls on campus."

"It's a nice campus. I stayed there for two weeks, diving in summer school."

"Where?"

"A dorm." The changeling knew where Jimmy Coleridge's students stayed now. Where would it have been eleven years ago? "Maybe Conway? Conroy."

"Oh yeah. That's close to where I stay." He used tongs to rotate the hot dogs 180 degrees, then went to the cooler. "Beer? Or a glass of wine."

"You have wine in there?"

"No, back in the fridge. Only take a minute."

"That would be good. I'm not much of a beer drinker. Maybe when the dogs are done."

"Keep an eye on 'em." He jogged away.

The changeling considered its position. This was a cusp. If it began a love affair with Russ—or restarted one—it would probably kill its chances for the job. But the job was only a stepping stone to get close to the artifact. Maybe Russ's lover would have a better shot at that than the receptionist.

Why did it feel this drive to be in the physical presence of the thing? It had seen all the pictures, studied the data, read people's frustrated inconclusions.

It remembered the feeling when it swam from Bataan to California. The inchoate feeling, the hesitation, when it passed over the Tonga Trench.

It felt that now, more strongly than ever. Something was taking form.

Russell came back with two long-stemmed glasses of white wine, already misted with humidity. "Drink it while it's cold," he said, handing one to her, and drank off a third of his in a gulp. "Ready in a minute." He gave the hot dogs a quarter turn.

"So why didn't you just move the thing to Baja? Why start from scratch here?"

"I wish." He stared at the grill. "Partly the difficulty of moving the damned thing. Mostly political, though. Mexico's too close to the United States, not just in miles, but politically and economically. Jack didn't want Uncle Sam breathing down our neck. Mexican soldiers knocking on our door. *Down* our door."

"They could do that?"

"Sure they could. Threat to hemisphere security." He split two buns and set them on the grill. "Independent Samoa really *is* independent. And stable. Tonga was closer to the artifact's original position, but we didn't want to deal with the politics there.

"Jack studied surveys of the Samoan Islands, and wound up here by a process of elimination."

"The first factor being 'Is there a town?'"

He nodded. "They call it the only city in Samoa, but as you know, it's not exactly Hong Kong. It's really just a bunch of towns crowded together, but it does have a pharmacy, hardware store, and so forth." He gestured toward the main building. "And this patch of land: it was undeveloped, privately owned, and on the water. Jack got in touch with the *matai* of the family that owned it and arranged to lease it. He even became a Samoan citizen."

"Did he join the family, the *aiga*?"

"No, although he didn't rule out the possibility. Technically, he'd have to share all his wealth with the family." He raised an eyebrow. "That's not in his nature."

"You've known him a long time?"

"No. Not until . . . he got in touch with me about the submarine disaster that led to our finding the artifact." The changeling knew, as Rae, that there was something secret going on there. Maybe it could tease the truth out of him in this incarnation.

"We never would have met, in the normal course of things. He was born into money, but chose a military career. I'm pretty far from either of those." He inspected the hot dogs. "These two are done." She held out paper plates and he installed buns and dogs on them, then repositioned the remaining two according to some arcane thermodynamic principle, and split two more buns to toast.

They silently went about the business of mustard and ketchup and relish, all out of small squeeze packets that Russell had liberated from various airports.

The changeling took a bite. "Good." Bland, actually.

Russell shrugged. "Sometimes I'd kill for some plain American sidewalk vendor food. Bacteria and all."

"You *made* money, though. As opposed to being born with it. You didn't raise the *Titanic* with spare change."

He shook his head, chewing. "Always use other people's money. Sometimes I feel more like a pitchman than an engineer." He paused to squirt another envelope of mustard into the bun. "Jack thinks, or claims to think, that there's a huge fortune in this. Maybe someday, but probably not for him. He's got a zillion eurobucks to earn back—and he's old."

"How about you?"

"I'm not so old."

"I mean money. Do you expect to make a fortune yourself?"

"No; hell, no. I'm in it for the game."

"That's what I thought. Hoped."

"Biggest thing in the twenty-first century. Maybe *the*

biggest thing, all the way back." He stared at the containment building. "Even if it's not from another world. That
would mean that our view of reality, our science, is wrong.
Not just incomplete, but wrong."

"Isn't that true, no matter where it comes from?"

"In a way, no. Last century, a guy pointed out that a sufficiently advanced technology is indistinguishable from
magic. . . ."

Arthur C. Clarke, the changeling didn't say. It had met
him at an Apollo launch in the 1970s.

"And that gives us an out. Our science could still be a
subset of theirs. Like going back to Newton and showing
him a hologram."

He was so absorbed in his explanation he wasn't aware
of the man walking quietly up behind him. His shadow fell
over him and he jumped, startled. "Jack!"

"Sorry. Didn't mean to sneak up on you."

"This is Sharon Valida. Jack Halliburton."

The changeling extended its hand. "We've met, briefly.
I work at the Pacific Commercial Bank."

"And have a good memory for faces."

Especially yours, the changeling thought.

"Hot dog?" Russell said.

"No, I'm headed for the hotel. I saw you here and wondered whether we might get together a little earlier tomorrow morning, before the . . . thing."

"Like what, eight o'clock?"

"Eight would be fine. I'll leave a message for Jan." He
nodded at the changeling. "Miss Valida. See you then,
Russell."

When he was out of earshot, the changeling said, "He
always dresses like that?" White linen suit, Panama hat,
Samoan shirt.

"Yeah, when he's not working in the lab. Maybe a century out of date."

"A few other rich old guys who come into the bank dress that way. My boss calls them his Somerset Maugham characters. Was he some actor?"

"Writer, I think." He ate the last bite and stood up. "Ready for another?"

"Let it get a little burnt. Try a beer, though."

"Excellent idea." He took two Heinekens out and popped them.

She drank off her wine and accepted one. "Here's to drunken debauchery on Sunday." They clinked bottles together. "So . . . showing Newton a hologram."

"Well, it's occurred to me that this thing might not be from another planet. It might be from our own future."

"Really? I thought you could only go the other way."

"You know about that?"

"I saw a thing on the cube. Particle accelerator."

"Yeah, they've been able to move a particle a fraction of a second into the future. Which is kosher; general relativity has always allowed that."

"But not into the past?"

"That's right—and it's not just relativity; it's causality, common sense. Cause and effect out the window."

"But you think—"

"I know it's like 'one impossible thing happens, therefore anything impossible can happen.' But it makes a screwy kind of sense. They sent this indestructible thing back a million years into the past, and put it where no one could find it. Then they went to dig it up . . ."

"And it wasn't there!" She nodded rapidly. "So they sent this kind of robot back here to find out what happened."

"Not a robot," he said. "Definitely not a robot."

"You knew her?"

He hesitated. "Pretty well. Or I thought I did. She was pretty human for a robot. Or transhuman, as I say, from the future."

"Evolved from humans?"

"Bingo. It wouldn't take millions of years, either. It's only law and custom, not science, that keeps us from directing our own evolution now."

The changeling considered this. It seemed to have memories going so far back that it always considered itself a visitor from the distant past. It *could* have been from the future, though, and lost the memory of that travel.

It knew that a way around the causality paradox might be that the time traveler not be allowed to take any information back in time. It had never thought of applying that to its own amnesia of the time before the centuries it had spent as a great white shark. It could have been sent back as a blank-slate creature that *needed* no memory to survive, and evolve.

"Have you talked this over with Jack?"

"Jack? No. He's all for aliens from another planet. Especially since the thing with Rae, our 'space alien.'"

"Which you don't buy."

"Well . . . I guess you can make a better scientific, or at least logical, case for extraterrestrial origin. But if so, why didn't she just come forward and say 'Take me to your leader'?"

"Maybe she was afraid."

"She wasn't afraid of me."

"Maybe Jack." The changeling smiled. "I take it she wouldn't be the only one."

"He's a little scary sometimes." He got up and turned the hot dogs. "Let's burn the other side."

She didn't say anything while he repositioned the meat and buns. When he looked up she was staring out to sea, an odd thoughtful expression on her face.

"Sharon?"

It was a song. *A song.*

The changeling never stopped manipulating the ones and zeros. Pretending to be human only used a small part of its intelligence, so while it was carrying on bank business or being social, even concentrating on Russ, most of its being was swimming through the binary sea of the message.

The message itself wasn't clear, but suddenly the changeling knew *what* it was.

A song in its native tongue. A language forgotten for a million years.

"Sharon? Are you all right?"

"Oh! Sorry." She rubbed her face with both hands. "Sometimes I do that."

He sat on the bench, not too close, and touched her hand. "Is it your parents?" She nodded her head in two short jerks. "I lost mine together, too, at least in the same week. I was quite a bit older than you, but it still hit me hard. Being alone."

Her eyes brimmed and she wiped them. "You're right. Alone." *He's a wonderful man*, it thought, *but he doesn't know what loneliness is.*

He wanted to take her into his arms, but restrained himself. "Let me take you home."

"No. It's passed." She flashed him a bright smile. "Let's have another hot dog." She peered into the empty beer bottle. "Maybe the beer makes me sentimental. I should have another."

"Your wish is my command." He opened two and passed her one. "Sentimental together."

A song. A song about home. "Are they burnt enough?"

He touched one lightly. "Done to a turn."

While they ate and chatted about deliberately inconsequential things, it made plans for the rest of the day and night. Especially night. Russell was in for a little surprise.

Tomorrow, they were almost certainly going to announce that the artifact had answered them, and perhaps release the binary sequence, so that a few million other people could try to figure it out.

People wouldn't. It would be like someone who didn't know what Braille was running a finger along a line of it, in a foreign language. A coded message, not coded for secrecy, but nevertheless unbreakable.

But by Tuesday, there would be outsiders all over the place. Reporters lucky enough to be in American Samoa would be on the spot by noon Monday. The Tuesday morning plane would be crowded with them, from America; Thursday, from Asia and Europe. Security would be tighter around the clock.

So it had until tomorrow morning.

"I don't want to rush things," Russell said, "but are you doing anything tonight? If I don't have an excuse, Jack's going to collar me at Aggie's."

She closed her eyes. Careful. "I wish I could. But I'm going out with a man from work." She patted Russell's knee. "Have to tell him I'm not interested. Free Monday and Tuesday, though."

"We already have lunch Monday," he reminded her.

"Dinner Tuesday, then."

"I'll make Sails reservations at eight, right away. There'll be a lot of hungry reporters in town."

The changeling nodded. "And I'll know the big secret by then."

"By ten tomorrow, if you listen to the news. Or you can wait and let me surprise you at lunch."

"Maybe I'll wait. I don't suppose you'll let me try to guess."

"Nope."

"You've discovered the president's an alien."

"Damn, you got it. Now we'll have to kill you."

"Oh, well. At least I found out early."

They pedaled around Apia after lunch, stopping at the Maketi Fou, the normally crowded central market, for iced coconuts. On Sunday it was pretty lazy, the vendors chatting in clusters in shady spots, reluctantly coming over to take their money. He bought her a mother-of-pearl neck-lace she admired. She bought him a garish silk crimson lavalava and dared him to wear it to dinner.

The changeling wondered whether there would be a dinner date. Their relationship was about to enter un-charted territory.

Maybe he *would* have to kill her, in a sense. In the sense that she was Rae, was Sharon.

Russell offered to let her keep the bicycle, but she said no, she was too contaminated by civilization, and didn't want to either leave it outside or lug it up the stairs to her small apartment. She left it at his cottage and kissed him good-bye, firmly, and walked the few blocks home with the kiss fading on her lips.

The changeling pulled the shutters closed over its win-dow and lay in the half-dark, listening to the click of the ceiling fan and the chatter of birds in the poinsiana tree outside.

It began to practice the language it didn't yet under-stand. With its glottis it made clicks exactly a twentieth of a second long, for ones, and carefully measured pauses, for zeros.

Early on in the message, there were three clusters of the sequence 000011110000, which were probably separators of some kind, and a fourth one just past midway. These di-vided the message into parts roughly 2:1:1:47:49. In anal-ogy to human music, perhaps it was a two-verse song, preceded by three packets of information: the first identify-ing it as a song, and the other two giving the title and some technical information, like tempo and key signature. Or fla-vor and electrical charge.

There was no obvious pattern to the two verses, though each one had imbedded the cluster, or word, 01100101001011—three times in the first verse and four in the second. There were no other long repetitions. Short ones, like 0100101, had no statistical significance, but if they represented words in a human language, they could be common ones like "a" or "the." You'd expect that with the high Shannon entropy.

Not much to go on, analytically, but to the changeling it had some intuitive or subliminal meaning, evocative but frustrating, like a melody heard in childhood and almost totally forgotten.

The ceiling fan made a click each three-quarter second. The changeling used it as a metronome, or rhythm section. Its human glottis could "speak" about a third as fast as the artifact had; it lowered the pitch of its sounds by a factor of three.

It practiced quietly enough so that someone eavesdropping would hear something that sounded like noise from the fan's motor, which was exactly what the CIA woman in the next room concluded. They had moved in a few hours after Sharon had her first lunch with Russell.

It didn't take long for the changeling to memorize the forty-five–second sequence of clicks and silences that it wanted to sing back to the artifact. But of course it couldn't get in there without Russell, so it had to wait until dark, and then some. If Russell had met Jack for dinner, he probably wouldn't be out too late. Would he then go to the lab, or home? Usually, it knew, he would go home for some light reading, listening to music, and since he'd be tied to the lab most of the next day, that was probably what he'd do.

At nine, it put on a cute black outfit, short skirt and a clinging buckyball top that shimmered shifting rainbows like a blackbird's wing. It slipped out quietly and with precise timing, when it heard the CIA agent go into the bathroom. By the time the agent suspected Sharon's apartment was empty, the changeling had quickly walked the half mile to the cottages.

The blinds were drawn on number 5, but the light was on by his easy chair. The changeling could visualize him sitting there with his book and glass of wine; a soft harpsi-chord tinkled the Goldberg Variations.

She stepped out of her shoes and tapped on the door. When he opened it, she slipped inside and eased it shut behind her. "I'm impulsive. Are you?"

It took him a couple of seconds to nod, staring. "With you I could be."

The cottage was one big room with a divider setting off the "bedroom"; she led him there, turning out the reading lamp on the way.

"Just a second." He stopped to light a candle, as expected. In its light, she stripped out of the skirt with a Velcro rip and pulled off the buckyball thing. Underneath, she was wearing nothing but the hummingbird tattoo.

She sat on the bed and pulled him toward her, unbuttoning his silly shirt while he fumbled with his cutoffs. He wasn't quite erect; she took him in her mouth immediately, to enjoy the change of state. She teased him gently with her teeth, as she knew he liked, and then took advantage of not having a gag reflex—the changeling had no reflexes, as such—to engage him deeply, cradling him with one hand and urging him down to the bed with the other.

It was what Rae had done with him, the first time. Would his brain be working well enough to make that connection?

He reached down to help her but she was already moist, in control of that function, too. She crawled up onto the bed and straddled him, helping him in slowly with a circling motion, sighing with genuine pleasure. Being with him as Sharon had not been enough.

She smiled down on him, playing with his hair while he moved up and down inside her, and after a minute said, "I have a little trick." She eased sideways and tilted a bit, raising her knee and straightening her leg, holding him in place. She slowly crabbed around, doing the same trick with the other leg, so that she was facing away, without having lost him in the process. "Still there?" Knowing that he was.

"How . . . did you do that?"

"Double jointed."

She knew he liked this aspect, and enjoyed the internal difference herself, but mainly wanted to be facing the other direction for a few minutes. He clasped her with his hands and she used hers in a practiced way, trying to control his progress while she worked on her face.

When the time was right, she had an enthusiastic orgasm, and he ejaculated with desperate eagerness right afterwards. She eased down to her side and he rolled over, holding her spoon fashion.

After a minute he somewhat surprised her: "Rae?"

She slowly turned around in the circle of his arms with her new face, the old face.

She ran a finger down the bridge of his nose while he stared. "'To see love coming, and see love depart.'"

"You . . . grew a new arm," he said inanely. "But you're the same inside." For ninety years, the changeling realized, it had always been nurse Deborah inside, whenever it was a woman.

He explored her face with his hands, and then drifted down to the tattoo. "But except for the face . . ."

"I'm still Sharon. Changing bodies takes longer, and hurts."

"Who . . . what . . ." He was still caressing her. "What are you?"

"'Who' I am is Sharon and Rae and a couple of hundred other people over the past century, and a number of animals and objects besides. The 'what' is difficult."

"Another planet?"

"I don't even know that. Your idea about my coming from the future isn't inconsistent with my memories, which are vague before 1931. I think that's when I first took human form."

"What were you before that?"

"A variety of creatures. I was always in the sea—great

white, killer whale; whatever was at the top of the local
biome's food chain. Pretty good survival instinct, I suppose.

"I could have been there as long as the artifact; the artifact might have brought me here—from the future, from
another star, another dimension. I feel a compelling attraction to it."

He nodded slowly. "So you seduced me, hoping I
could—"

She kissed him on the cheek. "Which doesn't mean I
don't love you," she whispered. "You can love someone
and use him. Or her."

He didn't say anything for a long moment. He smoothed
a strand of hair off her forehead, and smiled. "You seem so
feminine. As Rae, as Sharon, and now in between."

"I prefer being female. But I was a Marine in World War
Two, a male juggler in the circus. In the seventies I was a
male astronomy graduate assistant at Harvard, a few years
ahead of Jan; I graded Jan's papers when she took Atmospheres of the Sun and Stars. Small world."

"Did you ever meet Jack or me, before the project?"

"No. I knew about you, from the *Titanic* thing, of
course; I was a marine biologist."

"As well as a Marine." He shook his head in wonder.
"And now?"

The changeling pursed its lips. "Let me get us a glass of
wine." He shifted to rise and she put a hand on his shoulder. "I know where it is."

She crossed to the kitchenette and felt his eyes on her;
knew how she looked in the candlelight. "I wanted to take
more time. Wanted you to fall in love with me as Sharon."

"You were on the right track."

She filled a crystal glass with red wine in the darkness.
If he could have seen her face he would be startled, irises
the size of quarters. "But I had to force the issue, I thought.
Because of tomorrow."

"You know what's happening tomorrow?"

"Easy to guess. I know about the artifact's response, of course, as Rae. You decided to go public. I suppose to lure me out of hiding." She handed him the glass.

He took it without drinking. "Also to get a few million more people working on the sequence. Bigger computers." He sipped and handed the glass back to her. "Why didn't you just identify yourself? You'd be part of the project in a nanosecond, and we'd protect you from . . ." With a jerk of his head he indicated the people who had shot her.

"If you could." With the back of her fingers she stroked the stubble on his cheek. "I know human nature, darling, maybe better than you do. An outsider with almost a century of observation."

"You know love."

"I've known it a few times. I know xenophobia, too. I've been black and Asian and Hispanic in America, in the times when white people could do or say anything to you. A white prisoner on the Bataan Death March. It was a powerful lesson, being hated and feared automatically because you're different." She sipped and put the glass on the end table by the candle. "There's nobody on this planet more 'different' than me."

That was the first thing the changeling had said that wasn't the truth. But it couldn't know that there was someone stranger nearby.

"I have the message partly figured out," she continued. "Not as a Drake algorithm; certainly not as a verbal translation. It seems to be something like a song, and I think it's addressed to me. I want to go answer it."

"Tonight?"

"It has to be tonight. That's why I rushed this."

Russell sat up slowly. "I suppose the guard would let me take you in. But then what? Most likely, nothing will happen. Will you join the team then? As our resident Martian?"

"Sure. But only you and Jack and Jan would know I

wasn't sweet little Sharon from Hawaii, sleeping with the boss."

He rubbed her back. "The night guard is going to be either Simon or Theodore. They'd both recognize Rae. Can you become Jan? Her face, that is?"

"Easy. Five minutes." She got up.

Russell touched her hip. "Wait. Can I watch?"

The changeling turned. "No one's ever seen me do it." Russell nodded. "Okay." It sat back down, facing him.

It winced and there was a slight grinding noise as the cheekbones became more prominent and moved in closer to the nose. The chin lost its dimple and elongated. Wrinkles and laugh lines grew, and the skin under the eyes sagged. The eyes snapped from pale blue to brown. The hair grew to shoulder length and turned white, and then spread out and wove itself into a French braid.

"How can you do that? The hair, it isn't living tissue."

"I don't know how I can do any of it." She stood and spread her arms. The skin of her beautiful body rippled and faded to dead white, and turned into a nylon jumpsuit. The skin on her hands grew age spots and wrinkles.

He rubbed the nylon on her arm between thumb and forefinger. "You can make synthetics."

"Metals, anything. Back in the sixties I spent a week as a motel television set. That was educational."

"Transmutation of elements?"

She smiled at his expression. "I know. I have a pretty recent doctorate in astrophysics. The wildest edge of physics can't explain it.

"I think the only constraint is mass. If I turn into a person or thing considerably heavier or lighter, I have to gain or lose flesh. You wouldn't want to watch me consume a leg of lamb. Or an unabridged dictionary."

"That's how you could lose an arm and keep going?"

"Yes. That hurt, because it was an outside agent, and a surprise. If I had to detach an arm to lose weight, it would take a couple of minutes, and look pretty strange, but it wouldn't hurt."

He leaned back and shook his head, staring. "Are there more than one of you?"

"If there is, I haven't found her. I can *become* more than one individual; given an hour, I could split this body into three children. But the personality, the intelligence, becomes distributed, and weakened. I made myself be a school of fish once. Each individual fish was pretty dumb."

"So you haven't reproduced that way. By fission, like an amoeba."

"In fact, I have some sort of instinct against it. When I'm split, I'm anxious to get back together."

"I've wondered sometimes how they do it at home—wherever or whenever I came from. Maybe they don't reproduce at all. Why would immortals have to?"

"You can't *know* you're immortal, can you?"

"Not until I survive the heat death of the universe, no. But I've been through a lot and always seem to recover." She stood and carried the candle to the bureau mirror, and inspected her transformation. "Shall we go?" she said in Jan's voice.

"In a minute. Some of us have to dress."

They were only ten minutes from the project site. They said hello to a few people out enjoying the night air or sitting on their porches, no doubt adding grist to the rumor mill—people did suspect a romantic attachment between the two senior researchers.

The guard was Theodore, a large cheerful Chinese-Samoan. "Nervous about tomorrow, Professors?"

"You know about tomorrow?" Russ said.

"Just that there's something; something big. Simon told me."

"They probably know in Pago Pago," the changeling said.

"He told me it was a secret."

"Still is, I hope." Russell gestured. "We're going into the artifact room."

"Okay." He reached down and clicked something. "It's clear."

They went in by the reception desk and walked down a silent corridor to a blast door covered with warnings. Russ unlocked it with his handprint, and the heavy door sighed open.

In the anteroom there were two complex data consoles. He sat down at the larger one and typed a few lines. "Okay . . . I've turned off the cameras for maintenance. That'll be fun to explain."

"I'll look at it on the way out," the changeling said. "I think I can cover it."

"Computers, too?"

"MIT. I've had a long time to study things." It opened a locker. "Should we suit up?"

"Don't have to. Nothing nano going on." He put his hand on another door. "Open for me," he said quietly, evenly, and it slid away into the jamb in absolute silence. It was an airlock chamber. An identical door, without the ID plate, was on the other side.

They stepped inside and he said, "Close."

The door behind closed, but the one in front didn't open. "There are two people in the airlock," the room said. "I need a speech pattern from the one who is not Russell Sutton."

"I'm Jan," the changeling said. "Open for me." The door slid open and they stepped into the long corridor that connected the artifact room to the main building. Fluorescent lights winked on as the door slid silently shut. The windowless metal walls were full of clutter; people had put up cartoons and drawings with refrigerator magnets, and a galaxy of magnetized words coalesced into clusters of poetry, not all of it obscene.

One block of wall several meters long contained 31,433 ones and zeros, patiently inked in black Magic Marker.

A final blast door, thick as a bank vault, that opened on to the artifact room, was halfway open. As they passed through it, a bank of floodlights over the artifact came on with a crackling sound. In bright relief, they saw the arti- fact on its pylons, the big laser, the two useless horizontal microscope machines, the array of communication de- vices—and a man standing with folded arms. The chameleon.

"Jack?" Russ said.

apia and beyond

The thing that was Jack nodded. "Please do come in." He clicked an infrared signaler, and the bank vault door boomed shut.

"The guard didn't say—"

"I asked him not to."

"You expected us, then." Russ put a hand on the changeling's shoulder.

"Oh, yes. In a way, I've expected you for a long time." He was looking at the changeling. "Jan. Sharon. Rae. You really were a television set once?"

They both stared at him, speechless.

"I've had a microcamera in your bedroom, Russell, since you first moved into the *fale*. It's often been entertaining, but never so much as tonight." Russ opened his mouth, twice, but no words came out.

The changeling crossed her arms. "So you know what I am."

"Actually, no." It spread its own arms, palms up, and in

an instant became a duplicate of Russell, still in Jack's shorts and T-shirt.

"My God," Russell said.

"That's good," she said.

"You can't do it, can you? I watched you take several minutes just to change your face. But you've only had a century of practice."

"How much practice have you had?"

"Since the Stone Age, I think. But I can't remember it ever not being instantaneous." It changed back into Jack and walked toward her.

"Do you know where we're from?" she asked.

"I don't think we're a 'we,' dear. I can't become a television set or a great white shark or even a female. I can look like any man, but that's my limit. We're two different species."

"But maybe from the same planet, or time."

"Or dimension, whatever." He stood directly in front of the changeling and studied her. "I've been looking for someone like you for thousands of years."

"So the project," Russell said, "it was just a lure, to find—"

"Yes and no. The artifact is real." He didn't take his eyes off the changeling. "I discovered it years before the submarine had its accident."

"Which was no accident," the changeling said.

"Go to the head of the class. A rear admiral with top-secret clearance can get a lot done behind the scenes. I had her vectored close to the artifact and then set off the charge that sank her."

"A hundred and twenty-one dead?" Russell said.

Jack gave him an amused look. "How long do you think it takes for a hundred twenty-one people to starve to death on this planet?"

"That's beside the—"

"A little over four minutes. If you're feeling all weepy,

go feed somebody." He gestured toward a work table. "Let's sit."

They followed him over. He sat and poured coffee from a thermos into a Styrofoam cup. "Coffee?"

The changeling took a cup but didn't drink from it. Russell sat down uneasily. "How long have you been Jack Halliburton? Did you write—"

"*Bathyspheric Measurements and Computation*? No. I've read it, of course. I took over Halliburton's identity in 2015, because he seemed like a logical person to 'discover' the artifact and hire you to retrieve it."

"You killed him?"

"What else could I do, adopt him? We went sailing together one evening and I broke his neck and sent his body down with an anchor. Be glad it wasn't you. Could've been."

"Are you always a scientist?" the changeling asked.

"Rarely. Usually I've been a soldier of some kind. You said you were on the Bataan Death March. Which side?"

"United States."

"That must have been . . . diverting. I would have chosen Japan."

"You decided to kill Halliburton," Russell said, "just like that?"

"No, not 'just like *that*.'" There was some exasperation in his voice. "Not that it was difficult, but I did have to study him first. As I have studied you." He pointed a finger. "You're about to attack me; I can smell the norepinephrine in your sweat. Don't do it. I could swat you dead like a fly."

"But you have to kill me eventually, anyhow," Russell said, "and her, too. To protect your secret—"

"Don't jump to conclusions, Russ. I have more interesting options than killing you." He turned his attention back to the changeling. "Bataan was terrible. You must enjoy pain."

"No, but I can tune it out. Sometimes we have to bear it, to know what it's like to be human."

"Why would you want to do that? That's like a human being wanting to know how it feels to be a turnip."

"Not at all."

He shook his head. "You like them. You think you love this one. It's like loving a turnip."

"You've never liked or loved anyone? Since the Stone Age?"

In an instant he changed into a burly thug, all scars and tattoos, and he had Russell by the wrist. "Tol' you," he said in a deep growl. "Don' do that." Russell dropped the pen he'd been holding like a dagger.

"Don't you hurt him!"

He turned back into Halliburton, the skinny seventy-year-old, still clutching Russell's wrist in an iron grip. "How would you stop me?"

With thumb and forefinger she pinched the edge of the table and twisted it. A long jagged piece of wood popped up, rifle-shot crack, and separated, screeching as she ripped it away. She held it out like an offering. "I could shove this up your ass and break it off."

He let go of Russell and leaned forward. "Is that a serious offer? I might enjoy it. I rather did the last time, back in the Crusades, though I had to pretend to die, along with the others."

He gently picked the long fat splinter from between her fingers and slowly slid it down his throat, like a sword-swallower. He closed his mouth, coughed once, and shrugged. "Do you want to threaten me with something more serious?"

She shook her head slowly. "I don't see why we have to be adversaries. We should learn from each other."

"I'm learning. You could be." He gestured at the artifact behind her. "What did you mean by a 'song'? You think you can communicate with it vocally?"

"Acoustic vibration. You've been doing that with your solenoid."

"Why don't you give it a try, then? Sing your little heart out."

She stood up slowly and backed away, toward the artifact, not taking her eyes off the chameleon and Russell. "If you touch him—"

"I wouldn't dream of it. Go ahead."

When she was next to the artifact, she reached up and touched its mirror surface—then recoiled, as if from an electric shock.

"What is it?" Russell said.

She shook her head and started to trill. It was an unearthly sound, and no human could have done it, glottal stops modulating one tone in rapid-fire Morse code.

It was over in forty-five seconds. All three stared at the artifact; nothing overt happened.

The chameleon rose and walked quietly over to stand next to her, Russell following just behind. "Looks like it didn't work."

"I felt something. Give it time."

"We have plenty of time. Don't worry." The chameleon reached out and absently stroked her arm; gently took her wrist. "The arm's all healed?"

She cocked her head. "Of course."

"Pity." He pulled down hard and the shoulder socket popped sickeningly, and the arm ripped off. An instant later her other hand came up and struck his face so hard the lower hinge of the jaw broke off and swung free.

He staggered back and threw the arm away, and used both hands to press his chin back into place.

"What are you doing?" she said. After an initial spray, the bleeding from her shoulder stopped.

It took a moment for the jaw to fuse back into place. "I'm doing . . . what I've lived for, for thousands of years."

"Why?"

"Only one of us per planet."

"I'm not one of you."

"But you are—" Russ leaped onto his back and put a scissor-hold on his throat. The chameleon threw him off like a doll, to crash against the heavy laser mount.

"You are my only rival here. This is not personal. You just have to die."

She sidled around to where Russ was lying still. "It became personal when you hurt him. And I can't die."

"I believe I can put you into a state equivalent to death. All I have to do is tear you into several pieces and make sure those pieces stay separate. For all time."

The changeling found a pulse in Russell's throat and stood between him and the monster. "I could do the same to you."

"Not with one arm, I think. You won't have time to grow a new one, and you can't leave this room to do so at leisure."

She looked at the walls. "You're wrong. I could be through that wall and in the water in seconds. I don't think you want to face me in the water. Even one-armed."

"Leave and I'll kill him. Your choice."

The changeling hesitated. Jack couldn't let Russ live, no matter what happened to her.

"Go ahead," the chameleon said. "I won't even try to stop you. You'll be back, and meanwhile I'll enjoy killing him slowly. He hasn't been easy to work with."

She tried another tack. "I don't understand you. You're like a scientist who's searched all his life for something, but when you find it, you want to destroy it without learning anything first."

"I learned enough before you left that bedroom to come here. And I'm no more a scientist than you are a woman." He suddenly looked left. "Well, isn't *that* cute."

The amputated arm was transforming itself into a weapon. The nails had become long metal talons and eyes had formed over two knuckles. Pseudopods along the sides were turning into insectoid legs.

He turned back to the changeling. "Let me show you what I looked like when I first started looking for you." He became more than a foot shorter, bulking out so much that his T-shirt and shorts split. Black hair bristled all over his body and his face coarsened into Neanderthal features. He tore the rags of clothing away to reveal massive ridges of muscle and prominent genitals, engorged.

She leaped at him and he casually kicked her aside, the rough horn of his toe claws ripping cloth and skin between her breasts with a crunch of broken bone. She rolled once and came up in a crouch, pale, uncertain.

He stroked himself for a moment, looking at her, and muttered, "No."

"Please try." She tensed.

Without looking at the target, he struck sideways with the speed of a serpent and snatched up the disembodied arm. Wriggling, it tried to fight, but he closed a hand over its claws and bent back until they broke. He threw them to the floor with a clatter and then stripped the legs off like someone cleaning a shrimp.

He bit at the biceps and tore off a strip of flesh and then, munching it, broke the arm at the elbow. With a long dirty thumbnail he daintily excavated the eyes over the knuckles, and popped them in his mouth.

He smiled, his teeth pink with her blood, and took another bite.

The changeling looked around the room for something it could use as a weapon. The place was too neat; there was nothing loose. The huge laser could certainly cut the creature into chunks, but it was immovable as a boulder and could only be activated remotely.

Russell had regained consciousness and was staring at the horrible scene. The chameleon had stripped almost all of the flesh from the bone above the elbow. It dropped the arm and spit out a large gobbet. "At this point I should say,

'You have wonderful taste, my dear,' but in fact you don't. I don't think I've ever eaten anything as vile as you."

"You're the first creature I've ever known to take a second bite. You're the one with no taste." She saw Russell fumble in his pocket and come out with his Swiss Army knife. "No, Russ!"

The chameleon turned to look at him and laughed. "Wrong tool, Russell."

"Oh?" He half-turned and jammed it into a high-voltage wall socket. There was a shower of sparks and the shock knocked him flat. The lights went out.

The backup, a large gasoline-powered generator, came on in a second. The lights flickered and then returned to normal brightness. Russ sat back up, cradling his injured hand.

"That didn't buy you any time."

"That wasn't the point. People will come to investigate."

"They'll find they can't get the blast door open."

"You really haven't thought this through, have you? You kill us and then what? Call a press conference?"

"I'll just leave the way she—" He turned, and she wasn't there anymore.

The changeling dropped from a ceiling girder just as he looked up. She landed on his shoulders and gave his head two twists, and his neck snapped. A third jerk and the head came off, with enough force to hit the ceiling. But he had hold of her leg by then, and spraying blood from his neck, flung her off in a high arc. She landed heavily and rolled to the base of the artifact, not far from Russell.

By the time she stopped rolling, it had grown a new head, a grotesque combination of the Neanderthal and Jack. "That did hurt. Shall we play pain?"

Pulling herself to her feet, the changeling reached up and touched the artifact.

There was a sound like a distant large bell struck once.

The changeling took its true form for the first time in a million years. It elongated until it was about eight feet long. Its face had only one opening, with no apparent sense organs. You couldn't focus on its body—it changed, moment by moment, colors shimmering all over the spectrum, limbs growing and fading and transmuting. It was inhumanly beautiful.

The artifact flowed off its stand as if it were mercury. It shot in one straight rivulet toward the chameleon and formed itself into a domed cage around him.

The changeling spoke to it, in colors.

The chameleon seized the liquid bars of its cage, but they wouldn't budge. Then it spasmed into rigidity, and then froze, literally, frost riming all over its body.

The artifact melted into a puddle all around the chameleon, and then re-formed as a large silver ovoid, three or four times the size of its original manifestation, with the deadly creature inside. Colors flashed all over the room, and then stopped, and the changeling became Jan again, flickered through Sharon, and settled on Rae.

She walked over to Russ, took his hand, and helped him to his feet. She embraced him.

"What was . . . was that you?"

"It's news to me, too, but yes. I guess that's what I look like when I don't have to look like something else."

There was a loud creaking sound, and a large part of the ceiling dropped a few feet, then stopped, turned sideways, and settled slowly to the floor, leaning neatly against the wall.

"The artifact is sort of like my partner, alive in its way. It didn't realize who I was until I sang and touched it. That changed it, too; woke it up. It's been in a kind of waiting mode, suspended animation, since I left it to explore."

"Ninety years ago?"

"More like a million." She looked at the ovoid. "It doesn't know what Jack is, but he obviously shouldn't be allowed to remain on Earth. We'll take him home for study."

"He's not dead?"

"No. He can't die any more than we can. But he's not from our world."

"Where is your world?"

"Ten thousand light-years away. A planet in a globular cluster—Messier 22, in Sagittarius." She gave him a long kiss. "Get a telescope and look me up sometime."

"You have to go."

"Yes. It's like a law. I've been here for too long. Done things I shouldn't have done. Like fall in love with a local, an alien."

"Well . . . I know how that feels." She squeezed his hand and started to say something, but turned and walked toward the ship. An entrance rippled open. "Could I go with you?"

"Still the astronaut." She blinked away tears and shook her head. "The journey's too long. And you'd have to learn to like chlorine." She looked at him for a long moment and stepped into the ovoid. The entrance resealed.

The ship silently rose toward the hole in the ceiling. But then it settled back down to the floor. It opened again.

The changeling was in its natural form, splendid, chaotic. It became Rae again.

"Actually, the ship says you *could* come. But not as a human. You'd have to let it change you into something like me."

"It could do that?"

"Nothing to it." She smiled at him, eyes glittering. "And you'd still be Russ. My Russ."

Suddenly, loudspeakers crackled. Jan's voice, painfully loud: "Jack? Russell? What the hell is going on in there?"

Russell shook his head and laughed.

"Russ, the guard says you went in there with me! What are you doing?"

"Just . . . taking a little trip." He paused, then stepped over the threshold and felt himself start to glow.